Ed –

I hope you enjoy

This crazy journey

courtesy of my wild

imagination

Ry

RISEN FROM THE DEPTHS

A Mystery Novel

Ronald Lamont

KITSAP PUBLISHING

Risen From the Depths
First edition, published 2017

By Ronald Lamont

Copyright © 2017, Ronald Lamont

Cover photo from "USS ENTERPRISE CVN-65 WESTPAC 1978 Cruise Book"
with special thanks to ENTERPRISE crewman MM2 David H. Adams
and the entire ENTERPRISE Photo Lab

Author's photo by Tara Templeton Photography

ISBN-13: 978-1-942661-44-3

Published by Kitsap Publishing
P.O. Box 572
Poulsbo, WA 98370
www.KitsapPublishing.com

Printed in the United States of America

TD 20170228

50-10 9 8 7 6 5 4 3 2

Acknowledgments

To Mother, James, Wendy, Judie, Donna, Ken, Jerry, David, and John. Life is always an adventure when you grow up with eight siblings.

And to the men and women of the United States Navy and Department of Navy civilians with whom I both served and worked alongside. I achieved many successes throughout my career, none of which I can claim as my own, but instead were a testament to the dedication, integrity, and character of all of you. It was an honor and a privilege.

PROLOGUE

His eyelids... he can't seem to force them open... like a bad dream where you want to wake up, but you can't.

He tries to speak. A low moan is all that he can muster.

He summons every ounce of strength to open his eyes – to awaken from the nightmare.

A faint glimmer of muted light seeps in. A semblance of reality appears, but the vista is perplexing...

"What's that in front of me? It looks like the end of a road, but there's nothing but boundless sky beyond it? Wait... that's not the sky... that's water... everywhere. Am I at the edge of a washed-out bridge? Am I trapped in the middle of a flood??"

His head suddenly snaps back...

1

A thirty year-old 76-foot fishing trawler bobs and weaves like a prizefighter on the waters of the mid-Pacific ocean.

The boat's winches whine as they struggle to haul in the day's catch.

The net breaks the surface and is lifted high by the winch and crane. The size of the load catches many of the crewmen off-guard... envisioning 'dollar signs' as a result of their biggest catch in weeks.

Observing the hovering load a crewman turns to the Captain and proclaims, "Holy crap Cap, we've hit the Mother Lode!"

The seasoned Captain knows better and chuckles to himself, "Ah, the optimistic naiveté of a rookie."

"Don't count your pay just yet there Duncan" responds the Captain, "for all we know we could be hauling-in a giant squid or some other Denizen of the Deep that's not a part of the menu, payload that broke loose from a cargo ship during a storm, or a big pile of trash from a cruise ship."

A few crewmen guide the load down to the deck.

"Something made a hard landing" replies one of the crewmen.

"I hope we're not looking at the proverbial *'boot hanging from the end of a fishing pole'*" says another in response.

The net falls away and an avalanche of fish spew across the deck, revealing an unexpected captive to the astonished crew... a 1960's era automobile.

The Captain is as surprised as the rest of the crew and mumbles under his breath, "That's neither the lost payload nor pile of trash I had in mind."

A closer look at 'the catch' reveals an unusual paint job - not unlike that of a military fighter jet, right down to a squadron insignia and the lettering *U.S. NAVY.*

Several of the crewmen approach the vehicle in a manner similar to a Sheriff approaching an abandoned car on a remote dirt road... a mixture of curiosity and trepidation.

The Captain approaches the passenger-side windows in an attempt to peer inside for a glimpse of the car's bounty, alas the windows are darkened with sea-growth.

One of the crewmen grabs the driver's-side door handle and tries to open the door - nothing. He takes a deep breath, tightens his grip, and follows with a hard yank.

The car door flings open and the crewman falls to the deck... gallons of fish and water cascading over him.

"Son of a bitch!" yells the crewman.

As the waterfall recedes he notices a body, sprawled half out of the door but held in place by the lap belt. The body is clad in an aviator's flight suit; a pilot helmet askew atop his head.

"What the fuck?" the crewman says as he picks himself up from the deck, flaps his arms and hands to shake off the water, and heads toward the body.

"Somebody's screwin' with us" he yells to the Captain, "there's a freakin' dummy behind the wheel!"

A closer look seems to confirm his suspicion... besides the flight suit the 'dummy' is wearing gloves, *"Surely to cover up mannequin hands"* the crewman thinks to himself. And the head is conveniently covered by the helmet with its visor down in order to hide his *mannequin eyes*.

"Oh here we go" the crewman says aloud in a confirming manner as he notices the 'pilot' is wearing a mask... a strange, almost human-like Halloween mask.

He raises the helmet's visor to get a closer look. As the visor passes the eyes the cavernous sockets reveal a grisly, semi-fleshy, skull.

The crewman jumps back in surprise and disgust.

"Holy Fuck!" he says as he looks toward the Captain, "We've got a problem."

2

Jake Levine's desk phone rings. He can see by the Caller ID that it is the Director on the com-line.

Levine figured the Director would be calling. Levine's desk is adjacent to the Director's office and, unbeknownst to the Director, Levine can hear snippets of the Director's conversations, especially when the Director is either agitated or trying to make a point and his voice rises to a crescendo.

Levine finds it rather amusing that the Director seems to think he has some sort of sixth sense... always showing up at his office doorway soon after the Director has finished-up an interesting or important conversation. In this case all that Levine could make out was that the discussion had something to do with the Coast Guard.

Levine picks up the phone and before he can say "Levine" the Director says "Hey Jake, can you swing by my office?"

"Sure" responds Levine.

Jake Levine is the Senior Field Agent in the San Diego NCIS Field Office. He is 6 feet tall with an athletic physique. His dark curly hair with greying temples is kept relatively short; not 'military short' but more like, as his wife calls it, *akin to a Caesar from the days of ancient Rome.* His almost-squinting green eyes can produce a piercing glare that lets you know you fucked-up without him uttering a word. Superiors, peers, and subordinates all refer to it as "The Look" - something you never want to see directed your way. With rugged good looks and his athletic build this man in his fifties is often mistaken for being eight to ten years younger. Not that his wife minds as she is a number of years his junior... they met at the gym and immediately clicked; a shared admiration for intellect, wit, a sense of humor, and a dedication to fitness. And although his wife is a beautiful woman, when asked as to what drew him to her his first response is always "we laugh our asses off." On the job he is something of a dichotomy... professional, to-the-point, with integrity and high standards, yet will attempt to zing you with a dose of sarcastic wit. His personal mantra: "If you don't find a slice of humor in the midst of the madness this job will drive you crazy."

Levine walks into the Director's office. The Director, Jonathan Grey, is a few years younger and a couple of inches shorter than Levine, with short straight hair befitting his name... completely grey. And not that the Director is necessarily a heavy man, but let's just say that his affinity for a morning mocha-java and maple bar are not exactly doing him any favors.

The Director was Levine's subordinate back in the day, but Levine never had the desire to deal with the politics of the Director's Chair, he'd much rather work the field than attend a myriad of meetings every day and hob-nob with other desk jockeys. Jonathan Grey had been a damn good agent, with a knack for dealing with the political side of the business, so Levine was more than happy to see Grey work his way up to the Director's Chair. And the feeling was mutual... Grey considers Levine the best Field Agent in the agency, and probably would not have 'put his name in the hat' for the Director position if he didn't have Levine as his Senior Agent. The Director knows Levine will cover his ass out in the field while he deals with the '24/7' stress and politics of the Directorship.

The Director looks up from his desk as Levine walks into his office.

Levine doesn't utter a word; he merely gives the Director a *"What's up?"* look and gesture.

"Got a call from the Coast Guard; apparently a fishing trawler dredged-up a car in the middle of the Pacific" says the Director.

"Surely you didn't call me in here to discuss debris from the Japan tsunami that's been floating around the ocean for years and just so happened to get caught in a fishing trawler's net?"

"No tsunami debris here; reports are that the car is a 1960-something American–made sedan."

"So what are we looking at, a load of loot and Janet Leigh's character from "*Psycho*" in the trunk?" Levine jokingly asks.

The Director, being a little *too* literal, replies "That was a '57 Ford, not a '60's…"

"You're kidding me, right? It's called *humor* John" responds Levine before the Director finishes his statement.

The Director gives Levine a half-smile and then responds, "No report about any loot, but good guess on the rest… there *is* a dead body behind the wheel."

"Now you've piqued my interest, but why is the Coast Guard asking *us* to take this case?"

"Two reasons… the car is painted-up like a Navy fighter jet; and its 'pilot'" says the Director with air-quotes, "is wearing a U.S. Navy flight suit."

"No shit? I'm in."

"That's good since I already told them we'd take it."

"I figured as much; what's the current status?"

"The trawler's on its way back to San Diego; they'll be tying up at Fiddler's Cove."

"ETA?"

"Tomorrow; 1100 hours. Some of San Diego County's Forensic team, including their M.E., will be meeting you there."

"Doctor Watson I presume?" asks Levine with a smirk.

"How long have you been waiting to use *that* line?"

"Hey, at least I didn't say, '*No shit Sherlock?*'"

The Director just shakes his head and replies, "To answer your question… yes, Doctor Jonas Watson will be the investigating Medical Examiner."

"Sounds good; any additional details on the victim or the crime scene?"

"Apparently the victim is still in the car."

There's a moment of silence as Levine expected more than this one additional tidbit. It was only a couple of seconds but it seemed like an eternity to Levine, who is now clamoring for more… like a chocoholic who had been given but a single square from a Hershey bar.

"Oh, and they *did* provide the coordinates of the location they found it" the Director finally continues, "but I haven't heard if the Coast Guard has identified ships that may have been in the area, so that's something for you to follow-up on."

"Hell, this thing could have been dumped years ago. Plus, if someone's dumping a body I'm thinking they're not going to be stupid enough to have their GPS turned on while doing it."

"We all know there's no such thing as the perfect crime. Besides, don't you ever watch those *'Stupid Criminals'* TV shows? Don't underestimate the ability of someone to be a complete idiot."

"Good point" responds Levine with a smile… apparently the Director hasn't lost his sense of humor after all.

3

Slade Conroy stands at the office coffee mess pouring his morning cup of Joe. He is seemingly barely awake... his eyelids intermittently cycle from almost-closed to a wide-open stare, and his body is swaying like a toddler trying to stand still after a game of *'spin yourself around in circles for no particular reason'*.

When not in a zombie-like morning stupor Slade Conroy's looks and sense of style actually made him *'The face of the local agency's website'*. He stands 6 feet 2 inches tall, medium build, a coif of dark straight hair with nary a hint of grey, and at 42 years old he represents a hint of youth along with experience and wisdom that comes with age - exactly what the agency wanted to portray to the public. With his 'poster boy' looks and a name like 'Slade Conroy' he is often mistaken for either an actor or a politician... neither of which pleases Conroy, who wants to be recognized for his abilities as an investigator and not something superficial like his *"Mister Hollywood"* appearance.

With his coffee mug topped-off Conroy starts to sleepwalk his way back to his desk when he notices Levine exiting the Director's office. This is an odd sight this early in the morning... the Director is usually in hermit-mode with his office door closed until sometime after seven-o'clock. Conroy, with a confused look on his face, glances down at his watch and then back toward Levine.

"Hey Jake, a little early for a convo with the Director isn't it?" asks Conroy as they cross paths and then walk together toward their respective desks.

"We've got a case... possible homicide" responds Levine.

"Yeah?" replies a suddenly perked-up Conroy, "Where're we headed?"

"Fiddler's Cove."

Conroy, now at his desk, grabs his gun and badge, and starts to head toward the door.

"Holster your weapon there sheriff!" says Levine.

Conroy... surprised... stops in his tracks and replies, "What are we waiting for?"

"The crime scene."

"Wha... Wha... What???" replies a totally-confused Conroy.

Levine explains the situation.

Conroy is even more confused now, and responds in a rather animated manner, "A car painted up like a Navy jet... with a body inside wearing a flight suit... found out in the middle of the Pacific... how the hell is that even possible?? It makes no sense!!"

"Would you rather be doing the Annual Meth-head Training at the Navy bases... showing those pathetic *'before and after'* photos of sunken-faced, gnarly-toothed meth-heads in order to educate the sailors on the hazards of meth? If so I can arrange that for you instead."

Conroy knows Levine is just screwing with him and replies, "As entertaining as it is to hear the moans of disgust from the audience - I'll pass. I'm just blown away as to the oddity of this potential case."

"Tell me about it; I'm guessing it's going to get a lot crazier before it starts to make sense."

Special Agent Nicole McKenna has been sitting quietly at her desk soaking-in the conversation and is finally compelled to jump in. "I don't know about you guys" she says, "but I'm intrigued... this could be one of our more interesting cases."

"Beats the hell out of the typical stuff... drugs or liquor found stashed on the ship, drunken sailors or Marines duking-it-out at the Enlisted Club, theft of Government property..." replies Levine as his voice trails off.

Something dawns on Nicole, who says, "Hey, I remember a picture of a car being launched from an Aircraft Carrier that showed up on the internet several years ago."

Nicole starts pounding-away on her keyboard in an attempt to find the picture through the internet.

"That rings a bell now that you mention it" says Conroy, who then turns to Levine and, with a head-nod toward Nicole says, "There's that photographic memory of hers."

"Not to be confused with that *pornographic* memory of *yours* Slade" responds Nicole with a grin while she continues to type... not missing a beat.

"Damn, I forgot about that quick wit that goes along with your Halle Berry looks, your Degree from Stanford, *and* the fact that your expertise has made you the youngest Profiler in the Agency" replies Conroy.

Although Nicole is quite pleased with the zinger she threw Conroy's way, she is also a bit embarrassed by the compliments.

Conroy can read Nicole's body language and visual cues, and directs a statement toward Levine, "And look at her; all that and she's *humble* too!"

Nicole just shakes her head as she continues to search the internet.

Conroy adds... "It's pathetic; she's making us all look bad."

"Questioning your self-worth a bit Slade? And not to mention the fact that she was quite accurate in her assessment there '*Hef*'" adds Levine with a heavy emphasis on 'Hef'.

"You guys are never going to let me live down that ONE time I attended a Halloween party at the Playboy Mansion are you?" remarks Conroy, who then continues with an ill-fated attempt at defending that decision... "Do you know how hard it is to get VIP tickets to that thing? They're like twelve-hundred bucks a pop!"

"Twelve-hundred bucks a pop??!!" responds Levine, "At that price the ticket must have included a packet of little-blue-pills."

"Some of us have no need for an extra boost, thank you very much" replies Conroy, "But here's a humorous nugget for you along those lines..."

Levine immediately thinks to himself, *"Oh crap, where is Slade going with this?"*

"Back when the pills first came on the scene" Conroy continues, "one of the guys in my dorm said *"Oh man, I've got to try one of those... in the name of research of course... my girlfriend is totally down"*, and we're like *"Oh sure... 'research'."*

"I'm afraid to ask" responds Levine.

"So the next day we all asked him how his *'research'* went" Conroy continues, "and he responded: 'Two words - *Diamond Cutter'."*

Levine 'loses it' and almost spits up his coffee; Nicole breaks out into laughter. Conroy can't hold back either and joins in the hilarity as he re-lives the *Diamond Cutter* moment from his college dorm days.

Nicole finally regains her composure and then proclaims, "Ah, here it is" as she brings up a picture of the launch on the computer screen.

Levine and Conroy realize they need to get back on-point, and gather around Nicole's monitor. On the screen is a car flying off the front of a ship's flight deck, seemingly floating in mid-air, a trail of steam wisping behind it – following and encompassing the full length of the catapult trough.

"Yeah, that's it" responds Conroy, "I remember it was touted as the Navy's *'Al Qaida Terrorist Catch & Release Program'* ...gotta give the guy props that came up with that one... freakin' hilarious!"

Nicole looks toward Levine and asks, "What do you think Jake? Could this be our mystery car?"

"I like your 'thinking outside of the box' Nic, but see the *'65'* here on the flight deck?" says Levine as he points to the numerals on the front of the Carrier's flight deck, "That tells us this Ship is the USS ENTERPRISE."

"Okaaayyy??" responds Nicole in a *What's your point?* manner.

"It just so happens that this photo is from their 1978 WestPac Cruise where they launched the car during their Tiger Cruise as part of the entertainment for the 'Tigers' riding the Ship on its return to homeport" responds Levine.

Conroy turns to Nicole and asks quietly, "Tigers?"

Nicole simultaneously shrugs her shoulders and raises her eyebrows - she has no idea.

Levine, getting a gist of the hushed conversation, provides a response… "Dependents of the crew got to ride the Ship from Hawaii back to Alameda with their Sailor or Marine family member."

"Oh yeah, I've heard of that" remarks Nicole, "but I understand no wives or girlfriends were allowed?"

"The Captain didn't want half of the crew disappearing for 'conjugal visits'" replies Levine with air-quotes and a wink.

"Ahhhh… 'Conjugal-visit Sex'… that's got to be even more intense than make-up sex" says Conroy as he peers off into space; surely imagining such a scenario.

"As titillating as your observations are Slade… if we can get back to the case for a moment…" responds Nicole as she shakes her head and rolls her eyes.

Nicole then turns to Levine and asks, "You don't think it's possible that this could be the car from the Enterprise thirty-whatever years ago?"

"That would be a million-to-one shot" responds Levine, "But no matter the genesis of this thing we could be uncovering one hell of a mystery."

4

Levine heads up the walkway of his 1930's Art Deco style home... hardwood floors, plaster walls, archways, coved ceilings, built-in hutch in the dining room, mahogany interior doors, and large picture windows to take advantage of the views looking-out over the Pacific Ocean. It's a relatively modest home by today's standards, but was definitely upscale back in the 30's. Levine and his wife Elise have always had an appreciation for the classic style of the era, so when they found this little gem after the housing market took a dive it was as if they had discovered their own little piece of paradise.

Levine walks through the door clad in his gym clothes; it's Tuesday and, along with Thursdays, means *'work off your frustrations from* the daily-grind *at the gym'*. In Levine's case it's *'get your butt kicked in boot camp'* day. Levine loves the idea of getting a total-body workout... upper body, lower body, core, and cardio... all in a single one-hour session.

Being a gym-day for Levine means Elise has dinner almost ready to be served... as soon as Levine gets his sweaty ass out of the shower. Levine and Elise have alternating dinner-duties during the week; Levine gets Mondays and Wednesdays while Elise gets Tuesdays and Thursdays. Weekends are wide open... dining out, entertaining friends or family, cooking-up something together... whatever their moods strike them. Elise loves to cook, and even graduated from culinary school; not so much as a career possibility but to broaden her culinary talents, especially for entertaining guests, which is fairly often. Needless to say she would gladly do most of the cooking around the house, but she adores Levine's attempt to share the load, even if his abilities don't extend much beyond spaghetti, pork chops, or his signature dish - Tuna Mac.

Levine greets Elise with a kiss... not full-on passionate but with an obvious hint of intimacy, one that plants the seed for *'later'*.

"Ooh I love your scent after a vigorous workout" says Elise immediately following the kiss, "but we'll definitely have to do something about this" as she rubs the stubble populating his face.

Levine gets the hint... the seed he planted with his kiss is starting to germinate... he is now thinking of *'sooner'* rather than *'later'* and responds, "Well, I better get my ass into the shower!"

Levine emerges from the shower wearing only his towel, in guy-mode of course, wrapped around his waist.

Elise walks over and rubs her hand across his smoothly-shaven face, "Now that's more like it" she says with an impish grin.

"It was a *'shaving cream free-for-all'* in there!" says Levine.

Elise looks confused and starts to giggle as she tries to imagine what the hell he could be talking about, and laughingly responds, "Whaaat?"

"Well, I have a brand new can of shaving-cream, and I make *one minor touch* to the nozzle and *"poof"*... it ejected enough foam to shave a werewolf."

Elise starts to laugh, but Levine isn't finished...

"And I'm thinking *'what the hell am I going to do with all of this shaving cream?'* Soooo... I'm sporting a *'Brazilian'*" says Levine with a shit-eating grin.

Elise's laughter goes full-on hysterical.

"You're so ridiculous!" she manages through the laughter.

Levine responds with a goofy-ass smile and something akin to a disco move.

"And that dance!" she says as her laughter continues.

"That's what you get for making me watch those *'Dancing with Semi-celebrity Has-beens'* shows" responds Levine, now overemphasizing his ridiculous moves with pelvis gyrations.

"OK Elvis" says Elise as she rips off his towel and focuses on his 'equipment'... "You lied about the *'Brazilian'*."

"Yeah, but I got ya thinkin'" says Levine with a wink.

Elise smacks him in the ass with the towel and says, "Put something on and get your butt to dinner... it's getting cold."

"Good point; I *hate* shrinkage" replies Levine while looking down toward his crotch.

"I was talking about your dinner you knucklehead" she responds as she throws his towel at him.

"You never know what crazy-ass remark is going to come out of this mouth do you?" says Levine as he finally heads toward the bedroom.

"Five years and you never cease to surprise me" she replies.

"And you love it" says Levine.

Elise doesn't respond, but she realizes he is right.

5

Levine pulls into the parking area of Fiddler's Cove Marina. He cruises around the lot while scanning for the *'San Diego County Crime Scene Investigation'* van, or more specifically, Doctor Watson and his team. Considering the CSI van is on par with a medium-sized U-Haul truck there is no missing it when present - obviously they have not yet arrived.

Levine eyes a spot near the access gate to the Marina. He wheels his car into the space and pops the trunk. Conroy and Nicole exit the vehicle, with Levine immediately following.

Looking out toward Silver Strand Blvd, Conroy and Nicole expect to see the CSI van approaching at any moment. Levine does the same while simultaneously heading toward his car's open trunk.

Levine reaches into the trunk and pulls out a metal briefcase. It's their *'On-Scene'* kit; stocked with the necessary accoutrements to assess the crime scene while awaiting the much more extensively stocked CSI van.

Levine makes one last scan of Silver Strand Blvd as he closes the trunk – nothing.

As Levine, Conroy, and Nicole start walking toward the Marina's access gate Levine hits the speed-dial on his phone, listens for a moment, and then utters, "Hey Doc; you guys on your way?"

"I guess we miscalculated the drive time and associated traffic from Kearny Mesa" replies Doctor Watson.

Levine hears "You mean *YOU* miscalculated" in the background of Doctor Watson's cell phone.

"I stand corrected... *I* miscalculated the drive time" Doctor Watson clarifies, and then continues... "We considered driving around the south end of the bay and coming up through Imperial Beach, but figured Coronado would be a safe bet this time of day. Needless to say we got stuck in a long backup on the bridge for some unknown reason."

Levine provides the answer to Doctor Watson's quandary, "There's a Change of Command ceremony at North Island; on the Carl Vinson I believe."

"Just my luck. Anyway, we'll be there post-haste... we are just passing Hotel del."

"No problem; the trawler is at the end of Pier Bravo, we'll meet you there. We're going to get started by interviewing the Captain and crew."

"Understood."

Levine, Conroy, and Nicole start their trek down Pier Bravo. It's a medium-length pier with multiple branches extending perpendicularly on both sides, with distances between the branches accommodating small–to-medium sized pleasure craft. The pier ends in a "T" – one long pier capable of mooring much larger vessels; this is the location of the fishing trawler.

Levine leads the team up the gangway of the trawler, looking to be received by the Captain. Conroy and Nicole are not even thinking about the trawler Captain, the expectation of actually seeing the infamous sea-life encrusted sedan, otherwise known as *the crime scene*, has their curiosity piqued.

The trawler Captain steps forward to greet Levine's team as they step off the gangway and onto the boat. Levine can't help but think of the character *"Quint"* from the movie *"Jaws"* as he reaches out to shake hands with the Captain. Conroy and Nicole are almost oblivious to the introductions as they are rubbernecking around the deck of the trawler for signs of the sedan – nothing obvious, but there *is* a tarp that appears to be covering a *sizable something* up near the bow.

"It was crazy enough just to reel in an old car... I mean are you kiddin' me? Out in the middle of the Pacific?" explains the Trawler Captain,

"And then to see that it was painted-up like a military jet… well, we were pretty much dumbfounded."

One of the crewmen approaches just as the Captain is finishing his statement.

"Jorgensen here was the one who discovered the body" says the Captain as he nods and thumb-points to the crewman.

Crewman Jorgensen has the look of a seasoned deep sea fisherman; he also has the look and smell of someone who has been wearing the same clothes for a week… or five.

"The guy was wearing a pilot helmet with the visor down, so of course I thought it was just a dummy" says Jorgenson. "When I got up close I thought *"Holy crap, this is an old man in here!"* until I realized that what I thought was an old man was really just a very lifelike mask. In fact, it reminded me of *'the old white guy'* bank robber a few years back where it turned out he was really a young guy wearing a human-like *'old man'* mask."

"I remember seeing that on the news" responds Conroy. "They had BOLO's out describing him as a man in his seventies and even nicknamed him *'The Grandpa Bandit'*. When they caught him in the act it wasn't until they removed his sunglasses that they realized he was wearing a mask. Talk about an unveiling… it was like the *'audience shocker'* in a motion picture."

"That's exactly how it was with me" responds Jorgensen, "I start to pull off the helmet and staring me in the face are eye sockets… and nasty, gnarly, gruesome ones at that."

"That's when we realized it really *was* a dead body behind the wheel" says the Captain, "So, we immediately got on the horn to the Coast Guard. I guess since his flight suit said *U.S. NAVY* they called you folks."

"Anyway, we haven't touched anything since then" remarks Jorgensen, "so your pilot-dude is still behind the wheel."

Conroy turns to Levine and says, "I'm sure this is a long-shot, but I'm going to see if I can find the maker of the mask used in those bank robberies."

"You're thinking maybe the killer saw the same news report?" asks Nicole.

"I figure even if it's not the same source they might be able provide us names of other mask-makers" responds Conroy.

"You know that either the Doc or the lab might find a business logo or some other identifier embossed on the mask" replies Levine.

"True, but if not then whatever I come up with might help their investigation" responds Conroy.

"The ultimate team player - I knew there was a reason I've kept you around all these years" says Levine.

Nicole gives Conroy an *'attaboy'* nudge. Conroy cracks a smile – beaming like a 2nd grader who just received a gold star on his homework.

While Levine, Conroy, and Nicole are getting details about the discovery of the victim, Doctor Watson and Forensic Scientist Brandi Matthews are stepping onto the deck of the trawler.

6

Doctor Jonas Watson, age 51, has the build of a long-distance runner. He's a daily jogger and enters several 10K runs throughout the year, often finishing near the top of his age group ever since he became AARP eligible. With a balding head he sports a buzz-cut, figuring it is a much better look than the comb-over that many of his peers somehow convince themselves '*is not obvious whatsoever*'. His closely-shorn appearance may not be in the league of Sean Connery, but then again is not that of *Larry* from *The Three Stooges* either. His work clothes always include a pair of chinos, usually navy blue or khaki, with a color-coordinated shirt and tie; in fact he often looks like he's wearing military khakis, right down to the dual creases in his shirt running vertically through the chest pockets. Levine figures he must get them professionally pressed at the dry cleaners on Rosecrans Avenue down the street from the Naval Training Center, where ninety percent of their business is serving the military and the dual-crease-technique is '*standard operating procedure*'.

Doctor Watson joined the U.S. Navy Medical Corps directly out of medical school. His assignments included the Naval Region Northwest Medical Center in Bremerton Washington, the National Naval Medical Center in Bethesda Maryland, the Naval Medical Center Balboa Park San Diego, and tours on the Hospital Ship USNS MERCY and the Aircraft Carriers USS NIMITZ and USS ABRAHAM LINCOLN.

Aboard the ABRAHAM LINCOLN Doctor Watson served as the Chief Medical Officer. Such a responsibility is unique in and of itself, but during a deployment this responsibility is even greater as the Medical Department on an Aircraft Carrier serves as the Central Medical Facility for the entire Battle Group. It was during his Carrier deployments that Doctor Watson honed his skills in forensics and investigative techniques; after all, with limited resources afforded a floating medical center in the midst of the ocean, a Carrier's medical team must develop skills beyond those of a typical facility that can call-in experts on a moment's notice. As a forensic pathologist for San Diego County, Doctor Watson is the *'Go-to Guy'* for investigations involving the Department of the Navy.

Brandi Matthews' expertise is anything automotive. She may not exactly fit the typical *'forensic expert'* profile, but in this day and age the lines are rather blurred between typical and non-typical. Brandi has been a car-geek since she was a kid, showing a unique grasp of a vehicle's make and model at the tender age of five-years old. On family road trips, while her parents and siblings were calling-out license plates... "Oregon"... "Montana"... "Mississippi", Brandi was pointing-out "'56 Chevy"... "'40 Ford"... "'65 Pontiac." Needless to say she had a thing for the older classics just like her Dad, who considered most vehicles from the 1980's and 90's, the era of Brandi's youth, to be nothing more than clone-mobiles.

Brandi's father was an automotive machinist and mechanic, and it was no surprise to him that by age ten Brandi was chomping at the bit to help him work on his latest project. Her first was Mom's '62 Chevy Biscayne station wagon sporting a six-banger and three-on-the-tree: It was a relatively simple job of replacing the clutch disc, pressure plate, and throw-out bearing. Go figure it would later become Brandi's first car when Dad decided to upgrade Mom's ride to a mint condition 1966 Oldsmobile Vista Cruiser. The kids loved the small pseudo-sunroof running virtually the entire border of the Vista Cruiser's roof, so that even if you were the unlucky child that got stuck in the middle of the backseat you still had a view of the outside world... very important on a long road trip. But as cool as Mom's old classic cars were she finally decided to try something totally new, and surprised both husband and children alike with her choice... a 2009 V W Beetle... a far cry from V-8 power moving two-tons of classic American automotive steel down the road. But Brandi's Mom enjoys her new toy, saying that the dome-like roof makes you feel like you're driving around in a little bubble car... a description that Brandi immediately jumped on, teasingly responding "Oh, so it's your 21st Century *'AMC Pacer'*."

After Brandi's first sojourn into automotive troubleshooting and repair it wasn't long before she was juggling her schoolwork around pistons, crankshafts, intake manifolds and carburetors... *"A chip off the old engine block"* her Dad would proudly proclaim to friends and family alike. But being an everyday mechanic was not in her DNA; the intricacies of Forensic Science called her name... nothing was more gratifying than solving the mystery behind a motor vehicle accident or crime scene.

On the job Brandi is just 'one of the guys', but on weekends her favorite pastime is taking her '32 Ford roadster retro-rod to various classic car and hotrod shows, and even the occasional *'pinup girl'* photo shoot. Her roadster is right out of the 50's genre, complete with ultra-wide whitewalls and baby moon hubcaps, no fenders, no hood, and a flat-black paint job with a matte clearcoat finish.

Brandi stands 5-foot 9 inches tall with dark brown hair. She is always professional and modestly dressed when on the job, but when off-the-clock it is evident that she is quite proud of her voluptuous figure... *"All the right curves in all the right places"* as she describes it... often dressing the part of a pinup girl when attending events in her roadster. At thirty years-old Brandi often says that she was born in the wrong era.

While Doctor Watson is gathering up his medical kit, Brandi notices Levine heading their way.

As Levine approaches he directs a comment toward Brandi... "I see we've been assigned the A-Team."

"I wish I could say the same" responds Brandi in a sarcastic tone accompanied by a 'Got ya' smile.

"Can't even make it through greetings and salutations without you flipping me crap."

"If I didn't you'd think something was up."

"Good point."

Doctor Watson finds the conversation between Levine and Brandi rather amusing, and says to himself, *"These two never change – they're like siblings trying to 'one up' each other."*

Brandi gets down to business with her first question directed to Levine, "So I understand you have a classic car for me to defile?"

"I don't know about it being a classic, but I was hoping we'd get your automotive expertise on this thing; who knows what's lurking behind the sheet metal."

"Other than fish, sea critters, barnacles, seaweed and other organic gunk that's outside of my forensic sphere?"

"Exactly. One of the thoughts is that it might have been launched from an Aircraft Carrier."

"Launched from an Aircraft Carrier??"

"I know it sounds crazy but it's been done before, back in 1978."

Brandi, trying to make sure that Levine has not *'gone off the deep-end'* responds, "You're not thinking that *this* is *that* car are you?"

"Highly unlikely, but at the very least perhaps you can determine whether the vehicle is basically factory-stock, or has been modified for such a purpose."

"I'll give you what I can based on a cursory inspection here, including whether the chassis has been modified, but I'll need to dissect the slimy rust-bucket back at the garage to determine if any modifications might have been intended to support a launching."

While Levine and Brandi are exchanging verbal jabs Nicole notices that crewman Jorgensen is unveiling the prize beneath the tarp, and just as she suspected, it's the car. She makes a bee-line toward it... heading directly to the driver's-side door.

Nicole notices that the car door is slightly ajar; as if someone had attempted to shut it using too little force and it didn't fully latch. She turns around and makes eye contact with the trawler Captain - giving him a *"what the heck?"* look combined with a head nod toward the car door.

The Captain gets the hint – the female agent giving him '*the stink-eye*' is wondering why the car door is ajar.

"We couldn't just leave the guy hanging half out of the door, so we closed it just enough to catch the first latch" responds the Trawler Captain to Nicole's non-verbal question.

"Understood... thanks" replies Nicole.

Nicole unlatches the car door and gets her first real whiff of the victim and crime scene... *"putrid"* is the first word that enters her mind.

"Man this guy is ripe!" Nicole proclaims, and then turns toward the Trawler Captain, "Couldn't you have stored him in a freezer or something?"

"And screw up your crime scene?" responds the Trawler Captain "No ma'am."

Levine, being directly in the path of the conversation between Nicole and the Trawler Captain, smiles and shakes his head. He then turns toward Nicole and relays a statement, "You're going to like him even better when you get to frisk him."

"Frisk him??!" replies Nicole in a questioning manner awash in surprise and disgust.

"Check his pockets for ID" Levine clarifies.

"Aww crap!" responds Nicole as she starts to put on rubber gloves.

"*After* we get him out of the car" responds Levine, "Right now just get some detailed pictures of the scene."

Nicole mumbles to herself aloud, "I'm beginning to rethink my level of intrigue on this case."

Levine turns back to continue his conversation with Brandi, who decides to give him a little advice: "You realize Nicole is going to kick your ass one of these days, or end up being your boss."

"Wouldn't be the first time" responds Levine.

Nicole is about to snap her first picture when something catches her eye.

"Hmmm... *Snuffy*" says Nicole while out of view from the rest of the team.

Levine, Brandi, and Conroy all have a very puzzled look, trying to figure out what the hell Nicole is talking about.

Conroy responds in Nicole's direction, "Say what??"

Nicole pops-up from the driver's side of the car and provides a response, "The name on the victim's flight suit."

"*Snuffy??*" replies Conroy, "Definitely not the same vibe as '*Maverick*' or '*Ice Man*'."

"I see what you did there Slade" remarks Brandi, "Nice *Top Gun* reference."

Conroy is rather pleased with himself, as evidenced by his Cheshire Cat-like grin directed back toward Brandi.

With a possible moniker associated with the victim, Levine issues his first directive, "Hey Nic, when we get done here see what you can find out about that name."

"How's that?" replies Nicole.

Levine, mildly annoyed at Nicole's apparent lack of comprehension, provides clarification... "Check with the Carrier Air Wings out of Lemoore for an Aviator with a call-sign of *Snuffy*."

"That's exactly what I was thinking; but you know there's a high possibility that the flight suit was picked-up at a military surplus store or even a costume shop and the name means nothing."

"Yeah, and a lead that goes *nowhere* is one more step toward *somewhere*."

Nicole ponders Levine's statement for a second, then, hoping she had gotten his meaning, questions... "It narrows the focus of the investigation?"

"Now you're reading me."

"You've got a way with words, Jake."

Levine smiles... his protégé is learning.

"And I'll follow that up with a call to Pac-Fleet to see if there's been a recent launching of a car at sea" adds Nicole.

"Always one step ahead of me... now you're talkin'."

Levine turns back toward Brandi and is surprised to see that both she and Conroy are no longer there. He realizes the same thing that they apparently did - it's time to stop *talking about* the investigation and to actually start investigating.

7

Nicole, Brandi, and Conroy are crawling-over the crime scene; not so much like ants, flies, or maggots on road-kill, but more like judges at a car show assessing a restoration in order to determine if it meets *Top Flight Award* criteria.

Nicole is photographing the victim, paying particular attention to the positioning of his hands and feet, and looking for evidence that he is, or was, held in place by something other than merely the lap-belt.

Brandi, down on all fours with a flashlight in hand, is focused on the car's undercarriage.

Conroy, being a fairly typical guy, has his head under the hood.

"I can tell you one thing" Conroy proclaims, "it didn't *drive* off the end of a flight deck... someone forgot the carburetor."

Levine, as he is approaching the vehicle, comments... "Looks like an early-60's Plymouth."

"You're exactly right Jake" responds Brandi as she stands up and brushes-off the dirt from the knee-area of her trousers, "1963 to be exact."

Brandi looks at Levine and head-nods toward the front of the car. Levine had the same thought: *"Let's see what's under the hood."*

Levine and Brandi join Conroy at the engine compartment, with Conroy and Levine across from one another at each fender, and Brandi at the grille. They look like three buddies either admiring the car's engine, or trying to figure out why the damn thing won't start.

"What do you think Brandi?" asks Conroy.

"Wow, behind the sea-growth this looks like it's the original 361 cubic inch Commando B-series engine" responds Brandi, "Most car aficionados these days consider the old 361 to be good for nothing more than a boat anchor" she continues, "kind of ironic under the circumstances."

"I'm assuming that, other than being a bit of trivia, it doesn't really tell us anything" remarks Levine.

"That's true" responds Brandi.

Conroy speaks up about an observation he made when he first approached the car, "Hey, I noticed there are no license plates, but I was thinking maybe we can find a VIN number to trace."

"You really think you're going to be able to trace this thing? It most likely came from a wrecking yard" responds Levine.

"You're probably right Jake, but if we *do* find a VIN let's go ahead and run it… you never know" adds Brandi.

Conroy turns to Brandi and asks, "I don't suppose you have any idea where to look?"

"I'd start with the front edge of the driver's door frame" says Brandi, "Look for a stamped steel tag."

Conroy recalls what appeared to be a small plate etched with a myriad of letters and numbers; at least that's what stood out to him through the corrosion and sea sludge when he first popped the hood on the car.

"Now where the hell was that thing?" he says to himself.

Leaning across the driver's side fender he scans the engine compartment starting from the radiator and associated subassemblies to his left – nothing there. Moving clockwise to the opposite fenderwell, then the firewall to his right, and finally the fenderwell beneath him continues to be a fruitless endeavor. He follows the fenderwell up to the inner fender lip, and literally six inches from his fingers - there it is.

He thinks to himself *"It's always the last place you look"*, and then realizes what a ridiculous statement that is… *"Of course it's always the last place you look, what idiot keeps looking after they've found what they were looking for?!"*

Conroy looks toward Brandi, "Isn't this a stamped steel tag right here?" he says as he head-nods and points toward the metal plate. "Could *this* be the VIN?"

"That's the fender tag" replies Brandi, "It will only tell us the car *as-built.*"

"As-built?"

"Yeah, you know… the model, interior and exterior paint colors, engine, transmission, options like power windows and power antenna… stuff like that."

"And you need a super-secret decoder-ring to decipher it all" adds Levine.

"Either that or an Enigma Machine" Brandi proudly counters – she's been waiting for an opportunity to use that line.

Levine is surprised by Brandi's quick wit and knowledge of a decades-old device.

"Enigma Machine?" replies Levine, "I'm impressed."

"Classic cars and *anything World War Two*" responds Brandi, "Plus I've studied a bit of cryptography in my day."

"Cryptography?" replies Levine, who then adds with a smirk, "You shouldn't use those fancy words around Slade here, you'll have him all confused; he thinks '*crypt*-ography' is the study of graveyards."

"And that '*crypt*-ology' is 'talking to the dead'?" says Brandi as she decides to add to Levine's joke at Conroy's expense.

"You two are a regular '*Sonny & Cher*'" responds Conroy.

"Those two didn't tell jokes" says Levine.

"*Exactly*" replies Conroy with a shit-eating grin.

Levine and Brandi look at each other – they can't believe Slade just one-upped them.

"Touché, Slade" replies Brandi.

Levine decides to get back to the matter of the fender tag, and provides a final clarifier on the subject to Conroy, "Anyway Slade, none of those codes will get us any closer to identifying the owner of the car, so don't waste any of your time on *that* tag - just the VIN if you find it."

"Well, there's no getting to the driver's door frame with Nic clicking-away at the victim behind the wheel" says Conroy, "So I'll focus on the rest of the scene in the interim; starting with the engine compartment here."

Brandi steps away from the engine compartment and surveys the side of the car, contemplating the paint scheme.

"Painted-up like a military jet" says Brandi toward Levine, "Now I see how being launched from a Carrier is on your list of possible options."

"The launching back in 1978... the one I was talking about earlier... well, they painted the car like one of the squadron jets and launched it during the ship's Tiger Cruise" says Levine as he adds to the conjecture about a launching.

"You're thinking one of the west coast Carriers decided to do the same?"

"Gotta start our investigation into the source somewhere; and I'd rather start with confirming or eliminating six aircraft carriers than trying to do the same with several hundred, if not several thousand, commercial vessels."

"Makes sense, I guess that's why they pay you the Big Bucks" replies Brandi with a wry smile.

"I'm a government employee, remember? And I don't have the title *'Congressman'* next to my name."

"Hey, now *that* could be your next career move" replies Brandi sarcastically.

"A politician???" replies Levine with disbelief at such a thought, "I'd rather clean-out and scrub-down chicken coops using a pair of tweezers and an old worn-out toothbrush."

"That's a description I wasn't expecting."

"What can I say, I grew up in..."

"A small cow-town outside of Victorville?" interrupts Brandi.

"A small *chicken*-town north of San Francisco" Levine corrects, "Hence the *chicken coop* analogy."

"I had no idea there was a chicken-town north of San Francisco."

"I don't know about today, but *'back in the day'* it was called *'The World's Egg Basket'*."

"You're not talking about *Petaluma* are you?" says Brandi with a bit of surprise accompanied by a smile, "I drive my roadster up there every Spring for the *'American Graffiti Cruise'*."

"That's the place."

"And how cool that they filmed the movie there?"

"Yeah, not only getting to see some of the filming going on downtown, but especially to see it all on the big screen... pretty awesome for us local kids."

"That would have been the highlight of *my* youth."

"A nice trip down memory lane" says Levine, "but back to the task at hand..."

Levine turns his focus to the squadron insignia... a cartoon-like character of a tiger with a large head and over-exaggerated chin like a caricature drawing. The tiger is wearing a pair of boxing gloves and holding up its dukes like Muhammad Ali posing for a photo-op. A combination of letters and numerals are scrolled below the tiger character; they are deteriorated and minimally legible, and as near as Levine can tell it appears to read *RVA11-17*, but that's nothing more than a best guess at this point. Levine figures it must be the identifier of the squadron, if in fact such a squadron actually exists.

Conroy, with camera in hand, has moved away from the engine compartment and is now taking multiple photographs of the car's exterior from various angles. He's bounding-about and clicking-away like a professional trying to get the perfect shot of a bikini-clad model in hopes of making the cover of the *Sports Illustrated Swimsuit Edition*.

"Hey Slade" says Levine as he points to the passenger-side door, "Get some close-up shots of this squadron insignia."

Conroy crouches-down and zooms-in for *"his model's"* close-up. Click-click-click-click...

"There, that should do it" says Conroy as he returns to a standing position.

"Now add that to your 'To Do' list" says Levine.

"Add *what* to my 'To Do' list?"

"The insignia… find out if it belongs to an Air Wing squadron."

Conroy's a bit confused regarding such a directive and replies, "I could see if this was an actual jet plane, but what could some insignia painted on a car tell us?"

"If it's a legitimate insignia it might give us a lead as to the identity of the victim. You know… we find the squadron… they report that they've got a missing crewman… that gives us a name… it also provides us with coworkers that are now potential suspects…"

"I see what you mean."

Overhearing Levine and Conroy's discussion, something comes to mind that Nicole believes might be pertinent. She pops up from the driver's-side door and looks across the car toward Levine and Conroy.

"Hey!" she says to catch their attention, "Doesn't the Air Wing disappear at the end of a deployment?"

"Yeah" replies Levine as he's wondering what Nicole has in mind.

"So that could be a reason the murderer assumed they wouldn't get caught" responds Nicole.

"How's that?" asks Conroy.

"If investigators focused solely on the crewmembers *shipboard* and didn't consider Air Wing personnel that are no longer part of Ship's company" Nicole clarifies.

"Good point" says Conroy, "Plus I guess another possibility would be someone with a vendetta against the squadron."

"I like the way you two are thinking" says Levine "Keep it up."

8

Doctor Watson, wearing coveralls, approaches the car with his foot locker-sized Medical Examiner kit rolling behind him like a piece of luggage. He has a specific mission in mind… assess the victim to the maximum extent practicable at the scene before body-bagging him up and hauling him off to autopsy.

As the Doctor nears the driver's-side door he sees that Nicole is leaning into the car taking photographs, left hand against the dashboard to brace and hold her position, obviously being careful not to end up on the victim's lap. Although the Doctor is pleased with Nicole's apparent concern of ensuring she doesn't contaminate the scene and the victim, he's thinking that her concern has more to do with avoiding any chance whatsoever of coming in contact with a rotting corpse.

"Excuse me Agent McKenna" says the Doctor as he steps up behind her, "Mind if I take this guy off your hands?"

"It will be my pleasure Doctor, *believe me*" responds Nicole.

With the body still behind the wheel, and held in-place by the lap belt, the Doctor surveys the situation and makes an observation… "I've been on the scene of dozens of automobile accidents over the years, but *this* is a first."

"And here I thought you'd seen it all, Doctor."

"That makes two of us."

Doctor Watson turns back away from the victim, kneels down, and opens his medical kit. He retrieves, and commences to unfold, a large plastic sheet - 5 mils thick. As he gets the sheet completely unfolded, Nicole grabs one end. The two lay the sheet down adjacent to the driver's-side door.

Doctor Watson reaches into the car, unbuckles the victim's lap belt, and grabs the victim as he starts to fall out of the car. Positioning himself behind the victim, the Doctor slips his left arm under the victim's left arm pit, and then his right arm under the right arm pit – looking as if he is about to perform *The Heimlich Maneuver*. The Doctor then turns his head toward Nicole…

"Can you help me get him out of the vehicle?"

"I was afraid you were going to ask me that."

"The hazards of the job I'm afraid."

"What would you like me to do?"

"As I pull him out of the vehicle, grabs his legs and help me guide him down onto the sheet."

"Got it" replies Nicole as she positions herself between the hinge-area of the open car door and the victim.

The Doctor starts walking backward while holding the victim. Nicole grabs the victim's legs just above the knees as they slide off of the car seat and through the doorway; she then helps the Doctor lower the body onto the sheet.

Returning to a standing position Nicole looks down, scans her clothes from sternum to stilettos, or in this particular case… steel-toed shoes, and sees that she is now completely covered in slime and filth.

Nicole makes a mental note to herself, *"Disgusting. As soon as I get home the shoes are getting hosed-off, and everything else is going directly into the trash can."*

Doctor Watson scans the body and makes an initial observation aloud, "I can see why everyone thought this guy was a dummy, every inch of his skin is covered… flight suit, gloves, mask…"

"Hey Doctor" says Nicole, "Not that I'm looking forward to it, but Jake asked me to check his pockets for any possible ID."

"I can help you with that."

"Thank God."

The victim is on his back, with Nicole on her knees to the victim's left and Doctor Watson similarly positioned to the victim's right.

Nicole's first thought is to come up with a way to avoid, or at the very least reduce, the potential of actually having to reach inside the victim's pockets. Her brainstorm – the patented pat-down technique, not unlike the 'frisking' that Levine jokingly suggested - she figures a simple pat-down should let her know if there's anything in the pocket to retrieve.

While Nicole is contemplating her 'plan of attack' the Doctor gently uses his right index finger to lift up the edge of the victim's right pocket in the area of the flight suit that would equate to a front pants pocket. The Doctor then slowly slides his left hand into the pocket, gently feels around for any objects, and then removes his hand.

"Nothing in this one" states the Doctor.

"I was wondering" says Nicole, "couldn't we pat-down the pocket first to see if we feel anything, and if we do *then* check the inside of the pocket?"

"I don't want to introduce any possible impact to the body that could interfere with my ability to determine the cause of death. In fact, it's highly likely that the victim's body has been completely untouched since whatever event caused his demise… there could be a litany of evidence for me to discover that I want to ensure remains undisturbed."

"I hadn't thought of that" replies Nicole, who then says to herself somewhat dejectedly, *"So much for my brainstorm…"*

The Doctor continues checking the one remaining frontal pocket on his side of the victim - the right chest pocket. Nicole follows the Doctor's lead with the pockets on her side of the victim… hip pocket, chest pocket, and on her side only… a pocket on the upper left sleeve near the victim's tricep. All pockets checked thus far are empty.

"Before we roll him over to check the back pockets I'm going to unzip his flight suit" says the Doctor.

"Why's that?"

"Primarily to look for any obvious signs of trauma such as a gunshot wound, knife wound, visible blunt force impact like broken ribs - that sort of thing."

"I guess we'd also be able to see if he's wearing pants or a shirt underneath with pockets we'll need to check."

"True, but if that's the case I'll wait until I get him to autopsy to go through them."

"I like the sound of that."

The Doctor grabs the zipper up near the victim's throat and slowly starts to unzip his flight suit.

Nicole watches, albeit with a look akin to a grimace, as Doctor Watson unzips the flight suit down to the victim's waist. It turns out Nicole's anxiety was based more on anticipation of something completely grotesque than on reality – the victim is wearing a T-shirt and tighty-whiteys. *"A scary sight under normal circumstances..."* Nicole thinks to herself concerning any visual of tighty-whiteys, *"but a thousand times better than the gruesome slimy flesh of this poor guy."*

The Doctor examines the limited visible areas of the victim – nothing obvious as to the cause of death.

With the Doctor back out of the way Nicole takes this opportunity to capture more pictures of the victim.

"Time to turn him over" says the Doctor. "Let's roll him over in my direction, but I'll come over to your side so we can roll him together... you push from under his hips and I'll do the same from underneath the shoulder blade and upper back."

The Doctor and Nicole roll the victim over and then check his two back pockets – nothing.

Nicole captures a few more shots of the victim, and then the Doctor and she roll the victim back on his back just as Levine is approaching.

Nicole looks up toward Levine and says, "No ID on him – we checked every pocket."

"I had a feeling we weren't going to be that lucky" says Levine, "I guess we'll just have to wait for DNA results."

Nicole returns to capturing photos of the inside of the car, specifically the areas that are now uncovered where the victim had been located.

Levine turns his attention to Doctor Watson, "What do you see Doc?"

"There's nothing evident on his clothing like a bullet or knife wound" responds the Doctor.

"So nothing suspicious then... death by natural causes?" responds Levine sarcastically.

The Doctor grins and replies, "As always Jake, your sense of humor never fails to make its presence known."

"I wouldn't want to disappoint. Besides, you know I'm a totally different animal when it comes to hunting down a perp."

"That's true; I'd say you're like a police dog – loyal and even playful with their handler, but ruthless in their dedication to the pursuit and take-down of a perpetrator."

"You know me well Doc, and I like that analogy."

Levine thinks for a moment and then adds... "But I hope you're not implying that *the Director* is my *handler*."

"Well 'playful' is not the proper adjective when it comes to your coworkers... more like throwing zingers and flipping them crap, and I'm sure the Director gets his fair share just like everyone else."

"I have to agree with you on that."

"No, I was thinking more along the lines of *your wife* being your handler."

"Now *that* makes sense; and I'm sure *she* would agree."

"Most anyone that knows you two would agree."

"What can I say; I'm a lucky man."

Brandi walks up behind Levine and slaps him on the back, saying, "I'm guessing she's feeling pretty lucky as well."

Levine is surprised and turns around; he has a *"Brandi paying me a compliment??"* look of disbelief on his face.

"And don't tell anyone I said that" adds Brandi.

"They wouldn't believe me anyway" replies Levine.

Levine turns back to Doctor Watson and says, "So Doc... back to our vic?"

"I'll know much more once I get him to Autopsy, but there is *one* thing that's curious."

"What's that?"

"There appears to be some type of residue on the inside of the mask."

"Sea-growth?"

"No, this is a man-made substance... perhaps a lubricant, adhesive, or something toxic used against the victim. We'll need a chemical analysis to determine the specific compound."

"The guys at the lab will be looking forward to solving *that* riddle" adds Brandi, "This case is getting more interesting at every turn."

9

Conroy and Nicole have taken enough pictures of the crime scene that, between the two of them, could fill a family photo album. With this in mind they head over to Levine to give him a status report.

"Hey Jake" says Conroy, "We've covered every accessible square inch of the crime scene."

"Including as much of the vic as possible within the confines of the situation" adds Nicole, "You know... before the Doc gets him to autopsy."

Doctor Watson, still kneeling next to the victim, looks up and gives Levine a thumbs-up to indicate that he agrees with Nicole's assessment, followed by, "I concur."

"Sounds good" replies Levine, who then directs a statement to Conroy and Nicole, "But you two look like you have something else on your minds."

"Well, there's been all this talk about the vic being launched from an Aircraft Carrier" responds Conroy, "But what if the car was dumped from another vessel?"

"And they were hoping that if it was ever found they'd think it *had* been launched from an Aircraft Carrier?" adds Nicole.

"The Coast Guard is supposed to be looking into other ships within the area that they reeled-in the car" says Levine, who then makes eye contact with Nicole, "But if we find out that there were *no* launchings of a car from an Aircraft Carrier then how about following-up on that?"

"Will do" responds Nicole, who then pulls out her smart phone and jots-down this additional task.

"If this thing *was* launched from an Aircraft Carrier the killer went to a hell of a lot of trouble to pull it off" remarks Conroy.

"No kidding" says Nicole "Murder the guy, drag his body into the car, stuff him behind the wheel in full regalia like he's a NASCAR driver, get the car out to the catapult, and get him launched."

"All without being noticed while within the confined acreage of a ship" adds Levine; "*And* while surrounded by *who-the-hell-knows* how many people."

"To have everything fall in line *just right*" says Conroy, "you'd likely need an accomplice, if not more than one, to even have a *remote* chance of achieving your objective."

"The difficulty of successfully pulling off a scheme of such complexity sure seems to lend credence to the idea of the car being dumped by another vessel" says Nicole.

The wheels are turning inside Conroy's head, who responds, "You know who'd be the *perfect* vessel to pull this off?"

"Who's that?" asks Levine.

Conroy looks around to make sure no one other than the investigating team is nearby, and then says somewhat quietly, "The one who *discovered* it" he replies, with air-quotes on the word 'discovered', "No one would suspect *them*."

"You make a great point Slade" responds Levine, "but it seems unlikely based on reports I got from the Coast Guard."

"You've already gotten reports from the Coast Guard on this trawler?" replies Conroy.

"Yeah, I wanted to know *who* and *what* we might be dealing with – a part of my preliminary investigation" says Levine. "They said that they had performed a pre-underway inspection *and* that they have all of the trawler's movements tracked via GPS... from hoisting anchor to docking at Fiddler's Cove - nothing suspicious." And then he adds... "But we'll do our due diligence and keep them on our list as possible suspects until we can officially exclude them."

"So, if it *was* launched from a Carrier why would someone go through such a high risk series of actions?" asks Nicole, "Why not just kill him and throw him overboard in the dark of night?"

"Although about a hundred times less complex and equally less risky than the idea of a catapult launch" says Levine, "just throwing someone overboard is not as simple as it might seem."

"No?"

"Well, first of all you've got to be *out of sight & sound* of anyone else… not an easy task by itself… *and* it creates a potential problem of its own."

"What's that?"

"If there is *seemingly* no one around it also means the victim and you are essentially the *only* ones around; thus you'd be *the central focus* of any person that might happen your way, let alone someone you are completely unaware of because they are outside of your line of sight."

"So you're saying that to murder and throw the victim overboard is virtually impossible."

"Nothing's impossible; but I'm thinking about the *only* way would be a crewman getting their prey out on a catwalk, kill them, toss them overboard, and then hope that no lookout watches hear the splash as they hit the water."

"There are lookout watches to contend with as well?"

"Yep" says Conroy as he interjects himself into the conversation, "They're stationed round-the-clock."

"Plus, if a body *had* been successfully dumped overboard the Morning Muster would identify not only that *someone* was missing but exactly *who* that someone was" says Levine, "And then a full-scale investigation would ensue."

"*And* the killer would still be onboard… not a great 'get-away plan'" says Conroy, who then adds… "About your only hope would be convincing authorities that the person *accidentally fell* overboard, and that no one saw you with the victim at or near the time they went overboard, *and* that the body is not recovered."

"All of that *and* you'd have to rely on the body *not* being recovered?" asks Nicole.

"Hard to explain that it was an accident if they had a knife wound, evidence of strangulation, blunt force trauma, or whatever method was utilized to kill them" responds Conroy.

"Unless you managed a drug overdose that didn't look suspicious" adds Levine.

"Geez... considering all of the pitfalls we've discussed, how would murdering someone during a Tiger Cruise be any less risky?" asks Nicole.

"On a Tiger Cruise you've got hundreds of additional personnel who are not necessarily involved in a rigorous daily muster" responds Levine, "and thus easier to hide that someone was missing."

"But in order to ensure your victim is not identified as *missing*" says Nicole, "wouldn't the killer have to be their *sponsor*?"

"Nic makes a great point Jake" adds Conroy, "Even if they avoided detection while on the ship someone would surely file a *Missing Persons Report* at some point afterward, and the sponsor would automatically be the prime suspect."

"We're *way* off on a tangent here" responds Levine, "We *know* that *this guy* was strapped behind the wheel of this car and *not* tossed over the side of a ship, so '*Man Overboard*' scenarios may be something to consider on a future case, but they have no validity whatsoever in regards to *this one*."

"But checking Missing Persons Reports is in order, correct?" asks Conroy.

"Absolutely" responds Levine, "Add that to your list."

Conroy nods and starts to add it to his list of tasks. As he is writing he ponders the discussions of various scenarios for a moment. He stops and says, "Here's a crazy thought for you... how about a *suicide*?"

"Suicide??" says Nicole, "The only crazy thing about *that* idea is you bringing it up as a possible option."

"Maybe, but hear me out on this" responds Conroy. "We know that about a dozen things need to go *just right* for one person to kill the guy, load him in the car, and get him launched without being noticed."

"Yeah" replies Nicole.

"What if the guy wanted to off-himself and decided to dress up like a dummy and play dead, so to speak, long enough to get launched?"

"The guys involved in the launch are going to *know* it's *not* a dummy" Nicole counters.

"Remember, the Doc said every inch of his skin was covered" responds Conroy.

"Yeah, but you can't fake 'not breathing' or the total flaccidity or rigidity of your body - depending on a dummy's construction - needed to make it *appear* you're a dummy" Levine interjects.

"Flaccidity? Is that even a word?" replies Conroy.

Brandi, while overhearing the conversation, has been mum up to this point as none of the subject matter has pertained to her area of expertise. However, she can't resist such a perfect opportunity to make a smartass remark aimed directly at Conroy...

"Yeah Slade, that's what happens to *you* when you've had too much to drink... or so I've heard" she says with a shit-eating grin.

Nicole and Levine give Brandi a funny look, then Conroy, then back to Brandi... it's a *"what the heck's been going on between you two?"* kind of look.

"Don't give me that look!" says Brandi "It's a joke! Sheesh, what's wrong with you two?!"

Conroy gives Brandi a 'furrowed-eyebrow with a half-smile' acknowledgment of a well-executed slam, and then gets back to making his point... "Okay, well maybe an *assisted* suicide then" he replies, "After all, we're supposed to investigate ALL possibilities, not just the typical or convenient ones, right?"

"Yes Slade, we'll keep all options open" responds Levine.

"If the guy *was* launched" says Nicole, "well, hiding a body in a car that is to be catapulted overboard... I must say it seems like they'd figured-out the perfect disposal of the body."

"Or so they thought" counters Levine.

"Yeah, I guess you're right" says Nicole as she realizes it *wasn't* the perfect disposal of a body after all – considering the circumstances.

Brandi reaches into her 'Bag of tricks' as she calls it, and pulls out a large round mirror attached to a rod. She grabs the rod and extends it telescopically to approximately four-feet in length. She then starts to run the mirror underneath the car, like a SWAT team scanning for a bomb or other hidden device at a high-security installation. She starts just forward of the rear wheel on the passenger-side, extends it directly across to the driver's-side, and then starts to zig-zag her way forward. She gets to the forward cross-member, near where the engine and transmission connect, pauses for a moment, and then moves backward to where the driveshaft enters the transmission spleen, and then forward again; and stops.

"Hmmm... this is interesting" says Brandi.

"What's that?" asks Levine.

"There *is* a hook-like mechanism... or at least it could be. But I'll need to match it up to an actual catapult launch-chock to determine if that's the intended purpose."

"If this thing really *was* launched they're lucky the catapult didn't rip the car apart and reveal the body right there on the Flight Deck."

"How's that, Jake?" asks Nicole.

"Have you ever felt the force of a catapult launch?"

"I can't say that I have."

"We're talking several hundred pounds of steam pressure launching a thirty-thousand pound aircraft designed to handle such a force."

Conroy intercedes... "And it feels like your head's about to be ripped off as you go from zero to 175 miles per hour in 2½ seconds."

Levine continues to make his point... "This car weighs what, three-thousand pounds maybe?"

"I see what you mean" replies Nicole.

"So, do you think they got lucky? Or could it be someone that worked with the catapults?" asks Conroy.

Levine gives Conroy a glance that almost qualifies as '*The Look*'.

"Catapult operators" says Conroy as he jots down another task... "Got it."

"And Engineering" Levine adds, "They supply the steam to the catapults."

Conroy nods... and jots.

"There also appears to be some extra bracing under here, likely to make the chassis more rigid" says Brandi. "I'll be able to make a detailed analysis of it once we get it to the CSI garage."

"It's looking more and more like this thing actually *was* launched from an Aircraft Carrier" says Conroy.

10

Levine walks into the office and takes a glance at the triad of analog clocks on the wall: One to the far left for East Coast or "Headquarters" time with a label underneath it that reads "D.C."; one to the far right with "Pearl" underneath it stipulating "Hawaii" time; and one in the middle stipulating the West Coast, or more specifically "Pacific", time. The middle clock is larger than the other two, *"apparently so you don't forget where the hell you are"* Levine thinks to himself while shaking his head. According to the large clock, and Levine's watch, it is zero-six-thirty. The shift doesn't officially start for another half-hour, but Levine always likes to get a good thirty minutes or more of prep time before starting his work day so that he can efficiently and effectively mete out assignments at the 7:15 team meeting.

Barely ten minutes have passed when Levine's cell phone rings - it's Brandi.

"Hey Brandi, what's the good news?" asks Levine as he answers his phone.

"I just saved a ton of money by switching my car insurance" responds Brandi in her typical smartass way.

"You know they haven't been running those commercial for eons now, right?"

"Yeah, but you still got the joke."

"I'll give you that one. But know that my brain is not fully engaged enough for witty banter at this time of morning."

"Sounds like *someone* is in need of a triple-shot espresso."

Levine figures there must be a purpose for Brandi's call other than giving him crap before he's even had his morning coffee.

"I'm assuming you have some initial info on our Seagoing Sedan?" asks Levine.

"I figured you'd want an update for your morning meeting" replies Brandi, "and I've done enough research for you to eliminate the ENTERPRISE 1978 WestPac cruise as your source car."

"Yeah? How'd you determine that?"

"I thought your brain wasn't functioning well enough to comprehend details?"

"Witty banter – No; but comprehension - I can handle that."

"Well, I tried to find information... specifically pictures... of what a car submerged for thirty-some-odd-years in seawater might look like. Eventually I found an interesting corollary, the 'Underwater Car Cemetery' at Legrena, Greece."

"I'm guessing these underwater graveyard cars were in much worse shape than ours?"

"Oh yeah, after *that* amount of time it would be much more deteriorated, and fully engulfed in sea-life. I'll be able to give you a more definitive estimate as to how long it's been submerged after I analyze the metallurgical impact of various corrosive properties, the breakdown of soft goods, the extent of sea-life, and other such parameters. But I thought you'd like this piece of info for starters."

"You know me well... thanks!"

"And while you're continuing to try to get your brain engaged I'm off to attempt to exorcise more demons from this rust bucket."

"Sounds good; keep me posted."

Levine hangs up and immediately grabs the list he had started. He lines out *'Possibly launched from the Enterprise?'* and then continues to add tasks, questions, and actions:

~ *Aviator with the call-sign of Snuffy? - Nic*

~ *Any recent launchings of a car from a Carrier? – Nic*

~ *Ships in the area if not launched from a Carrier - Nic*

~ *Info / maker of the mask used in bank robberies – Slade*

(coord w/CSI lab for mask source)

~ *Substance inside the mask – CSI lab*

~ *Squadron insignia - Slade*

~ *Missing Person's report? – Slade*

~ *Hook-like mechanism vs. catapult launch-chock – Brandi*

~ *Victim's flight suit and helmet – CSI lab*

~ *Victim's cause of death – Doc*

~ *Victim ID – CSI lab*

Levine starts the meeting by informing Conroy and Nicole the update from Brandi: No Enterprise launching for this particular Plymouth. He begins to address the next item on the agenda when Nicole's cell phone rings. She looks at the caller ID and then looks back to Levine and says, "Pac-Fleet." Levine gives her the raised-eyebrow *"well answer it"* look.

"Special Agent McKenna" says Nicole into her phone. She gives a few head nods, raised eyebrows, and several murmurs of comprehension, ending with "Thanks Commander."

Nicole hangs up and relays to Levine and Conroy, "Pac-Fleet reports there was a launching of a car from the USS SEADRAGON six weeks ago."

By the look on his face it is evident that Levine likes what he's hearing. He then takes his list and lines-out the associated entry about a possible Carrier launching.

"Our first stroke of luck on this case" responds Conroy, "That's *got* to be our source."

Nicole's optimism perks up as well, figuring they've made a major leap in their investigation… "So, if the Ship reported a missing crewmember then we've likely ID'd our vic" she proclaims with a high level of confidence.

"And if *not*, then he must be one of the 'Tigers'" adds Conroy, "Either way, we've whittled it down to a couple of possibilities."

"You've narrowed it down to those two options, have you?" replies Levine.

"What other option could there be?" asks Nicole.

"Yeah" adds Conroy, "either a missing crewmember or a missing Tiger… that pretty much covers who could have been launched."

"Well, for one" adds Levine, "you forgot about a crewmember who was *supposed* to be on *leave* in order to make room shipboard for the Tigers."

"You mean they were supposed to be on leave but instead were murdered and launched?" replies Nicole, "And thus they would *not* have been listed as a 'Man Overboard' or 'missing' because they weren't supposed to be on the ship at that time anyway?"

"You've got it" says Levine.

"You're right" says Nicole, "I hadn't thought of that possibility."

"So, someone who was supposed to be on leave, when in reality they never left the ship" remarks Conroy, who then thinks back to Nicole's image of a car being launched from an Aircraft Carrier and adds "Well, technically they left the ship, just not in the usual manner."

"Yeah" adds Nicole, "Behind the wheel of an old Plymouth."

"Before we start dotting the "i's" and crossing the "t's" on this case" remarks Levine, "realize that just because the SEADRAGON launched a car doesn't mean that *this* is the car they launched. Right now all we've got is the next step in our investigation."

"So what's our next step?" asks Conroy.

"For you two it's *continuing to work on your list of tasks*" replies Levine.

"Alright" replies Nicole, "I'll start with the Carrier Air Wings out of Lemoore for an Aviator called '*Snuffy*'."

"And I'll see if I can find anything on that insignia" says Conroy. "What about you, Jake?"

Levine grabs his cell phone, scrolls through his contact list, and hits '*Send*'. On the other end of the line he hears… "*Quarterdeck USS*

SEADRAGON... Officer of the Deck, Lieutenant Briscoe speaking... how may I help you Sir or Ma'am?"

11

Levine and Conroy approach the Entry Gate at Naval Air Station North Island. After a vehicle and ID check courtesy of the gate guard, Levine and Conroy motor through the entryway and immediately observe the USS SEADRAGON moored bow-south at the pier adjacent to Quay Road.

Levine finds a convenient parking spot near the bow of the ship; it is marked with a small sign *USS SEADRAGON - Commanding Officer's Guest*.

"That would be us" remarks Levine as he pulls into the spot, "It's nice to have friends in high places."

"You're friends with the CO?" asks Conroy with a smattering of surprise in his voice.

"Seriously Slade?" responds Levine in a tone of disbelief, "It's a figure of speech – we're official guests."

Conroy feels a bit *'the fool'*... not the first time while working with Levine, and mentally adds it to his list of *'learning experiences'*.

As Conroy exits the car he pauses for a moment, scans the Ship from bow to stern, and proclaims, "I never lose my sense of awe at the sight of these Aircraft Carriers... unbelievably majestic."

"You've got to love the beauty of ninety-thousand tons of diplomacy" adds Levine.

Levine and Conroy travel past the Enlisted Brow – a dual gangway located on an aircraft elevator that has been lowered to the level of the hangar bay. There's a mass exodus of sailors filling the gangway like cattle being funneled through a gate... it is 1600 hours and the liberty bell has rung.

"Thank God we don't have to make our way through *that* stampede" remarks Conroy.

"Rank has its privileges" says Levine.

"And a Federal Agent's badge doesn't hurt" adds Conroy.

Levine and Conroy make their way up the Officer's Brow - a single gangway leading to the Ship's Quarterdeck. At the end of the gangway is a Petty Officer, clad in his service dress whites, poised to greet personnel requesting permission to come aboard.

To the petty officer's left is a Lieutenant – the Officer of the Deck… more commonly known as the 'O-O-D' as the seemingly-required military acronym would dictate. He is also clad in his service dress whites. The Lieutenant is standing behind a podium constructed of wood, unstained but varnished, with the ship's logo as its centerpiece. He is surveying all who approach the Ship's Quarterdeck, like a bouncer stationed at the entryway of an exclusive club to ensure that no malcontents shall enter. In the O-O-D's case it's not about malcontents, at least not officially, it's about rank… and you must have the proper pedigree to pass through this hallowed entryway.

Levine and Conroy are met with a snappy salute from the Petty Officer as they step off of the gangway and onto the Quarterdeck.

"NCIS Special Agents Levine and Conroy; we have a meeting with the Captain" states Levine as both Conroy and he flash their badges and ID.

"Yes Sir" responds the Petty Officer as he drops his salute.

The Lieutenant gives a nod of approval aimed toward Levine and Conroy, or perhaps it was toward the Petty Officer, Levine isn't quite sure.

Immediately following the Lieutenant's nod of approval, a young and sharply-dressed Marine, a Lance Corporal, emerges from behind the Lieutenant. The Lance Corporal steps forward to address Levine, "The Captain is expecting you, Sir - If you will follow me, please."

Levine notices the Lance Corporal is wearing an epaulet on one shoulder; apparently denoting him as being in specific service to the Ship's Captain.

Levine and Conroy follow the Lance Corporal from the Quarterdeck inboard onto the hangar bay, and then almost immediately back outboard toward a closed hatch-door with a sign *Admiral's Passageway: 0-5 and above only.* The military translation: Commander and above for the Navy and Coast Guard; Lieutenant Colonel and above for the Army, Air Force, and Marines; GS-14 and above for Department of Defense Civilians.

The Lance Corporal opens the hatch, holds it while Levine and Conroy enter, and then re-closes the latch behind them.

Conroy looks around for the so-called 'passageway' - noting that the area is more like a vestibule, essentially void of anything except a ladder to the immediate left.

Levine can see the confusion on Conroy's face and provides clarification, "It's essentially a vertical passageway – a stairwell if you will - heading up to the Oh-Three level."

The Lance Corporal heads up the ladder – Levine and Conroy right behind.

It is not your typical ship's ladder... every inch of metal is polished, with solid-wood handrails that look like stained and varnished teak, and each end of the handrail is wrapped in nautically-styled braided rope.

At the Oh-Three level the Lance Corporal leads Levine and Conroy through a couple of turns, and then through a door into the Captain's In-Port Cabin.

The Captain's In-Port Cabin is certainly befitting the Man and his position... the leader of a crew upwards of 3,000 men and women assigned to the ship itself... 5,500 strong with the Air Wing aboard. Pristine and well-appointed, the area receiving guests consists of a large table near the cabin's entry, and a lounge-area to the far end. The table is not unlike what you'd expect to see in the White House Situation Room… formally attired and seating twelve, with the Captain at the head of the table, and the Executive Officer, referred to by Captain and crew alike as 'the XO', to his immediate left. Remaining seats are typically filled by other Senior Officers and high-ranking guests, whereas additional attendees would be seated in less-formal chairs placed around the periphery. The lounge-area consists of a sofa, coffee table, lounge chairs, a formal cabinet graced with mementos of the Ship, a large picture of the Ship lighted by sconces on either side, and three port-hole style windows in an homage to Naval vessels of a bygone era. Not 'opulence' by any stretch of the imagination, but the Captain's In-Port Cabin is definitely *'U.S. Navy protocol'* at its finest.

12

Two Commanders clad in their khakis walk into the Captain's In-Port Cabin. As Levine and Conroy approach to greet the officers, in walks the Captain, also dressed in khakis. The two Commanders pop to attention.

"Carry on" states the Captain.

At age 49 the Captain seems almost too young to hold a position of such high authority, but then again most Commanding Officers of an Aircraft Carrier have been on the advancement *'fast track'* since they were junior officers, being recognized as having *'the right stuff'* early-on in their career. And although he may seem a bit young for such a high level of responsibility, he exudes what the military calls *'Command Presence'*. It is no surprise that a high percentage of Aircraft Carrier CO's go on to achieve the rank of Admiral.

As the Commanding Officer of an Aircraft Carrier the Captain is an Aviator... a 'must' if you are going to command a vessel whose primary mission is to launch and recover aircraft in support of sorties in the defense of your country. And, as all current Carriers are nuclear-powered, the Captain is also a graduate of the Navy's Nuclear Power School and Prototype Training. After all, an understanding of the propulsion system driving one of your country's most important assets is critical.

The Captain approaches Levine and reaches out to shake hands. "Special Agent Levine?" he says, "Dan Sheridan."

"Captain" responds Levine as they release their grip. Levine then nods toward Conroy and introduces him to the Captain, "Special Agent Conroy."

"Agent Conroy" says the Captain as he shakes Conroy's hand.

"Captain" responds Conroy.

The Captain then turns to his left to introduce his subordinates.

"My XO, Commander Burke" he says, "And the Air Boss, Commander Williams."

The XO is an up-and-coming version of the Captain. He's age 46, is also an Aviator, and has just completed his Naval Nuclear Power and Prototype Training. It's always obvious to staff and students at the Navy Nuclear Training facilities when an aviator is assigned to the program; after all, they are in their 40's with the rank of Commander while their fellow students are mid-twenties Ensigns and Lieutenant J.G.'s that were selected for the Naval Nuclear Power Program right after receiving their commission. Another difference is that young Nuclear Officers will become Watch Officers – overseeing operations of the reactor plant of a nuclear-powered vessel, while the periodic aviator in the program is there simply to understand the nuclear power plant of the Aircraft Carrier that he or she will one day command.

If the XO does well during this assignment he will receive his promotion to the rank of Captain, obtain command of a deep-draft vessel, and will one day take command of his own Aircraft Carrier.

The Air Boss, age 54, is the oldest of the three - and he looks it. Greying, balding, and not as spry as the Captain or XO he looks like he's been run through the ringer a few times over the years. Although obtaining the position of Air Boss is a great achievement, this is surely his last assignment before retirement.

Levine, understanding the hierarchy of the Ship's command, reaches out to shake hands with the XO.

"XO" he says as he shakes hands and releases his grip.

He then reaches his hand out to the Air Boss and acknowledges him as well... "Air Boss" he says.

Conroy then steps forward to shake hands with the XO and Air Boss.

Now that pleasantries have been exchanged the Captain gets down to business...

"I understand a car was fished out of the ocean that you believe might be our Tiger Cruise launch?" says the Captain to Levine.

"Yes, Sir" replies Levine.

"And there was a body inside?"

"Wearing a flight suit with the name '*Snuffy*'... we're assuming an Aviator's call-sign."

The Captain looks toward the XO and Air Boss.

"Snuffy??" replies the Air Boss with a hint of surprise, "Uh... no Aviators with that call-sign, Sir."

"And we had no missing members of the crew during the Tiger Cruise" adds the XO.

The Captain looks back toward Levine and asks, "What if it came from another vessel trying to mimic our launch as a means of diversion?"

"We're looking into that Captain, but it *does* seem to have a hook-like mechanism attached to the chassis that could provide a connection-point for a catapult."

"So, if it *is* our launch, then someone managed to get a body inside without being noticed."

"The victim was wearing a mask, likely to hide that it was a real person rather than a dummy."

"Since we had no unaccounted-for crewmembers you must be assuming it was one of the 'Tigers'?" asks the XO.

"Or a crewmember who was supposed to be on leave" responds Levine.

"Assumed to be on leave when in fact they were murdered and launched?" asks the Captain.

"That's one of the possibilities, Sir" replies Levine; who then asks... "Has anyone gone on leave that has not returned?"

The Captain looks toward the XO.

"We have two sailors currently listed as UA" responds the XO, "Petty Officer Jamison and Airman Apprentice Sewell."

"Coincidentally" adds the Air Boss, "both sailors are assigned to the Air Department as part of aircraft launch and recovery."

"So they could have been involved in your Tiger Cruise launch?" asks Levine.

"That's entirely possible" replies the Air Boss.

"One of them could be the victim" proclaims Conroy.

"Or one or both could be the perpetrator" adds Levine.

The Captain looks toward the Air Boss and says, "Airman Apprentice Sewell... the name sounds familiar."

"I believe he may have been up to see you for Captain's Mast during the deployment, Sir" replies the Air Boss.

The Captain nods his head with a look of recollection; along with a hint of displeasure. He then looks back toward Levine...

"We'll give you anything you need on our missing sailors" says the Captain, "What else can we do for you?"

"We'll need a list of the 'Tigers' that rode the Ship" responds Levine, "With any luck a 'Missing Persons' report may have been filed which could provide us investigative avenues beyond our forensic analyses."

"XO can get that list for you, along with any other riders we may have had... local politicians, vendors, contractors, the Channel 5 News team... you name it."

"I appreciate that, Captain."

"Anything else?"

"The car has, what appears to be, a squadron insignia" says Levine as he shows a picture of the insignia to the Captain. The XO and Air Boss move closer to view the picture as well.

"That insignia does not match any of our squadrons" says the Air Boss, "but I couldn't tell you exactly what insignia the launch team used, it simply had to be approved by the Tiger Cruise Launch Coordinator."

"I'd like to interview the crewmen involved in the launch" says Levine.

"They should all be on-duty. I can escort you to their work area when we're done here" replies the Air Boss.

The Air Boss suddenly realizes he has inadvertently broken protocol and turns to the Captain, "If that's alright with you, Captain?"

"Make it happen" says the Captain.

"Yes, Sir" responds the Air Boss.

Levine holds up the picture again, pointing to the area beneath the cartoon-like tiger and asks, "What about these letters and numbers underneath… they appear to read *'RVA eleven tack seventeen'*… does that mean anything?"

"It's *similar* to the nomenclature for a Navy squadron identifier" says the Captain, "but it doesn't follow the specific format."

The XO takes a closer look and says, "If someone was going to *invent* an insignia they'd likely come up with something similar to a real one; I'm thinking it's something like that."

"Mind if I take a closer look?" asks the Air Boss.

Levine hands the picture to the Air Boss.

The Air Boss pulls out his reading glasses, scans the picture closely and says, "You know… if what appears to be an *'eleven'* is actually an *'H'* *then* the formatting would be in line with a Navy squadron."

The Air Boss hands the picture, and his 'readers', to the Captain.

"I see what you mean" says the Captain, "There are no *current* squadrons using that designation, but some of the old Reconnaissance Fighter squadrons might have used it – I'd start there."

"I appreciate that" replies Levine, who then adds… "I'm curious Captain, what was the impetus for the launch?"

"It was just one of many activities performed to entertain the Tigers" responds the Captain, who then turns toward the XO and Air Boss.

The XO and Air Boss understand the Captain's non-verbal directive… *'provide details to Agents Levine and Conroy'*.

"Nightly Navy-themed movies like 'Top Gun' and 'The Caine Mutiny' on a large screen in the hangar bay" says the XO.

"Observing flight ops from both the Island and catwalks around the flight deck" says the Air Boss.

"A flyover representing all of our aircraft: Helo's, fighter jets, bombers" says the XO, "With one of the Super Hornets breaking the sound barrier at the moment he flew over the Ship."

"And most everyone's personal favorite" says the Air Boss, "a couple of the Super Hornets flying a few miles off of the ship's port side and dropping live ordnance in the ocean."

"The explosions... the shockwave... they loved it" adds the XO.

"Wow" says Conroy, "How does one get to be a guest on a Tiger Cruise?"

"I'm sure we can arrange something on return from our next deployment Agent Conroy" says the Captain.

"That would make my entire year Sir, thank you" responds Conroy.

"The Air Boss here gave us the idea for the car launch" says the XO as he head nods toward the Air Boss.

"The picture of the ENTERPRISE launch was all over the internet, I wasn't the only one familiar with it, so I can't really take the credit" responds the Air Boss.

"I'm guessing we saw the same picture on the internet" replies Levine, "The one showing the car flying off the front of the flight deck?"

"That's the one" responds the Air Boss.

"Although it was extremely unlikely to be the car *we* found, we *did* include the ENTERPRISE launching as part of our initial investigation, but our automotive forensic expert has been able to eliminate that car as the source" adds Levine.

"I see that you're attempting to cover all bases" says the Captain.

"Yes, Sir" responds Levine.

"Anyway" says the XO, "we thought a launching would be a great homage to the ENTERPRISE launch back in 1978."

"And with the ENTERPRISE's fairly recent inactivation it seemed like a fitting tribute" says the Captain.

Once again nodding toward the Air Boss, the XO adds... "Air Boss said he was sure his guys could pull it off."

"All we needed was the go-ahead from the Strike Group Commander, Admiral Pierce" says the Captain, "And he gave us the thumbs-up."

"It was a great morale booster for the crew after such a long deployment" says the XO.

"And the Tigers loved it" adds the Air Boss.

"Needless to say, if it turns out that there was an actual person behind the wheel it would be an absolute travesty" says the Captain.

"Yes, Sir" replies Levine.

"And we will keep this under wraps while you investigate… *correct* Agent Levine?" asks the Captain, with an obvious hint behind the question.

"Of course, Captain" replies Levine, "And I'm hoping that word has NOT gotten out that a body was found in the launch car."

"No one beyond the three of us" responds the Captain, who then looks toward the XO and Air Boss with more of a warning than a question… "Correct, gentlemen?"

The XO and Air Boss respond in unison, "Yes, Sir."

"In order to maintain the integrity of our investigation I'd like to keep it that way" replies Levine.

"You have my word on it" responds the Captain.

"I appreciate that" says Levine; "Thanks for your time Captain." He then looks toward the XO and Air Boss, "Gentlemen."

The Captain, XO, and Air Boss all give a nod of acknowledgment, and then Levine turns to make his exit.

"Agent Levine" says the Captain.

Levine turns back around and responds, "Sir?"

"If anyone *did* commit such a heinous crime on *my* Ship" says the Captain, "Well… you know where I'm going with this…"

"Yes, Sir" responds Levine, "We won't stop until we get the bastard."

"Probably better for you to find him than me" replies The Captain.

Although Levine is sure the Captain would *not* actually take matters into his own hands if given the opportunity, Levine gets the point and responds, "Understood, Sir."

13

Levine, Conroy, and the Air Boss step out of the Captain's In-Port Cabin. Standing there waiting for them is Brandi, with a small metal briefcase in hand.

"I see you got my voice mail" says Levine to Brandi, and then points to her briefcase, "Your launch-chock assessment kit?"

"You know it" replies Brandi as she holds it up.

Levine then proceeds to make introductions... "Forensic Scientist Brandi Matthews, this is the Air Boss - Commander Williams."

"Ms. Matthews" says the Air Boss as he reaches out to shake hands.

"Commander" responds Brandi as she acknowledges him and then releases her grip.

Levine turns to the Air Boss and says, "Brandi is our forensic expert on *everything automotive*; she's going to help us figure out if the Plymouth that she has at the CSI garage is the same car you all launched."

"Along with any trace evidence that might help us identify our killer" adds Brandi.

Levine turns back to Brandi and says, "The Commander is going to escort us to the *'Cat Shop'* to talk to the launch crew, and will also set you up to check out a catapult launch-chock, and Slade to talk to the catapult operators."

The group traverses their way through the series of 'knee-knockers' – the slang for the oval pass-throughs, or portals, that define the Oh-Three level bow-to-stern passageways at each port-starboard bulkhead. Although Levine is quite familiar with the slang, as he passes through the portals he notes that *'shin*-knocker' would be a more appropriate term based on the height of the lower lip the oval.

Unscathed by the knee-knockers at the Oh-Three level passageway, the group arrives at the Catapult Shop, more commonly referred to as the 'Cat Shop'.

Entering the Cat Shop, Levine sees a Chief Petty Officer at the forefront, and a number of crewmen in the background. From the looks on their faces they all appear to have been awaiting the arrival of Levine and his team.

The Air Boss introduces Levine, Conroy, and Brandi to the Chief Petty Officer - Chief Greene. Chief Greene is wearing khaki pants that are the standard working uniform for all Chiefs and Officers, but in lieu of a matching khaki shirt the Chief is clad in a long-sleeve pullover that matches his name - green. All Air Department personnel have specific-colored pullovers that identify their associated duty, and for Chief Greene's Division, Aircraft Launch and Recovery, that color is green.

The Air Boss explains to Chief Greene the desires of Levine, Conroy, and Brandi.

The Air Boss then turns to Levine and says, "Chief Greene here will take care of all your needs."

"Thanks Commander" replies Levine.

The Air Boss departs and Levine, Conroy, and Brandi exchange greetings with the Chief.

"Agent Levine, I understand you wish to talk to our launch crew?" says Chief Greene, who then turns to Conroy, "Agent Conroy, you wish to talk to our catapult operators?" and then turns to Brandi, "And Ms. Matthews, you wish to assess and measure a catapult launch-chock?"

Brandi immediately interjects, "Except that I also need to be in attendance for at least a portion of Agent Levine's interview with the launch team... there may be aspects of the vehicle and the launching that could be vital to my portion of the investigation."

"Understood, ma'am" replies Chief Greene.

"And you're spot-on with everything else Chief" says Levine.

"Great" replies the Chief.

Chief Greene then turns to the sea of sailors of varying shirt colors... some green, some blue, some yellow... and bellows, "Petty Officer Cruz!"

Petty Officer Cruz, one of the many sailors wearing a green pullover, looks toward Chief Greene to see that the Chief is giving him the 'come over here' finger gesture.

"Yes, Chief?" responds Petty Officer Cruz as he approaches.

Chief Greene looks at Conroy, "Agent Conroy" he says, "Petty Officer Cruz will take you to the Cat Spaces and go over all of the actions that occurred in support of, and during, the launch of the car."

"Thanks Chief" responds Conroy.

Petty Officer Cruz then says to Conroy "If you'll follow me, Sir."

Petty Officer Cruz and Conroy exit the Cat Shop.

Chief Greene then addresses the rest of the crewmen, "I'm sure you are all wondering why you're here."

"Yes Sir" replies one of the more senior Petty Officers.

"A fishing trawler dredged-up a car in the middle of the ocean" the Chief responds, "and Agent Levine and Forensic Scientist Matthews are investigating this occurrence. Specifically, they are trying to determine if the car that was reeled-in is the car we launched during our Tiger Cruise."

Chief Greene then looks at Levine and asks, "Does that pretty much sum it up, Agent Levine?"

"Yes Chief" responds Levine, "And of course we will be looking for details surrounding the launch as well – a necessary part of our investigation."

Levine then addresses the crewmen... "I understand you all were involved in the launch of the Tiger Cruise car" he says.

Third Class Petty Officer Simmons, age 23 African American male, wearing a green pullover, looks around at his fellow shipmates and responds, "In one manner or another, Yes Sir."

Levine hands out pictures of the car, including a close-up of the squadron insignia, and says, "Could this be the car?"

The crewmen pass the pictures amongst themselves.

Airman Styles, age 22 Caucasian male, and wearing a blue pullover, responds as he looks at the full-view picture, "Looks like it."

Airman Jones, age 21 African American male, also wearing a blue pullover, has the picture of the squadron insignia in-hand, "Yeah, that's the insignia."

The crewmen hand the pictures back to Levine, who then directs a question to all of them... *Who* did *what* as part of the launch?"

"We all had a hand in painting the car" responds Airman Jones, "and I did the squadron insignia."

Airman Diaz, age 21 Hispanic American female, wearing a blue pullover, responds, "I towed the car with my tractor: From the Hangar Bay, up the Elevator, and out onto the Flight Deck."

Third Class Petty Officer Red Elk, age 24 Native American female, wearing a yellow pullover, responds, "I directed Airman Diaz in the movement of the car."

"Once the car was up on the Flight Deck" says Airman Styles, who then points to Airman Jones, "both Jonesy and I pushed it into position while Petty Officer Simmons steered from outside the driver's-side door."

"Once we had it aligned with the catapult, I hooked it up to the launch-chock" adds Petty Officer Simmons.

Brandi, showing a picture of the hook-like mechanism on the car asks Petty Officer Simmons, "This area here" she points, "is that where you connected the car to the catapult?"

"Yes, ma'am" replies the Petty Officer.

"And then what happened?" asks Levine.

"Petty Officer Jamison did a last check of everything" replies Airman Jones, "and then gave the LAUNCH signal."

"Where *is* Petty Officer Jamison?" asks Levine.

"Nobody knows, Sir" replies Petty Officer Simmons, "He took leave when we got back to port and hasn't returned to the Ship."

"And Airman Apprentice Sewell is also missing?" says Levine, "What's his story?"

"He screwed-up during deployment" replies Petty Officer Simmons; "Got arrested in Singapore for fighting outside a club."

"Yeah, we thought he was going to get 'caned'" says Airman Jones, "If they still do that kinda thing."

"Div-Oh... um, the Division Officer, had to try to save face with the Singapore authorities" says Petty Officer Simmons. "Man was Div-Oh pissed; he put Sewell on restriction for our next port visit - Hong Kong."

"You'd think Sewell would have learned his lesson" says Airman Styles, "but then in Australia he got 'into it' with a Bouncer. Petty Officer Jamison tried to break it up and ended up getting cold-cocked."

"Jamison was often coming to Sewell's rescue" adds Airman Jones.

"After *that* fiasco Sewell got sent up to see the Captain" says Petty Officer Simmons. "He got busted down to Airman Apprentice and missed the next two port visits."

"He took leave in Hawaii and we haven't seen him since" says Airman Styles.

"Do you think Jamison and Sewell planned to go UA together?" asks Levine.

"I can see Sewell saying *'screw this shit!'*" responds Petty Officer Simmons, "But Jamison? No way."

"Although he was acting strange the rest of the Tiger Cruise" adds Airman Jones.

"How so?" asks Levine.

"Quiet... kind of withdrawn" responds Airman Jones.

"Yeah, not like his usual self" adds Airman Styles.

"Not what you'd expect from someone coming home after seven months at sea" adds Petty Officer Simmons.

Levine thinks for a moment. He has noticed that the sailors were somewhat nervous when he first started questioning them, but over time they have become fairly relaxed and at-ease… just as he had hoped. He thinks it is now time to shake them up… to make an attempt to determine if any of the sailors knew that an actual person was in the launch car. He figures if any of them were involved it shouldn't be too hard to trip them up. With that in mind he's not even going to segue, he's going to jump right in…

"Tell me about the dummy" Levine blurts out to the crowd.

"The dummy?? Sir?" responds Airman Jones.

"Yeah… there was a dummy in the car, right?"

"Yes Sir."

"So tell me about it."

"Well, it was lifelike-sized and pretty realistic."

"And the Halloween mask was cool" adds Airman Styles.

"*Realistic*?" says Levine in response to Airman Jones' statement, "How do you mean?"

"It was kinda like a mannequin" replies Airman Jones, "but instead of hard plastic skin like a mannequin, the skin was more human-like… you know, sorta soft and squishy… like you'd see at Disneyland or Universal Theme Park or something."

"Yeah" adds Airman Styles, "And it had eyes that looked *real*. In fact, when we put the Halloween mask on, it was like a real person staring out at you from behind the mask… it kinda creeped-me-out the first time I saw it."

Petty Officer Red Elk looks at Styles with disbelief and says, "You were creeped-out by a *dummy*? What are you, some kind of a wimp or something?"

"What?" replies Airman Styles, who can't believe the Petty Officer is essentially questioning his manliness, "You weren't creeped-out when you saw it?"

"Of course not" responds the Petty Officer - the tone of her voice and her furrowed brow clearly indicating that she is almost offended at such a thought.

Levine wasn't expecting the dummy to be so intricate; he figured the launch guys would just stuff a flight suit with rags, fashion some appropriately-sized orb to use for the dummy's head that they'd throw the mask over, and then top it off with a helmet. Now he has a whole *new* list of avenues to consider: The killer either knew *where* to find, or figured out *how* to find... a high-quality dummy, and the killer had the money to *spend* on a high-quality dummy. However, the *big* item that he was hoping might fall into his lap: Perhaps the *real* dummy is stashed on the Ship somewhere? If so, then it could be a treasure-trove of evidence.

"That doesn't sound like your everyday dummy" says Levine, "Where did you all get it?"

"No clue Sir, I think Willie picked it up" replies Airman Jones.

"Willie?" asks Levine.

"Petty Officer Sewell" responds Airman Jones.

Airman Styles nudges Airman Jones and says quietly, *"Airman Apprentice."*

"Oh yeah" says Airman Jones, who corrects himself, *"Airman Apprentice* Sewell."

Levine thinks to himself, *"Of course it had to be one of the* missing *sailors."*

"I'm guessing that the dummy wasn't loaded into the car until right before the launch... is that the case?" asks Levine.

"That's correct, Sir" replies Petty Officer Simmons.

"Then where was the dummy kept in the meantime?" asks Levine.

"It was kept in a crate in an office area just off the hangar deck" says Airman Styles.

"Any chance the crate is still around?" asks Levine.

"I don't see why it would be" replies Petty Officer Simmons, "It was more than likely hauled off the Ship with tons of other junk when we returned to port."

Levine turns to Chief Greene and says, "Hey Chief, when we're done here I'd like to have someone take me down to the space off the hangar deck where the dummy was stored."

"I can take you there myself, Sir" replies the Chief.

"I'd appreciate that, Chief" says Levine.

Levine gets back to his line of questioning... "Who placed the dummy in the car?" he asks.

"I assume the Chief Warrant Officer" replies Airman Styles.

Levine notices several other crewmen nodding in agreement.

"Chief Warrant Officer?!" replies Levine. He is *not* happy that this is the first time he has heard of another person being involved in the launch, *and* the fact that they are not present for this interview.

"Chief Warrant Officer Bauer" replies Airman Styles, "The Tiger Cruise Launch Coordinator."

"Where do I find the Chief Warrant Officer?" asks Levine.

"This was his last deployment, Sir" responds Petty Officer Simmons, "He retired the day we got back."

"How convenient" remarks Levine in a sarcastic tone.

"What's that, Sir?" asks Petty Officer Simmons.

"Oh nothing" responds Levine.

Levine realizes he needs to put this piece of news behind him and get back to his series of questions. "So how did you guys come up with the paint scheme and squadron insignia for the car?" he asks.

"Chief Warrant Officer gave us the details" replies Airman Styles, "Showed us a picture of some old jet from the 1960's or 70's and said *'paint it like that'*."

"And he gave me a squadron insignia to copy" adds Airman Jones.

"Of course he did" replies Levine with his frustration starting to get the better of him.

Levine continues with his line of questioning, "So where did the car come from?" he asks.

The crewmen look at each other with an *"I don't know? ...do you?"* look on their faces.

Finally Petty Officer Simmons responds as he looks around at his shipmates, "It had to be the Chief Warrant Officer... *right?*"

The crewmen collectively nod in agreement, intermixed with a "yeah", and a "had to be" among them.

Levine provides an open question to the sailors... "Is there anything that you all want to share with me? Or any questions?"

The sailors all look around at each other and finally one of them half-raises their hand.

"Yes?" says Levine.

"Are we in some kind of trouble for launching the car into the ocean?" asks the sailor.

"Not at all" responds Levine, "The launch was approved by the Captain and even his boss, the Admiral." Levine then continues, "Like the Chief said, we're just trying to find out if the car we found is the one you guys launched."

The sailor exhales with a sigh of relief.

Levine scans the room and asks, "Anything else?"

The sailors remain silent as they collectively nod their heads indicating 'No'.

Levine then looks to Chief Greene and says, "Well, that's all I had Chief; can we head down to that space on the hangar deck?"

"Yes, Sir" replies the Chief, who then directs a statement to Petty Officer Simmons... "Petty Officer Simmons, escort Ms. Matthews up to the flight deck so that she can check out a catapult launch-chock."

"Aye-aye, Chief" responds Petty Officer Simmons.

"And the rest of you..." says the Chief, "Dismissed!"

14

Levine meets Conroy and Brandi on the hangar deck near the access hatch to the Quarterdeck. Conroy has a couple of file folders in hand.

Levine points to the folders and asks, "I don't suppose those are files for the missing crewmen?"

"Yep" replies Conroy, "It will be interesting to see what we can learn from them."

Levine then turns to Brandi and asks, "So did you and your '*launch-chock assessment kit*' have any success?"

Brandi opens up her metal briefcase and pulls out a tubular device.

"It matched up perfectly" she says as she waves it around like a trophy.

"What the heck *is* that thing" says Conroy as he peers at the device.

"It's my mock-up of the hook-like mechanism on our Plymouth" replies Brandi with a proud smile.

"It looks like the cardboard insert of a paper-towel that has been wrapped in duct tape" responds Conroy.

"Well Slade, forensic science is not about *fancy*, it's about *accuracy*" replies Brandi, "And I engineered this baby to the exact circumference of the hook-like mechanism."

"I'd say you're using the term '*engineered*' rather loosely" responds Conroy, "But whatever gets you a ribbon at the Science Fair..."

"You should know better than to mess with a forensic scientist, Slade" says Brandi, who then adds with a wink... "We know how to make you disappear without leaving a trace."

"Point taken" replies Conroy.

Levine waits for a moment to ensure that Brandi and Conroy have finished-up there little tête-à-tête; he then turns to Conroy and asks, "So, what did *you* find out?"

"I found out that *'Engineering'* provides steam to the catapults on the *ENTERPRISE*" says Conroy, "but on *NIMITZ-Class* Carriers like the SEADRAGON, it's *'Reactor Department'.*"

"Okay smartass, did you get anything useful or not?"

"Not really; at the catapult control room… or whatever it is that they call it… they explained how it was pretty much a standard launch but at a reduced steam pressure for the car; which is also where I learned that the steam was provided by the Reactor guys."

"Okay, I get it; I was wrong about *Engineering.* Anything else?"

"Then I went down to the Reactor Office" responds Conroy, "and talked to the ARO…"

"Assistant Reactor Officer?" Levine interrupts.

"Yeah – Commander Stone; and she confirmed the operation as told to me by the catapult guys… at least as much as she could without getting into the classified Nuke-stuff; but the overall operation from the two perspectives were in-sync."

Conroy throws it back to Levine, "What did you find out from the launch guys?"

"I came away with almost as many questions as I got answers."

"How do you mean?"

"Well, one of the missing sailors the XO told us about… Petty Officer Jamison… provided oversight of the launch, including giving the 'Launch' signal, *and* was acting suspicious after the launch."

"Suspicious? Do you mean the launch guys suspected something fishy… no pun intended… about the launch and this guy's actions?"

"Actually *'suspicious'* is my word… they said he was *'acting strange'.*"

"Like he was hiding something?"

"That's my take on it."

"Any of them tip their hand regarding the body?"

"No; I tried to trip them up, but they all seemed to think it was just a dummy behind the wheel. And I let them go on thinking that way; after all, I don't want to tip *my* hand."

"You don't want to tip *your* hand?" asks Conroy, unsure of Levine's meaning.

"Right now *only* the killer knows that there was an actual person behind the wheel, so if word gets out about the body... well, that means the killer screwed-up and opened his trap."

"And once there's chatter out there it could invariably lead us back to the source?"

"You've got it."

"Did any of them actually *see* the dummy?"

"Apparently a number of them."

"Damn this killer is smart; he makes sure a number of the crewmen see the dummy so that no one is the wiser when he dresses up his victim *as* the dummy."

"Yeah, I think we've got our work cut out for us trying to catch *this* son-of-a-bitch."

"But hey, if there really *was* a dummy, and it was never launched, then maybe it's still on the Ship somewhere?"

"That was exactly *my* thought, but I had the Chief take me down to where they had been storing it prior to the launch – not even a trace of the damn thing."

Conroy can tell by the look on Levine's face that the wheels are turning in his head. "I get the feeling there's more" says Conroy.

"Oh yeah" says Levine in a *'You better believe it'* tone, and then clarifies "That would be the guy who, at this moment, appears to be the prime suspect."

"Who's that?"

"The Launch Coordinator" says Levine, "A Chief Warrant Officer who told them how he wanted the car painted, gave them the squadron insignia to copy, *and* apparently loaded the 'dummy'... a-k-a *the victim*... into the car."

"Then why aren't we bringing him in for questioning?"

"He *conveniently* retired the day the Ship returned to port."

"Convenient for the other guys too… maybe they're throwing the Warrant Officer under the bus in order to throw us off their tracks, or to at least buy some time?"

"Yeah I thought of that, but seeing and hearing their responses as I grilled them…"

"Or maybe they're covering for the missing Petty Officer?" says Conroy before Levine has a chance to finish his statement.

"Could be, but they'd be taking one hell of a risk covering for a guy that might be a murderer" replies Levine, "Setting themselves up to be charged as accomplices, or at the very least – with obstruction."

"So, our two frontrunners are the missing Petty Officer and the Warrant Officer?"

"You've got that right. And since the Warrant Officer orchestrated the entire launch… and *especially* since he allegedly loaded the victim into the car… that puts him at the top of our *'suspect food chain'*."

A light bulb goes off in Conroy's head. He lifts up the file folders, opens them, and starts scanning. "What was the name of the Warrant Officer?" he asks as he flips through the files.

"Chief Warrant Officer Bauer" replies Levine.

Conroy scans the files; first flipping through Petty Officer Jamison's file and then Airman Apprentice Sewell's…

"He's the guy that did *both* Jamison's *and* Sewell's 'Evals'" says Conroy.

"Anything of note in there?" says Levine.

Conroy flips to Petty Officer Jamison's file, "Pretty much all positive comments for Jamison."

"And Sewell?"

Conroy then focuses on Airman Apprentice Sewell's file, scanning through one page then another before saying, "Not a flattering picture, especially all of the stuff that led to him getting sent up to see the Captain and subsequently busted down to Airman Apprentice."

"So, like the Captain and I were alluding to, perhaps everyone *thinks* Sewell took leave in Hawaii and went UA when in fact the reason he's missing is because he got murdered, strapped into the Plymouth, and launched?"

"Sewell took leave in Hawaii?"

"That's what the launch guys said."

"Did anyone actually *see* Sewell while they were in Hawaii?"

"Don't know; that's something we'll have to look into."

"So, if we don't find any trace of Sewell in Hawaii then it looks like he's our victim, and that Bauer and Jamison are the perpetrators."

"Maybe... but the launch guys said Jamison was always coming to Sewell's *rescue*, so why would he do an *'about face'* and then be an accomplice in his murder?"

"Maybe he'd had *enough* of trying to save Sewell's ass and finally hit the breaking point?"

"Yeah? Well what's *Bauer's* motive?"

"Judging by Sewell's Evals he was a major pain in Bauer's side."

"Even so, that's hardly a motive for murder."

Conroy thinks about that for a moment and then responds, "Hell, with Sewell's apparent hot temper we'd have a better motive for *him* to kill *Bauer*... talk about a conundrum."

"Good point, but we're getting ahead of ourselves here; we're only *speculating* on the identity of the victim, so trying to come up with a motive at this point is futile... let's see what the Doc's autopsy results give us."

"And I'll see if I can find some activity by Sewell in Hawaii after the Ship got underway."

Levine's cell phone rings – it's Doctor Watson.

"Hey Doc" says Levine. He listens for a moment and responds, "That would be great; I'll see you at 0900" and then hangs up.

"What's up, Jake?" asks Conroy.

"The Doc's going to give me some preliminary results of the autopsy in the morning. Perhaps he'll be able to give me an idea as to whether or not Sewell is the victim."

Levine turns to Brandi and says, "While I'm over there I'll swing by your area to see how things are going with the car."

"Sounds good" says Brandi.

"I'll fill Nic in on everything we learned here today" says Conroy, "and get an update from her on the stuff she's been working on."

"And keep plugging away at *your* list of tasks... including the ones we added today" remarks Levine.

"Of course."

Levine looks at his watch and says, "Time to call it a day; let's get the heck out of here."

Levine, Conroy, and Brandi enter the Quarterdeck, receiving a "Have a nice evening" from the Petty Officer as they pass by him and onto the gangway.

"You as well" replies Levine, Conroy, and Brandi in unison as they head down the gangway in single file.

Heading toward the parking area Levine turns to Conroy and says, "Let's get you back to your car at the office."

"I like the sound of that" replies Conroy, "I'm beat."

"See you in the morning" says Levine to Brandi.

"Ciao guys" replies Brandi.

15

Levine walks into the Autopsy room of the San Diego County Medical Examiner's Office. Doctor Watson is in full regalia... scrubs, rubber gloves, even a rubber apron. Levine is familiar with the routine when Doctor Watson is assessing a body... grab a lab coat off the rack and don a pair of rubber gloves from the wall dispenser.

The victim is lying supine... on his back... on the autopsy table with his chest cavity opened in the typical Y-pattern to support an internal inspection. A series of X-rays are posted on a trio of adjacent computer screens nearby.

"What have you got, Doc?" asks Levine while donning his gloves as he approaches.

"Nothing good" replies the Doctor, "At least not for this poor bastard."

Levine is a little surprised at the colorful 'matter of fact' bluntness of Doctor Watson's response.

"The job taking its toll on you, Doc?" asks Levine.

"How's that?" replies the Doctor... not realizing how blunt his statement had come across.

I don't recall you ever getting so gruff when talking about a vic" explains Levine.

"Oh *that*" says the Doctor, "Sorry; I just feel for the guy" who then explains, "Considering the circumstances surrounding his death."

"It's that bad??" says Levine. "At the marina you said there were no obvious signs of his cause of death, so I figured it couldn't be *too* brutal or savage?"

"The *brutality* is the fact of being *alive* when he was launched."

"*Whoa!* I know you're good Doc, but how can you tell something like *that*?"

"Well, he died from a broken neck" replies the Doctor as he points to one of the X-rays.

"Uh-huh" responds Levine as he peers at the screen – the break being obvious at the spot where the Doctor is pointing.

"But when an assailant *purposely* breaks their victim's neck" continues the Doctor, "they tend to do so in a twisting-rotational manner."

The Doctor positions himself behind the victim's head, and then, without touching him, he places his left forearm across the throat such that his left hand is near the right-side of the victim's lower jaw. The Doctor then places his right hand across and behind the back of the victim's head near the left temple. The Doctor subsequently demonstrates such a move – his left hand moving back toward his left while his right hand simultaneously moves back toward his right.

"Yeah" replies Levine, "Twisting his head until his neck snaps."

"Well, instead of a rotational fracture of the cervical vertebrae and associated ligaments, our victim here has atlanto occipital dislocation."

"You're getting all *'medical technical'* on me Doc."

"It occurs when severe flexion or extension exists at the upper cervical vertebrae" explains the Doctor as he demonstrates a head way-down *'chin-to-chest'*, then way-back *'eyes-to-ceiling'* motion.

"Whiplash" responds Levine.

"Yes, but much more severe than a whiplash; atlanto occipital dislocation involves *complete disruption* of all ligamentous relationships between the occiput and the atlas."

"That sounds pretty bad."

"Oh it is; death usually occurs *immediately* due to stretching of the brainstem, which causes respiratory arrest."

"So, how does that all fit-in with the thought of the victim being alive?"

"Such dislocations typically occur from a tremendously-high impact, such as an automobile accident, where even if you see it coming the force is so strong you cannot prevent the dislocation."

"But the force of the catapult launch was relatively minor; a pittance in comparison to launching a plane, and I've never heard of anyone dying from a catapult launch?"

"Which is why I'm almost positive he was *alive*... passed-out behind the wheel when he was launched, and thus the fully-relaxed neck muscles made the cervical spine much more susceptible to the force of the launch."

"Hmmm... I see what you mean."

"And even more so the slamming force of the car hitting the water... sufficient to cause such an injury" adds the Doctor.

"And with him wearing the helmet?"

"That would have magnified the force due to the additional weight on the head and neck" replies the Doctor, "Possibly being the difference between a whiplash and the complete disruption the victim suffered."

"Not that it would have made a difference in the end" says Levine.

"That's an unfortunate truth. Even though it appears he was alive when he was launched, at least he died almost immediately thereafter – a much better end than plunging to the bottom of the ocean while still alive."

"Any idea how long the guy has been in the water?"

"I'd estimate a couple of months."

"That's in line with the SEADRAGON's launching."

"I thought that might be the case."

"And speaking of..." says Levine, "they have two missing sailors; any chance the victim could be one of them?"

"Unless the missing sailors are middle-aged I'm afraid not; he appears to be somewhere in his mid-fifties to mid-sixties."

"Ages 24 and 25. Their status just changed from possible victim to potential suspect."

"I'm guessing you had already prepared yourself for that possibility?"

"Oh yeah; and since you haven't given me a name to this point I assume we have no DNA hit on the vic yet?"

"Actually we struck-out... no match in the database."

"How is *that* possible? I thought all members of the military had their DNA on file?"

"I'm sure you considered the victim might be a civilian and was only dressed as a Navy pilot as part of a ruse?"

"Yeah, but after winning three bucks on Lotto yesterday I thought my luck had turned around."

"I'll give you a call once I hear from Doctor Leland, our forensic odontologist."

"Thanks Doc. If you don't have anything else for me I'm going to stop by the garage and get an update from Brandi on the car."

"In that case you might as well hang on to the gloves and lab coat" says the Doctor just as Levine is starting to remove his rubber gloves.

"Good point" says Levine as he ceases his glove-removal action, and then exits the autopsy room.

Levine makes his way to a separate wing of the facility. Reaching the CSI garage he stops at the access door and presses the button adjacent to the door. A buzzer sounds and Levine opens the door to the garage.

As Levine enters Brandi notices he is wearing rubber gloves and a lab coat. She gives him a stern look. "Did you just come over from Autopsy?" she asks.

"You have a unique grasp of the obvious" replies Levine.

"You didn't just get *cadaver gunk* on my buzzer did you?" Brandi says in a displeased tone.

"*Cadaver gunk*... is that a *technical* term?" replies a smart-assed Levine.

"You know what I mean" says Brandi, who is not in the mood for Levine's hijinks.

"No, these were just precautionary; I didn't lay a finger on the victim."

"That's good; you were about to become the CSI garage custodian."

"It probably pays better" responds Levine.

"You're in rare form today, Jake."

Levine smiles, and then decides it's time to get back to the task at hand and says, "So, anything to report?"

"Only one thing at this point" Brandi replies, "But I have a few irons in the fire, so I may have more for you as early as this afternoon."

"Sounds good; what's the *one thing* you have for me right now?"

"It's nothing earth-shattering, but I've figured out how the victim was held in place."

"I'm assuming something beyond just the lap belt?"

"If solely the lap belt he would have been slumped over – indicating that he was either passed-out or dead and *not* the dummy that the crew believed was behind the wheel; so I knew there had to be an additional restraining device."

"But there wasn't a separate device holding him in place at the scene" states Levine.

"That's because it had broken free."

"So, what was it?"

"You know how the early version of a shoulder belt was merely a second seat belt anchored at the pillar near the roof?"

"That latched into a second clip next to the lap belt clip to the right of the driver" says Levine with recollection, "I had forgotten all about those."

"That was the device used here as well. And since it had broken free from the pillar, but was still attached to the clip at the seat, it *appeared* to be the passenger's seat belt."

"Stupid question, but how did you figure that out?"

"The passenger lap belt is still intact – it was just tucked between the seat cushions so it wasn't visible. And there's a stripped hole in the pillar and a similarly chafed bolt I found on the floorboard."

"I'm guessing the shoulder belt was jerry-rigged by the launch guys and not a factory-installed device?"

"That *has* to be the case; it was much too small of a bolt, and based on wear patterns it was barely screwed-in... only a few threads."

"Alright" says Levine, "Another mystery solved; only nine hundred ninety-seven more to go."

"You're figuring this is a 'thousand mystery' case?"

"It's a nice round number."

"With a number that large it sounds like you're setting yourself up for failure."

"It's not about solving all one-thousand mysteries; it's about solving *just the precious few necessary* to connect the dots."

"Like '*Wheel of Fortune*'" responds Brandi.

"I was thinking more like '*Name that Tune*'" replies Levine, "But I guess that shows our generational differences. And in either case, it fits."

16

Conroy and Nicole are comparing notes on their collective progress on the case when Levine walks into the office.

"What have you two come up with so far?" asks Levine.

"Nic got info on a number of our items while you and I were on the Ship yesterday" responds Conroy.

"Yeah?" says Levine, "Let's hear what you have, Nic."

"For starters, I talked to the Carrier Air Wings and none of them have an Aviator with a call-sign of *Snuffy*... they checked both Active Duty and Ready Reserve."

"It was a long shot; I guess I'm not really surprised."

"And the SEADRAGON provided us the list of all of the 'Tigers' that rode the Ship" Nicole continues, "I compared it with the list of missing persons throughout Southern California that Slade came up with this morning – no matches, unfortunately."

"So, we're running into dead ends."

"True" interjects Conroy who then turns to Nicole, "But Nic, tell Jake what you came up with that we hadn't thought of."

"I was thinking that maybe the Ship had captured the Tiger Cruise activities on video... you know... some great PR for them" says Nicole.

"And you found something?" replies Levine.

"Their website shows the launching; the Ship's Photo Lab is sending me the footage."

"That's great work, Nic."

Nicole smiles... recognition for accomplishments are always appreciated.

"And how about you Slade?" asks Levine, "Anything else to update me on?"

"Yeah... back along the lines of missing persons..." replies Conroy, "I have *not* been able to come up with an electronic footprint for Airman Apprentice Sewell - the missing sailor who was supposed to be in Hawaii."

"Being on restriction for most of their port visits means that Sewell had only a few opportunities to spend his money" says Levine, "So, he could have saved up a fair amount of cash during their deployment, but I can't imagine he could be living 'off the grid' for *too* long."

Conroy nods toward Nicole and says, "Actually we were thinking that if none of the 'Tigers' were reported missing, and the Ship reported no missing crewmembers during the Tiger Cruise, *and* there's no indication that Sewell is even *in* Hawaii, then *he* must be the victim."

"Sewell?" replies Levine.

"Yeah" says Conroy, "Like we were talking yesterday - that maybe everyone *thought* he was on leave when in fact he was murdered and launched?"

"There's a *huge* problem with that theory."

"What's that?"

"According to the Doc our vic is middle-aged. Plus the lab hit a dead-end on his DNA... no match in the database, and *all* active-duty military have their DNA on-file."

"Shit! Then who the hell *is* this guy?!"

"Unless we find some other means to identify him we're going to have to pin our hopes on dental records... and *then* try to figure out how the hell he got on the SEADRAGON."

"Damn!" says Nicole, "And here we thought for sure we had at least figured out the identity of the victim."

"But we *do* have more info for you" says Conroy, "After having gone through the missing sailors' files and talking to their superiors and fellow shipmates."

"Great" says Levine, "Let's hear it."

"Airman Apprentice William Sewell" says Conroy as he puts Sewell's Navy ID photo on the 42-inch screen; "Just as we had determined... pretty much the screw-up. Described as very intelligent, but has a problem with authority... from insubordination Shipboard to anyone else he sees as *'telling him what to do'*... hence the fights in Singapore and Australia. And, as you know, got busted down to E-2 during this deployment, and took leave in Hawaii and hasn't returned to the Ship."

Conroy then nods toward Nicole.

"Second Class Petty Officer Gerald Jamison" says Nicole as she puts Jamison's Navy ID photo on the screen, "A model sailor... made advancement on the first attempt all the way to E-5. Has a spotless record and is highly regarded at all levels. Everyone is baffled by his disappearance."

"So, we have the hot-tempered screw-up, but he *wasn't* there for the launch" says Levine, "And the guy that *was* there for the launch, and even provided *oversight* and gave the LAUNCH signal, is *'Mister Squared-away-Sailor'*."

"Yeah" says Conroy, "Every time we think we have an answer we find out we had the wrong question."

"Oh, we had the right question" replies Levine, "We just didn't get the answer we had *hoped*."

"Yeah, you're right" admits Conroy, "But it's still frustrating."

"Frustrating or not, we've still got a job to do" says Levine, who then looks to Conroy and says, "Any news on the squadron insignia?"

"Yeah, but basically a dead-end" replies Conroy. "The insignia matches an actual squadron, the *RVAH-17 Fightin' Tigers*, but the squadron was decommissioned back in 1979 when the Navy stopped using the RA-5 Vigilante jet on Carriers."

"So, apparently Airman Jones just copied an old insignia that the Warrant Officer happened to have" says Levine.

Levine's cell phone rings. He looks at the Caller ID and then answers, "Hey Brandi."

"Hey Jake, I've got an update for you if we can connect via video feed" replies Brandi.

"You've got it" responds Levine.

Levine then turns to Nicole, who still has Petty Officer Jamison's info on the 42-inch screen, and says, "Hey Nic, can you line us up a video feed with Brandi?"

"Sure" says Nicole.

Nicole makes the connection via her computer, and Brandi comes online on the 42-inch screen; she is in the CSI Garage and is using her laptop as the source of the video feed on her end. The Plymouth is visible in the background.

"So Brandi, what do you have for us?" asks Levine.

"Hey guys" says Brandi as she can see Levine, Conroy, and Nicole all gathered around to receive her info. "Well, for starters" she says, "I've got some news on the squadron insignia."

"Slade dug up some info on it as well" responds Levine, "It's a real squadron but they were decommissioned in 1979."

"I couldn't tell you anything about *that*, but I *can* tell you *this* crazy news… it's the *exact same* squadron as the one painted on the car launched off the ENTERPRISE back in 1978."

"No shit??" replies Conroy.

"And the car is a dead-on match" Brandi continues, "A 1963 Plymouth Savoy."

"How the hell did you figure out all of those details about the ENTERPRISE launch car?" asks Levine.

"There's a Navy Archive website that has about a kazillion pictures of virtually every Ship you can think of" replies Brandi, "And just our luck, they've got pictures of the ENTERPRISE Plymouth launch, so all I did was compare those with our car."

"Sheesh, this case is getting crazier all the time" proclaims Nicole.

"Hey Brandi, any idea how long the car was submerged?" asks Levine.

"Based on the amount of oxidation and seagrowth, or more accurately the lack thereof, I'd say it was only an artificial reef for a couple of months... tops."

"That agrees with the Doc's estimate as to how long the victim was submerged."

"Well, I've got something else here that's almost as strange as the car matching the one from the ENTERPRISE" says Brandi as she head-nods toward a table in the garage.

"You've got our attention" replies Levine.

Brandi grabs her laptop and walks over to the table. She holds it over what appears to be the flight suit the victim was wearing, laid out on the table.

"Forensic Scientist Alden analyzed the victim's flight suit... the style, the fabric, the weave... and concluded that it's from the 1970's" says Brandi, "The same era as the ENTERPRISE launch."

"What the hell??" responds Conroy.

Levine has an epiphany, and looks toward Nicole. "Hey Nic" he says, "The Carrier Air Wings said there were no *active-duty or ready reserve* Aviators called *Snuffy...*"

Nicole has a feeling she is thinking the same thing that Levine is thinking, and responds before he finishes... "See if they have records of *former* Aviators with that call-sign?"

"Have them start with the squadrons deployed with the ENTERPRISE during the '78 WestPac" replies Levine.

"Will do" responds Nicole.

Levine looks back to the screen and says, "Anything else for us?"

"That's it for now" replies Brandi.

"Great stuff today Brandi... thanks!" responds Levine.

The screen fades to black while Levine, Conroy, and Nicole quietly ponder the information that Brandi provided.

"Hey Nic, you're a Profiler..." says Conroy, "Any idea why someone might want to mimic the ENTERPRISE launching from thirty-odd years ago?"

"Well..." says Nicole as she contemplates the question, "Many of the psychologically-deranged are fixated by some specific event, and will often attempt to recreate that event."

"Or it could be a diversion" responds Levine, "Hoping that if the car was ever found it would be a rusted-out hulk that investigators would assume *was* the car from the ENTERPRISE."

"Or both" adds Nicole.

"It will be interesting to see if the call-sign *Snuffy* yields an aviator from back in the 70's like the flight suit" says Conroy.

"No kidding" responds Nicole as she picks up her phone and punches in the number to the Carrier Air Wings in Lemoore.

"Senior Chief; this is Special Agent McKenna" she says into the phone, "Remember the Aviator with a call-sign of *Snuffy* I asked you about? Well..."

17

With their list of tasks seemingly in the hands of others, Conroy and Nicole feel as if they are momentarily in *'wait and see'* mode... a term that they know Levine despises. Fortunately, the brief sense of purgatory is quickly ended with a simple chime from Nicole's computer.

"Hey Jake" says Nicole, "I just got the launch footage."

"Great" says Levine, "Can you put it on the screen?"

"I'm downloading it as we speak" replies Nicole.

The footage appears on the screen. It shows three sailors; two at the rear of the car in blue shirts, and one outside the driver's-side window in a green shirt who appears to be steering as they roll the car out to a designated spot... the catapult. A fourth sailor, wearing a yellow shirt, is clearly in charge of the entire maneuver, guiding them as they get the car into position.

The sailor at the driver's-side window then jumps underneath the front of the car and connects it to the catapult; and then gives a thumbs-up to the sailor who has been guiding them. That sailor does a quick check of everything, ending at the driver's-side door, then backs away and raises his hand as the other sailors also move back out of the way.

A fifth sailor, standing back and away from the rest of them, and wearing a yellow shirt but with khaki pants, raises and then drops his arm, and down the catapult trough and over the front of the Ship goes the car - like an airplane in slow motion...

Whoa, that was pretty impressive" says Nicole.

"Hey Nic" says Levine, "Go back to the beginning and slow it down, would you?"

"Sure" replies Nicole.

The footage starts to run again and almost immediately Levine says "Stop!"

Nicole freezes the footage.

Levine gets up next to the screen and points to the sailors at the rear of the car... "These are Airman Jones and Airman Styles."

Levine then points to the sailor by the driver's-side window and states, "This is Petty Officer Simmons."

Levine then turns to Nicole and says, "Go ahead, Nic."

The footage starts to run again.

As the footage is running Levine points to the sailor in the yellow shirt directing the maneuvers and says, "This must be the missing Petty Officer... *Petty Officer Jamison.*"

As the footage continues to run Levine now points to the sailor in khaki pants, "And this must be the retired Chief Warrant Officer" he says.

The footage continues to the end.

Conroy looks to Levine and says, "Looks like the launch-guys were telling the truth."

"Yeah" replies Levine, disappointed that they didn't learn anything new.

As the team contemplates their next move they are interrupted by the sound of Nicole's cell phone ringing.

"Special Agent McKenna" says Nicole as she answers her phone.

Nicole starts taking notes while she is listening. Her conversation consists mostly of "uh-huh" and "I see", but also includes "what number was that again?" and "how do you spell that?", and is concluded with "Thanks Senior Chief."

Nicole hangs up her phone and turns to Levine and Conroy. "Carrier Air Wing 21 reports there *was* a former Aviator with the call-sign *Snuffy*" she says, "A Lieutenant Commander Vincent Colletti, assigned to squadron RVAH-17 in the late 70's."

"Holy crap!" says Conroy, "That's the squadron painted on the car!"

"And no wonder they couldn't come up with a DNA profile" adds Levine, "that ability didn't exist back in the 70's."

"Hell, they couldn't even *spell* DNA back then" says Conroy in a smartass tone and accompanying smile.

"Hey Nic" says Levine, "Did they give you any details on this guy... what he did in the Navy... his various duty stations?"

"They're working on digging up his files, but all they had right now is name, rank, and squadron."

"Well, while we're waiting for Lemoore to dig through thirty years of old files let's get started on our own search."

"Sounds good" replies Nicole, who then turns to Conroy and says, "Hey Slade, I'll see what I can find through the *'Navy Records'* web portal if you want to try the Internet?"

"Can do" replies Conroy as he jumps on his computer and commences a 'people search' on the name *Vincent* followed by *Col...* before he stops and asks, "Hey Nic, is that one 'L' and two 'T's?"

"Two 'L's and two 'T's" responds Nicole.

"Thanks" says Conroy.

While Nicole is wading through a myriad of links via the Navy Records portal, Conroy gets a quick hit on *'people search'*... it's a minimal amount of information, but it's a start.

"So I've got a dozen total *Vincent Colletti's* here, seven of whom have the exact spelling" says Conroy.

"Start with those seven" responds Levine, "But don't discount the other ones yet, just in case those seven don't pan out."

"Here are the locations of the seven... Boston, Alexandria Virginia, Athens Georgia, St. Louis, Las Vegas, Sunnyvale California, and Honolulu."

"None in Southern California?"

"Nope; which would explain why we found no *'Missing Persons'* report."

"Honolulu is interesting though."

"Why's that?"

"Ummm... *that's where the Ship picked up their riders for the Tiger Cruise*" says Levine with emphasis and raised eyebrows showing disbelief that Conroy is not making the connection.

"Oh yeah... *Duh*" says Conroy in an '*I can't believe I'm such an idiot*' tone.

Conroy thinks for a moment and then says, "You know... in hindsight I focused on missing persons in Southern California, but in reality the 'Tigers' riding the Ship could have been from anywhere in the country."

"Considering every state in the Union is represented by the Ship's crew, we tripped-up on that one" responds Levine, somewhat annoyed at himself for not thinking of it earlier.

"Yeah, sailors could have a parent flying-in from New Jersey, or a sibling flying-in from Idaho, or a buddy flying-in from Oklahoma... you name it" replies Conroy.

"So, the common theme would be individuals with a one-way ticket to Hawaii, *and* a one-way ticket from San Diego *back* to their original location" adds Nicole.

"That's a good idea" says Levine, "but let's start with the name we *know – Vincent Colletti*."

"Well, I'm going to take a leap of faith and check *Missing Persons Reports* in Honolulu" responds Conroy.

"And who knows" says Levine, "depending on the results you might actually redeem yourself from your earlier 'brain fart'."

Conroy doesn't respond, but by the look on his face it's obvious that he's hoping for such a result.

"And while you two are doing *your* thing..." says Levine who then points to Conroy...

"Contacting the Honolulu Police Department to see if they have a Vincent Colletti listed as '*Missing*'" responds Conroy.

Levine then points to Nicole, who responds, "Continuing my Navy Records search on Colletti."

"...I'm going to give the Director an update" says Levine.

18

Levine, with a sandwich in hand along with what appears to be a latte', approaches his desk.

"I figured you couldn't have been updating the Director *that* long" says Conroy, "A quick trip to the *Gluten-Free Café?*"

"A BLAT" says Levine as he holds up the sandwich, "And a cup of their daily dark roast."

"A BLAT?" replies Conroy.

"Bacon-Lettuce-Avocado-Tomato" responds Levine.

"I had one of those yesterday" says Nicole, "They're awesome!"

"As soon as you're done we'll give you an update" says Conroy.

"I'm good" replies Levine, "Go ahead."

"I got hold of Honolulu PD and they *do* have an open Missing Persons case on a *Vincent Colletti*" says Conroy.

"Did you get any details?" replies Levine.

Levine's cell phone rings just as Conroy is about to speak; Levine immediately holds up his fingers in a *"halt"* gesture toward Conroy and says, "Hold that thought."

Levine looks at the Caller ID and then answers, "Yeah Doc, what have you got?"

"That substance I noted on the inside of the mask…" says the Doctor.

"Yeah?"

"Well, it was also found on the inside of the victim's gloves, and the lab analyzed it and determined that it's Super Glue."

"Super Glue inside both the mask and the gloves?"

"If I was going to venture a guess, I'm thinking that the killer wanted to make sure the victim would not be unexpectedly unmasked."

"Or the reality of human hands being uncovered" adds Levine.

"This news doesn't really help your case I realize, but I thought you'd be interested" says the Doctor.

"Every piece of information is one more brush stroke toward painting the picture... thanks."

"Well, I have another piece of news that I *know* you'll be interested in."

"You've got my attention, Doc."

"Doctor Leland made a Dental Record match on the victim."

"It wouldn't happen to be *Vincent Colletti* would it?"

"You came up with another method of identification?"

"Actually we had come up with a *possibility* but nothing positive. The name on his flight suit... *Snuffy*... matched a former aviator from the 1970's."

"I should have known. The flight suit was our *best guess* as well... considering the use of dental records is an inverse process."

"You can't use the records to determine the name of a victim; you have to start with the name of a missing person, get their dental records, and *then* compare to the vic, right?"

"Until we build a database of dental X-rays like those of CODIS for DNA and AFIS for fingerprints, you are exactly right."

"But we didn't have a name to start with?"

"We took a WAG on the flight suit... got the records for all Naval aviators assigned to the *Fightin' Tigers* squadron in the late 70's."

"Sometimes a Wild Ass Guess is all you've got to work with, and better yet when it reaps dividends."

"That's exactly right. Now you not only have a name, but a lead into his background as well."

"That's a fact Doc; some great news that should provide us with a very productive afternoon... thanks!"

Levine hangs up and says to Conroy and Nicole, "We've got a dental record match confirming our victim is Vincent Colletti... what do we know about him?"

"He was a navigator on the RA-5C Vigilante as part of the *RVAH-17 Fightin' Tigers* squadron" says Nicole as she reads from the *Navy Records* portal, "And it just so happens that he was deployed with the squadron during the 1978 WestPac cruise on the ENTERPRISE."

"Clues keep working their way back to the ENTERPRISE launch" says Conroy, "It's crazy!"

"He was subsequently transferred to Adak Alaska in 1979 when the squadron was decommissioned" adds Nicole.

"Adak??" replies Conroy while making a shivering movement and sound, "Who the hell did *he* piss-off?"

"After his tour in Adak he resigned his commission" says Nicole who then adds, "And that's the extent, Big-Picture wise, of what I gleaned out of Navy Records."

"I'll take it from there, Nic" says Conroy, who then continues… "After the Navy he moved to the San Francisco Bay Area, *Silicon Valley* to be specific, where he worked as a mid-level manager for a computer tech firm."

"Obviously at some point he moved to Hawaii" says Levine.

"Yep" replies Conroy, "In 2003 his mother passed away, leaving him a relatively modest inheritance, and he retired to Honolulu."

"And you were saying earlier that Honolulu PD *does* have an active Missing Persons case on him?"

"Yeah; he was reported missing six weeks ago by an acquaintance who claimed Colletti owed him money."

"That sounds like it's around the same time as the SEADRAGON's port visit?"

"That's exactly right; the report was filed two days after the Ship got underway, and the last known sighting of him was the day *before* the SEADRAGON's departure."

"So, did you get any details regarding their investigation?"

"They were coming up with dead ends: They found no signs of foul play in his home, his car was still in the garage, and there was no attempted use of his credit cards."

"As if he just fell off the face of the earth."

"That's how it looked. They canvassed the neighborhood, local establishments, his favorite watering hole... *Davy Jones' Locker*... and came up empty."

"His favorite watering hole was called *Davy Jones' Locker?*" asks Levine.

"Yeah" replies Conroy in a curious tone.

"The irony" says Levine, "is that *Davy Jones' Locker* is a euphemism for a sailor drowned at sea."

"Wow, that *is* ironic" says Nicole, "The oddities just keep piling-up in this case."

"That was his last known sighting" remarks Conroy.

"*Davy Jones' Locker?*" asks Levine.

"Yep; employees of the bar said Colletti had gotten into a heated argument with someone identified only as 'Willie', but he... the guy named Willie... left well before Colletti."

"And I assume nobody knew this guy 'Willie'?"

"Apparently not. They also checked flights off the island and cruise ship departures, and came up empty."

"Hmmm..." ponders Nicole, "If *I'm* Honolulu PD I'm looking into this guy *Willie*, and also the guy that reported him missing in the first place."

"You make a great point, Nic" says Levine. "Especially since a high percentage of Missing Persons were actually reported missing by the person that turned out to be their killer... usually a spouse, boyfriend, girlfriend, or even a member of their family."

"Yeah, but they couldn't rule out the possibility that he'd suffered some type of accident since they had no evidence otherwise" says

Conroy, "But the guy that reported him missing remained on their short list of suspects."

"Who else was on their list?" asks Levine.

"A guy they caught using Colletti's cell phone."

"Someone used his cell phone after he disappeared?"

"Very suspicious, right? But he claimed to have *found* the phone, and there was no evidence tying him to Colletti's disappearance, so he's nothing more than a *person of interest* at this point."

"So, I get the impression that their case had gone stagnant?"

"That would be an understatement. When I told them what *we* had it was a *huge* relief to them... a '*break in the case*' from their perspective... and thus they were more than happy to provide me with the details I just gave you."

Something dawns on Nicole and she picks up a sheet of paper from her desk and scans it, stopping to say... "The list of 'Tigers' riding the Ship shows a *Vincent Colletti*."

"Who's listed as his sponsor?" asks Levine.

Nicole runs her finger along the sheet to the '*Sponsor*' column and says, "Chief Warrant Officer Gordon Bauer."

"No fucking way!" responds Conroy as he realizes the tie to the person that *they* have considered a potential suspect – Chief Warrant Officer Bauer.

"What??" responds Nicole.

"He's the Tiger Cruise Launch Coordinator... the guy who allegedly loaded the dummy... a-k-a *the victim*... into the car."

"He's *that* Chief Warrant Officer?"

"Yep" says Conroy.

"Son of a Bitch!" says Levine, "Find his ass! And the rest of him!!"

Conroy smiles at Levine's quick-witted remark.

Considering the emphatic nature of Levine's directive Nicole completely misses the humorous aspect and immediately starts typing-away on her keyboard. It is only a matter of seconds before she pauses in disbelief.

"What the hell??" Nicole proclaims while still staring at her computer screen.

"What is it?" asks Levine.

"I started a web search on Bauer and the first thing that popped-up is his obituary."

"His *obituary?*" responds Conroy in disbelief.

"You're shittin' me?!" says Levine.

"According to his Obit he died three weeks ago" replies Nicole.

"Shortly after the vic... *Colletti...* was launched into the ocean" says Conroy as he realizes the coincidental nature of the timing.

"Do we know how he died?" asks Levine.

"Doesn't it say so in his Obit?" says Conroy.

Nicole scans the obituary and then responds, "Nope... nothing in here, not even a clue."

"They stopped putting the cause of death in obituaries years ago unless the family specifically wanted it identified" replies Levine. "Now the best you can do is see if they have one of those statements *'In lieu of flowers the family requests donations be made to whatever-the-hell-the-guy-died-from'* and thus you can *deduce* the cause from that statement."

"I'll try our intranet portal to the County Medical Examiner's secure website" responds Nicole, "Maybe they've posted the Death Certificate by now."

"And if you come up empty via that route let me know and I'll call the Doc" says Levine.

"Maybe Bauer actually had a conscience and his vicious crime ate-away at him until he couldn't take it anymore?" says Conroy, "Ultimately taking his own life to make amends for his egregious act."

"Whoa... *'To make amends for his egregious act'* ...what are you, Shakespeare or something?" replies Levine. "I think this *'poster boy - face of the agency's website'* crap is starting to go to your head."

Conroy reaches into his pocket and says, "Hey Jake, I've got something for you."

Conroy pulls his hand out of his pocket as Levine takes a look to see what it is... Conroy's giving Levine '*the middle-finger salute*'.

"Funny" says Levine sarcastically, "Right back at ya."

"Hey" says Conroy, "Maybe he was a witness or accomplice and was killed because he was a loose end?"

"Holy crap!" says Nicole as she stops typing and looks up from her computer screen... "His Death Certificate says *Cancer*."

This news surprises the entire team. Levine in particular has trouble coming to grips with the fact that his prime suspect is dead, especially with his death being due to cancer where he would have no trail of forensic evidence to pursue a possible homicide or suicide as the cause of his demise.

"Cancer?? Are you freakin' kidding me??!!" Levine blurts out.

"So much for being killed because he was a loose end" remarks Nicole.

"Speaking of loose ends, except for tying up a few ourselves it looks like we've got this case nailed" says Conroy with a certain sense of conviction.

To say that Levine has an issue with such a thought would be an understatement.

Nicole sees the look on Levine's face and says to herself, "*Oh crap... I'm glad Slade is the one who said that and not me.*"

"Really?" says Levine as he directs a stern look at Conroy, "Make your case for it."

"Bauer orchestrated the whole thing" says Conroy in a very positive matter-of-fact tone, following such a declaration with the list of damning evidence as he sees it...

"He told them how to paint the car" says Conroy as he holds up his thumb indicating the first item of note.

"He gave them the squadron insignia to copy and paint on the car" he says as he adds his pointer finger to his gesture to show that he is counting-up his *evidence*.

"He *provided* the car" he says as he adds his middle finger to his gesture.

"He could have been the one that purchased the dummy and merely had Sewell pick it up, especially since Sewell wouldn't have had that kind of money to spend on a dummy" he says as he adds his ring finger to his gesture.

"The *'clincher'* is that he loaded the guy into the car" he says as he adds his pinky finger to the gesture to make it appear as a *'High Five'*.

"And the *'nail in the coffin'* that ties it all together is that he *sponsored* Colletti" he says as he changes his gesture from a *'High Five'* to both hands *'Two-thumbs-up'*.

"That's an impressive list" responds Levine, "And many investigators might box it up, tie a ribbon around it, and file it away as *'Case Closed'*..."

"But..." says Conroy as he can tell by Levine's tone that there is more to the point he is apparently making.

"How's that?"

"I can tell by your response that there's a *'but'* following that statement."

"Hell yes there's a *'but'*!! The only thing on your list that is of major importance that we actually *know* is the fact that he sponsored Colletti on the Tiger Cruise."

"What do you mean? The launch guys gave us everything I mentioned."

"They *assumed* the Warrant Officer provided the car, they *assumed* that he loaded the guy into the car, and they've even got *you* taking a ride on the *'assumption train'* with your speculation about Bauer and the dummy."

"What about the car's paint job and squadron insignia?"

"So he told them how to paint the car so that it mimicked a squadron's jet plane; how does *that* make a case for murder? A Judge wouldn't even allow that to be introduced as evidence in a trial."

"Well shit!"

"Hey, I'm not saying that Bauer is *innocent*; hell, for all we know when all is said and done we may find that he *is* the killer, but that needs to be proven beyond a reasonable doubt and nothing less."

"So, now what?" asks a somewhat-dejected Conroy.

"For starters, I want to know *everything there is to know* about Chief Warrant Officer Bauer, and what ties him to Vincent Colletti."

"Since Slade's already been looking into Colletti I'll take the lead on Bauer" responds Nicole.

"Slade, get a copy of Honolulu PD's case file on Colletti… his last known sighting, if he knew anyone on the SEADRAGON" says Levine who then adds, "Anything we don't know yet."

Conroy nods with an expression of comprehension.

"And find out about the guy that had his cell phone" Levine continues, "Oh… *and* the guy that claimed Colletti owed him money."

"Got it" acknowledges Conroy.

"Hey Nic" says Levine, "Do we know Colletti's berthing assignment during the Tiger Cruise?"

Nicole scans through her paperwork and replies, "He was assigned a stateroom with Jason Kirkpatrick, a civilian contractor with *Tech-Star Avionics*."

"We're gonna need to talk to that guy" responds Levine.

"Agreed" replies Nicole.

"Hey Jake, when I was digging up info on Squadron RVAH-17 I noticed that they have a local alumni that meets every month at the *Flight Ops Café* in Coronado" says Conroy.

"Perhaps someone remembers Colletti, along with anyone from his past who might hold a grudge?" adds Nicole.

"That's exactly what I was thinking" responds Conroy.

"When's their next meeting?" asks Levine.

"Finally a stroke of good timing" replies Conroy, "Tomorrow morning at eleven."

Levine looks at his watch and says, "Okay, tomorrow you two go talk to the Contractor... see if he saw or heard anything about Colletti that might implicate Chief Warrant Officer Bauer beyond what we already know."

"I'll call *Tech-Star Avionics* and make an appointment" replies Nicole.

"Sounds good" says Levine, "And for the remainder of the afternoon, see what you can find out about Bauer... his background, any military or civilian police reports, non-judicial punishment... you name it."

"Will do" says Nicole.

"And I'll get on the horn with Honolulu PD and have them provide me a copy of their files on Colletti" adds Conroy.

"And while you two are visiting the Contractor I'll see what I can find out about Colletti, if anything, from his former squadron members" says Levine.

19

Conroy and Nicole enter the office space of *Tech-Star Avionics* and approach the receptionist at the Front Desk. The receptionist, Tara, age 23 and fresh out of Community College, is blonde and attractive, and has clearly taken notice of Conroy. She is hoping that the attractive brunette with him is his coworker and not his wife or girlfriend.

"We're looking for Jason Kirkpatrick" says Conroy as Nicole and he hold up their badges.

"Of course" replies the receptionist, who then grabs her phone, punches in three numbers, and speaks into the phone... "Sir, you have visitors."

The receptionist looks directly at Conroy, seemingly oblivious that Nicole is also present, and says, "He'll be right out."

Conroy and Nicole step back and away to a small waiting area just a few feet away from the receptionist. The area contains four armchairs with a small table between the two middle chairs. Taking a seat near the table, Conroy scans through the small stack of magazines in hopes of finding something interesting to peruse. *"Go figure it's all technical crap"* says Conroy to himself as he flips through the stack.

Nicole leans over and, with an ever-so-subtle head-nod toward the receptionist, whispers to Conroy, "It appears you have a fan."

Conroy gives Nicole the *"who me?"* look.

Nicole just shakes her head... she's sure that Conroy noticed the *'googly-eyes'* and *'1-900 voice'* the receptionist directed his way.

Jason Kirkpatrick, early forties, five-foot-ten, and dressed in Business Casual - slacks with a button-down shirt but no tie - approaches. Conroy and Nicole hold up their badges.

"Jason Kirkpatrick?" says Conroy, "NCIS Special Agents Conroy and McKenna."

Kirkpatrick has a confused look on his face. The first thought that enters his mind is that there is an issue with some of the contract work under his tutelage on one of the local Navy ships. He is hoping that it is not an act of vandalism by a disgruntled sailor, shipyard worker, or contractor... which is usually the case when NCIS is called to investigate.

"What can I do for you?" responds Kirkpatrick.

"You rode the USS SEADRAGON a couple of months ago?" asks Conroy.

"Yes, I conducted training of Air Department personnel on a system upgrade that was to start right after their return to port" replies Kirkpatrick.

"You shared a stateroom with a *Vincent Colletti*?" asks Nicole.

"Vincent?" replies Kirkpatrick, "Yeah, is he in some kind of trouble?"

"He's dead" responds Conroy, "Apparently launched off the Ship in a car."

"The Tiger Cruise launch car??" replies Kirkpatrick.

"Exactly" responds Nicole.

"How is that even possible?" asks Kirkpatrick.

"That's what we're trying to find out" replies Conroy.

"What can you tell us about him?" asks Nicole.

"Not much really" says Kirkpatrick. "I was conducting multiple training sessions daily... morning, afternoon, and evening in order to work around personnel watch-stations, so we hardly ever crossed paths; in fact, he was usually in his rack by the time I finished up my evening training sessions."

"Did he happen to share any info about his past" replies Conroy, "or his sponsor?"

"I remember him saying he used to fly jets in the Navy, and that he was a guest of Chief Warrant Officer Bauer, but that's about it" responds Kirkpatrick.

Nicole is somewhat surprised that Kirkpatrick mentioned Bauer, a name that was seemingly nothing more than the sponsor of a weeklong roommate from two months ago. She is hoping that it's not a matter of Kirkpatrick having a photographic memory, but instead that he can provide potentially crucial information about both Colletti *and* Bauer, and their possible relationship.

"He didn't say how they knew each other? Whether they had served together? Anything like that?" asks Nicole.

"I assumed it might be something like that... having served together" says Kirkpatrick, "Heck, he could have even been Chief Warrant Officer Bauer's uncle for that matter, but he never said."

"Did *you* know the Chief Warrant Officer?" asks Nicole.

"Sure, he was the Department '*Tech Assist*'" replies Kirkpatrick, "He was the person with whom I coordinated the training times, made sure the crewmembers were in attendance... that sort of thing."

"Were you aware he was also the Tiger Cruise Launch Coordinator?" asks Conroy.

"Yeah, I found that out when he had me schedule my training *outside* of the launch-time since he and some of his crew were involved in it, and so that the rest of them would get a chance to see it" says Kirkpatrick, "That allowed me to watch as well, which I thought was pretty cool at the time, now knowing that Vincent was behind the wheel... well, it just makes me sick to my stomach."

"When Colletti no longer showed up in the stateroom after the launch, didn't that seem strange?" asks Nicole.

"Not at all" responds Kirkpatrick, "His suitcase and personal items were all gone, so I just assumed he moved to Chief Warrant Officer Bauer's stateroom."

"Is there anything else you can tell us about the Chief Warrant Officer?" asks Conroy.

"He seemed a bit anxious" replies Kirkpatrick, who thinks for a moment and then asks, "You don't think he had anything to do with Vincent's death do you?"

"We're investigating all possibilities" responds Conroy.

"Did you know that Bauer is dead?" asks Nicole.

"What??!!" responds Kirkpatrick.

"Cancer" says Nicole.

"He appeared to be, well, not in the best of health" responds Kirkpatrick, "but having just met him I had no idea what was the norm for the guy."

"I understand" replies Nicole.

"Getting the news that two men I knew, albeit minimally and briefly, had recently passed..." responds Kirkpatrick, "Well..."

"Our condolences" says Nicole.

"I appreciate that" replies Kirkpatrick.

Conroy hands Kirkpatrick his business card. "If you think of anything that might help us, please call" he says.

"I will" replies Kirkpatrick.

Conroy and Nicole depart the building. As they're walking back to their car Nicole remarks, "I guess we couldn't have expected too much info considering he barely knew either of them."

"And from what he observed, everything between Colletti and Bauer seemed to be on the up-and-up, unfortunately for us" responds Conroy.

"Yeah, I was hoping he'd say *'this here seemed rather strange'* or *'there was something fishy about that'*... but no such luck."

"Well, a devious killer is going to make sure their prey is at ease and comfortable before they pounce, so it appears that's *exactly* how Bauer operated."

"Now we just need to figure out the tie between the two of them... Colletti and Bauer."

"And Bauer's motive."

20

Levine walks through the door of the *Flight Ops Café*. It's a medium-sized café with booths running along the two opposing walls, small tables in the middle of the café, and a lounge area at the far end that includes a number of chairs that appear to be right out of the *Ready Room* of an Aircraft Carrier.

The walls are adorned with photographs and memorabilia covering the spectra of U.S. Navy and Marine Corps aircraft from the early days of Naval Aviation: Biplanes landing on the deck of a converted surface ship, to F-18 Super Hornets landing on today's nuclear-powered Aircraft Carriers. Levine's personal favorite is the photograph of Doolittle's Raiders flying their B-25's off the flight deck of the USS HORNET in 1942.

Seated in the lounge area are a number of men in their 50's, 60's, and 70's, with many of them wearing their old Aviator jackets. They are hanging out, shooting the breeze, and reliving their Glory Days as former aviators and flight crew personnel.

Several of the men turn to see who has entered; they are surprised to see that it is not one of the regular attendees.

Conrad "Condor" Caldwell, age 75 but spry as a 35 year-old, and wearing a "U.S. Navy" Aviator jacket with an EAGLE on the lapels denoting him as a Navy Captain, decides to break the ice. "Hey Stranger" says Caldwell, "you a *Fightin' Tiger?*"

"Special Agent Levine, NCIS" replies Levine, "I'm hoping you might have information about a former Fightin' Tiger."

"No such thing as a *former* Fightin' Tiger" responds Caldwell.

Levine thinks to himself, "*I guess once you're in the club you're in for life.*"

Caldwell stands and reaches out to shake hands with Levine, "Conrad Caldwell" he says, "A pleasure to meet you."

"Captain" replies Levine, providing Caldwell with the courtesy he has earned in achieving the rank of Captain.

"Please, call me Conrad" replies Caldwell, who nods toward the entryway, "Rank disappears once we walk through the door here."

"Of course" says Levine, who then inquires of the group... "Any of you gentlemen remember a Vincent Colletti? Went by the call-sign 'Snuffy'."

"That S-O-B *Snuffy*?" replies Sam "Spades" Kozinski, age 64 and wearing a U.S. Navy Aviator jacket with the silver oak-leaves of a Commander on the lapels, "I think we can make a '*No such thing as a former Fightin' Tiger*' exception in *his* case."

"Commander is it?" says Levine as he reaches out to shake hands, "Agent Levine."

"Sam Kozinski" replies Kozinski.

"So you knew him?" responds Levine.

"A few of us had the pleasure... *so to speak*" replies Kozinski in an obvious sarcastic tone.

"When was the last time any of you saw him?" asks Levine.

"Not since the squadron was decommissioned back in 1979" replies Caldwell.

Several others in the group nod their head in agreement.

"So, is he in some kind of trouble?" asks Kozinski, "Screwed-over the wrong person and gone on the lam or something?"

"He's dead" replies Levine, "Launched off the SEADRAGON in a car six weeks ago... during their Tiger Cruise."

"Like we did on the ENTERPRISE back in '78?" asks Caldwell.

"Yes, in fact they mimicked the ENTERPRISE launch in every detail" replies Levine, "Same paint scheme, *Fightin' Tiger* squadron insignia, even the exact model of car."

"Holy crap!" says Kozinski, "Karma finally caught up with him."

"What can you tell me about him?" asks Levine.

Roger "Ramjet" Baldwin, age 62 but fit and chiseled like a modern-day Jack LaLanne, and wearing his Aviator jacket with 'USMC' and the gold oak-leaves of a Major, joins the conversation... "He was abrasive, verbally abusive, pretty much a jackass to be honest" responds Baldwin.

"He sure thought highly of himself" adds Kozinski, "Always bragging about how he consistently *saved the day while surrounded by incompetence'.*"

"When in reality all of the squadron's successes were achieved *in spite of* Colletti" adds Caldwell.

"Certainly not *because of* him" says Kozinski.

"He was particularly rough on the JO's – the junior officers" says Baldwin.

"Although there *was* that *one* enlisted kid he almost screwed over" adds Kozinski, "Airman Williams; the kid who'd been accepted to NESEP... you know..."

"The 'Seaman-to-Admiral' Program" responds Levine.

"That's it" says Kozinski. "Anyway, Colletti was constantly on the Airman's ass. I think he loathed the idea of a '*blue shirt*' getting the gift of a college education and commission."

"He was probably worried that the Airman would rise up the ranks and surpass him" says Baldwin.

"And Colletti would have to be licking *his* bootstraps" adds Kozinski, "Wouldn't *that* have been something?!"

"And the Airman wouldn't take it up the Chain of Command" continues Baldwin, "because Colletti would threaten to get his NESEP Acceptance revoked."

"If it wasn't for the Squadron Commander here..." says Kozinski as he nods toward Caldwell, "I'm sure Colletti would have screwed the Airman out of his schooling and ultimate commission."

"Luckily, I was able to jump in before he impacted the poor kid's career" says Caldwell.

"Since he ultimately got into NESEP" says Kozinski, "there's no real reason for the former Airman to hold a grudge; not to the extent of murdering the guy anyway."

"Yeah" adds Caldwell, "If I was him I'd be hoping to run into Colletti so that I could gloat and possibly even rub his nose in it, not to kill him."

"There *was* that *one* junior officer that he really had it in for" remarks Baldwin.

I remember that now that you mention it" says Caldwell, "Now what the heck was his name?"

"You talkin' about *'Rhino'*?" replies Kozinski.

"That's it" responds Caldwell.

"You're exactly right... a top-notch guy and smart as a whip" says Baldwin, "But when he'd point out that Colletti's orders were not in accordance with instructions or directives, well, Colletti wouldn't tolerate an underling embarrassing him in front of the rest of the crew."

"Colletti was so clueless he didn't realize that the only person embarrassing him was *himself*" says Kozinski.

"Pretty common for those types of personalities" adds Baldwin, "You know... those that put the blame on others when they actually stuck their head up their *own* ass."

"I remember it like it was yesterday" says Kozinski.

"Colletti being a complete and total ass?" asks Baldwin.

"Well, there's that of course" replies Kozinski, "but I was specifically referring to the fact of him screwing-over Rhino when he *knew* Rhino's lifelong dream was to have a career as a Navy pilot."

"Yeah, it's one thing to take someone to task because of a single incident" adds Baldwin, "but it's another thing altogether to ruin their career."

"Colletti ruined his career?" asks Levine.

"Thanks to substandard FitReps courtesy of Colletti" replies Baldwin, "Rhino was forced to resign his commission."

"Unfortunately, I was unable to salvage his Navy career" responds Caldwell, still feeling a bit responsible for such a travesty, even after all these years.

"You can't blame yourself Captain" replies Baldwin "After all, you *did* eventually see through Colletti's con-game."

"Yes, but I didn't really understand the extent of his act, and the impact on others, until I observed his tirade in front of all those kids during the Tiger Cruise" responds Caldwell.

"Yeah, I couldn't believe my eyes and ears" says Baldwin, "The looks on those poor kids' faces…"

"It tore your heart out" adds Kozinski, "To be honest I wanted to toss Colletti overboard right then and there."

"We all would have helped you" replies Baldwin.

"Needless to say that was the last straw" says Caldwell, "And I made sure his ass ended up in Adak for his next duty station."

"That explains something" says Levine.

"What's that?" asks Caldwell.

"Colletti's Personnel Record" responds Levine, "We've been reviewing it as part of our investigation and one of my Agents thought that Colletti must have pissed someone off to end up in Adak after his tour on the ENTERPRISE."

"Hopefully it taught him a lesson" replies Caldwell, "but I guess we'll never know."

"Anyway, if anyone had a reason to hold a grudge, it would be *Rhino*" says Kozinski.

"When it comes to former squadron members anyway" adds Baldwin, "Who knows how many others there are that Colletti crossed paths with over the years."

"None of you remember *Rhino's* actual name?" asks Levine.

"Could have been exactly how it sounds, you know… *R-Y-N-O*" says Kozinski.

"He was with the squadron so briefly, but *'Ryno'* doesn't sound right to me… are you sure it wasn't *Ryan*-something?" replies Baldwin to Kozinski.

"Hmmm… Ryan… that *does* sound kind of familiar" responds Kozinski, "*Rick* Ryan maybe?"

"Now *that* rings a bell" replies Baldwin, who then turns to Levine and says, "But I wouldn't quote us on it."

"What about his rank?" asks Levine.

"Either a Lieutenant or a JG" responds Caldwell.

"Well, I appreciate your time Gentlemen" says Levine as he reaches out to shake hands, first to Caldwell, "Conrad" says Levine; then Kozinski, "Sam" says Levine; then Baldwin, "Major" says Levine.

"Roger Baldwin" responds Baldwin.

"Roger" acknowledges Levine.

Levine smiles at the subtle way he managed to get the Major's last name; figuring it might come in handy during his investigation.

Levine exits the café and dials his cell phone. Upon hearing an answer he says, "Hey Slade, you two back in the office?"

"Got back a little while ago" says Conroy, "I'm going through Colletti's case file that Honolulu PD sent over."

"I've got another item for your list if you're ready to write."

"Go ahead."

"See what you can find on these four names, they were all part of the *Fightin' Tigers* squadron and served on the ENTERPRISE during the '78 WestPac."

"*Four* names?" replies Conroy, surprised at the number of potential suspects that Levine had come up with.

"Yeah" says Levine, "One who, according to the squadron guys, has the biggest reason to hold a grudge, but none of them could remember his name, only his call-sign *'Rhino'*. He was either a Lieutenant or Lieutenant JG."

"And the rest?"

"The other three are the guys I just spoke with; two of which *really* seemed to have a beef with Colletti, even after all these years."

"And they are??"

"Navy Commander Sam Kozinski, and Marine Corps Major Roger Baldwin."

"And the last guy?"

"He's a long-shot... the former Squadron Commander... but I figure *what the hell,* better to *verify* he's not a suspect than to *assume* he's not; his name is Conrad Caldwell – retired Navy Captain."

"But none of these guys were on the SEADRAGON during the Tiger Cruise, correct?"

"True, but one of them could have been *behind* it all."

"Understood."

"You got anything for me?" asks Levine.

"Something jumped out at me in Colletti's case file" responds Conroy.

"Yeah? What's that?"

"You're not going to believe who had Colletti's cell phone."

"Just cut to the chase Slade, I'm not really in the mood to play '*twenty questions*'."

"It was our UA screw-up, Airman Apprentice William Sewell. So it looks like the mystery man '*Willie*', and the guy that had Colletti's phone, are one in the same."

"Is Honolulu PD trying to track him down?"

"Better than that; he's back on the SEADRAGON."

"No shit??"

"*And* he's not going anywhere - they've got him on restriction."

"Well then..." Levine starts to say.

"I know..."interrupts Conroy, "Get my ass over to the SEADRAGON."

"And have Nic start looking into the names I gave you... including a back-trace on this '*Rhino*' guy like she did with '*Snuffy*'" says Levine.

"Got it" replies Conroy.

21

Levine looks at his watch; it's straight-up twelve-noon. He grabs his phone, does a quick scroll, hits '*Send*' and then says, "Hey Babe, whatcha doin' for lunch?"

"I've got a hot date with a tall, dark, and handsome gentleman" replies the sultry voice on the other end of the line.

"Oh yeah? Where's that?"

"How about *Spinnaker's?*"

"Twenty minutes?"

"See you there."

Levine pulls into the parking area of *Spinnaker's Restaurant*, a very nice yet relatively modest establishment overlooking San Diego Bay. The exterior is flagged by large spinnaker sails both street-side and bayside to make a visual statement to potential customers from either vantage point.

Levine sees Elise's car and wheels into the space next to it. She is still behind the wheel, visor down, apparently touching-up her lipstick.

As Levine pulls up next to her she flips up the mirror on her visor, looks over his way, and gives him a smile.

The two exit their vehicles and meet at the walkway in front of the restaurant.

"Ooh fresh lips" says Levine as he greets her with a delicate kiss - not wanting to smear her newly-applied beauty treatment.

"Puckerly-perfect" she replies as she puckers her lips.

"Hey gorgeous" says Levine as he extends his arm.

"Hey handsome" she replies, grabbing his arm as if he's her escort at a formal event – '*Walking the Red Carpet at a Hollywood Gala*' if you will.

The two of them walk through the door of the restaurant and are greeted by the owner, Katherine.

Katherine and her husband have owned the restaurant for twenty-odd years and often greet customers as they arrive; a way of portraying *"we're all a part of the family"* – an atmosphere they have successfully conveyed all of these years.

"Hey, it's the newlyweds" proclaims Katherine with a big smile - a moniker she has given Levine and Elise based on their appearance of being in the Honeymoon-phase of their marriage for as long as she can remember.

Levine and Elise both smile, with Levine responding, "We'll take that."

The restaurant is adorned in a nautical motif, the majority being pictures of sailing vessels of various types showcasing their spinnakers… from Clipper Ships, to local sailboats in the harbor, to action photos of high-tech sailboats competing in the America's Cup. An eclectic array of sailing equipment is also arranged throughout the restaurant… a small spinnaker sail in the waiting area along with a number of cleats, padeyes, a block and tackle, a wooden tiller, a winch, and an anchor among them.

Katherine shows Levine and Elise to their table, an intimate two-topper next to a window looking out toward the bay.

"Your server will be with you shortly; can I get you anything to drink while you peruse the menu?" says Katherine.

"Iced tea for me, thanks" replies Elise.

"A cup of your dark roast coffee would be great, thanks" says Levine.

Katherine departs and Elise looks to Levine, "So how was your morning?"

"I just spent the last hour with a cast of characters at the *Flight Ops Café* in Coronado" replies Levine.

"A cast of characters?"

"Yeah… *Grumpy, Dopey, Happy, Sleepy, Snuffy, Rhino, and Doc.*"

Levine thinks for a moment and adds... "Well, *Doc* was *technically* yesterday... Doctor Watson, our forensic pathologist working the case."

Elise responds in a somewhat giggling manner, "I don't remember the Seven Dwarfs including a *Snuffy* or *Rhino*."

"Actually those two were the only *accurate* names out of the bunch, along with *Condor*, *Spades*, and *Ramjet*; but *Grumpy*, *Dopey*, *Happy*, and *Sleepy* seemed fitting under the circumstances."

Levine and Elise are briefly interrupted by Katherine's return. "One iced tea for the lady; and a cup of dark roast for the gentleman" she says.

"Thanks" says Levine.

"So, what's with the goofy names?" asks Elise as they resume their conversation.

"Aviator call-signs" replies Levine.

"Those are the nicknames that Navy pilots use, right?"

"Marines and Air Force as well."

"I can see someone selecting a nickname like '*Rhino*'... *a large and powerful beast*... but '*Snuffy*'??"

"Yeah, we're a little perplexed at that one too, but unfortunately he's the victim so there's no telling why he picked the name."

"He's the victim?" she says as she puts her hand over her heart, "Wow, I feel bad saying anything."

"Not your fault my dear."

The two are interrupted by the server's arrival, "Good afternoon" she says and then realizes she recognizes them, "Oh hey, I haven't seen you two in a while, welcome back. Have you decided what you'd like for lunch?"

Levine and Elise look at each other – they haven't even picked up their menus let alone decided on their meal.

The two look back at the server and Elise says, "Oh Hi. Umm... just a sec" as she runs her finger down the menu - doing a quick check to see if a dish they had the last time they were there is still listed. She stops her scan and says, "Here it is" and then looks to Levine, "What do you think Hon, how about the Quinoa with veggies?"

"Sounds good to me" replies Levine.

Elise turns to the server and says, "Just one order for the two of us to share, please."

"Great choice" responds the server, "and I'll be right back with a refill for your iced tea and coffee."

"Thanks" replies Elise; who then looks toward Levine and asks, "So, how's your team doing?"

"They're great" replies Levine, "Although I don't always let *them* know that."

"You'd better! Good people need to know they're doing well."

"Actually I do, but I also have to keep them on their toes; and of course I have to flip them crap as well."

"Of *course* you do… that's the *Jake Levine* we all know and love."

"I doubt that's how *they* would term it, but one has to maintain some levity in this line of work or the nature of the beast will drive you nuts… especially when '*the beast*' is the investigation of a murder."

"Good point, but do any of them flip crap back at *you*?"

"Well Slade does somewhat, and *Brandi* is an *expert* at it."

"Brandi's working this case? I *love* her!"

"Yeah, since the crime scene is that old Plymouth."

"I forgot about the old car… that makes sense."

"And Nic hasn't thrown any zingers my way as of yet."

"No surprise since she's a newer Agent and you're her boss."

"True, but she *has* gotten Slade with a few good ones."

"Speaking of Slade, he's been like your *right hand man* for a while now, right?"

"Oh yeah, it's great to have someone you know you can always count on."

Lunch arrives for Levine and Elise; and they continue their conversation while they dine.

"So how about Nicole, she's kind of an *up and comer* isn't she?" asks Elise.

"She's been great as well, and impresses me more every day. What she may lack in experience she most certainly makes up for in drive, dedication, and intellect."

"Those are great qualities to have on your side."

"No kidding. And something that the rest of the office is unaware is that Nicole was a '*hot property*' coming out of college… with the FBI, DEA, and Homeland Security trying to land her services."

"And she picked *you guys*" says Elise, beaming with pride for her hubby.

"Yeah, she liked the idea of the wide variety of investigation modalities of NCIS: Navy bases, Marine Corps bases, ships, submarines, airplanes, nuclear propulsion plant prototypes, laboratories… almost anything you can think of."

"Another thing that I admire about her" says Elise, "is that although she's stunningly beautiful she seems to downplay all of that and focus on her abilities and achievements."

"I agree. She defines herself by her actions, her integrity, her character… the person within and not her outward appearance." Levine then adds with a smile and a wink, "Reminds me of *someone else* I know."

"Aww thanks Babe" she replies while almost blushing, "So I get the impression that at some point Nicole could be one of your best agents."

"She's probably at that point already. In fact, just a couple of days ago Brandi said I'd better not flip Nicole *too much* crap because she'll end of being my boss someday."

"That's exactly right, take a cue from Brandi and me, you'd better watch out when it comes to flipping us ladies crap."

"Well, I'd likely be retired by the time she works her way up to the Director's chair."

"Retired? But you *love* your job."

"It's more like a love-hate relationship" replies Levine somewhat sarcastically yet somewhat seriously.

"Who are you kidding; you *thrive* on these hard-to-crack cases."

"I have to admit, it *is* very rewarding to achieve success in the face of adversity."

"Besides, what would you do if you retired? You know *I'm* not ready for retirement."

"Well, maybe I could help you out at the Studio? After all, I can *'shuck and jive'* with the best of them" responds Levine with an over-exaggerated goofy smile and funky hip-twisting semi-dance move while he remains seated.

"Did you forget that I've seen your dance moves as recent as a couple of days ago?" she replies in a smartass tone accompanied by a wink.

"Ouch!" responds Levine.

"You know I'm just playing with you Babe; I know you can *'cut-a-rug'*, but I'm sure you have much greater interests than my dance studio."

"Hmmm... with *my* background maybe I could write True Crime novels?"

"I like the sound of that. You never know, it could be your true calling... your niche."

"Of course if I'm writing about *actual* cases then I'd need the agency's permission along with access to the files. I can see that being a major *pain-in-the-ass* right off the get-go."

"Well, how about coming up with crime dramas merely using your knowledge and expertise of solving such cases?"

"Like an amalgamation of crimes I've investigated over the years?" Levine replies as he ponders such a notion, "I like it!"

Elise responds while whispering in a breathy voice... "Ooh I love it when you use those fancy words... you know your intellect is a *huge* turn-on for me... too bad we don't have time to swing by the house for a *'nooner'*."

Levine looks at his watch and says, "Crap!" with an obvious look of disappointment, and then continues, "Well when I get home later just remember *one thing*."

"What's that?"

"It'll be the noon-hour *somewhere* in the world" he responds with a wink.

Elise smiles; and then, having finished her lunch, realizes it's time to get back to the studio. She gets up from her seat, bends over and gives him a kiss, followed by a corresponding wink and says, "Alright then... I'll see you at '*noon*'."

Levine attempts to respond, but he finds himself tripping over his own tongue.

Elise walks away, with Levine transfixed on her the entire time as she disappears from sight through the doorway.

Levine finishes his lunch and then heads to the counter to pay his bill. The cashier, who was also his server, asks him "So, how do you two do it?"

"What's that?" asks Levine.

"Keep your relationship so fresh."

"Oh that."

"What is it; '*Happy wife - Happy life*'?"

"In a sense I guess, but it's really what I call '*living the ideal life*'."

"What do you mean by '*the ideal life*'?"

"It's an unspoken promise we've made to each other."

"Unspoken?"

"Yes; we never specifically had the conversation, it's just something that evolved in our relationship."

"How do you mean?"

"It starts with communication and laughter of course; there's nothing like *laughing your ass off* on a seemingly daily basis."

"That is *so* true."

"It may sound cliché, but it's really about the simple things - letting them know that they are at the forefront of your mind, and how much they mean to you."

She ponders Levine's statement for a moment, trying to ensure she understood his meaning. Levine takes this opportunity to provide clarification...

"Each day you try to do a little something for them... it could be merely a heartfelt word or a small gesture, but it is given without expectation for anything in return except the gift of knowing you brightened their day... you made them feel special."

"Perfectly said."

"Thanks, but she's the one who deserves all the credit. It's how she has always treated me, and luckily I wasn't a complete dunderhead and figured it out... so I continue to try my best to live by this credo."

22

Conroy is escorted by a First Class Master-at-Arms into a Conference Room on the Oh-Three level of the USS SEADRAGON.

Airman Apprentice Sewell, clad in the orange jumpsuit that all sailors on restriction have the '*honor*' of wearing, is seated at the conference room table.

Conroy notices that Sewell is surprisingly unkempt considering that he undergoes a daily morning inspection and is escorted wherever he goes. He looks like a sailor who's been thrown in the brig and restricted to a bread & water diet, but the Navy doesn't do such a thing these days so Conroy figures this is just Sewell's *preferred look*... his *personal sense of style*.

Conroy pulls up a seat across the table from Sewell. The Master-at-Arms says, "I'll be right outside the door, Sir."

Conroy replies, "Thanks."

As he prepares to start questioning Sewell, Conroy knows that the best way to get a Hot-Head to screw up and implicate oneself is to get them riled-up. Conroy figures he'll start off by merely flipping Sewell some shit, and then '*ratchet it up*' over the duration of his interview.

"Nice poopy-suit Airman" says Conroy as he scans Sewell's outfit.

"I dress according to the occasion... I figure it's a step up from the '*Got it at Goodwill*' look *you've* got going on there" responds Sewell, "and it's Airman Apprentice."

"That's right... Airman *Apprentice*."

"So, who the hell are you?"

"Special Agent Conroy, NCIS" replies Conroy as he flashes his badge and ID.

"NCIS is investigating a sailor who had gone UA? Nice expenditure of the taxpayer's money."

"We don't care about your going UA; we're more concerned about your relationship with Vincent Colletti."

"Who?"

"The owner of the cell phone you were using in Hawaii."

"The old dude that calls himself '*Snuffy*' and hangs out at *Davy Jones' Locker?*"

"See... you *do* know him."

"Like I told the Honolulu cops, I didn't steal the guy's phone; after he left we noticed the phone where he was sitting."

"I thought you told them you *found* the phone?"

"Yeah, I *found* the phone on the guy's *seat*."

"And who's the '*we*' you are referring to?"

"Jerry and me."

"'*Jerry*' as in '*Petty Officer Gerald Jamison*'?"

"Yeah" responds Sewell, noticeably getting a little frustrated, "Do you want to hear about the old fart or not?!"

"By all means."

"So we're hangin' out at *Davy Jones' Locker* and there's this old guy nearby just talkin' away, sea-story after sea-story, to anyone who'd listen... I swear he had about a hundred of them, he had the two of us bustin' a gut."

"So you decided to join him."

"Sure; we figured the old geezer was good for a few laughs, so we bought him a brewski and sat down to hear more of his stories."

"What kind of stories?"

"Crazy stories about port visits in the Philippines."

"*Crazy* stories?"

"Yeah, like some port city where apparently the main source of income was '*Servicing the Sailors*' if you get my drift."

"What else?"

"And he was telling us... well actually *bragging about*... how he was the 'Head Honcho' for the Plymouth launch on the ENTERPRISE back in 1978."

"And you told him you guys were going to do your *own* Plymouth launch?"

"Oh yeah, he was blown-away by that news, you'd think we made his whole year."

"Yeah?"

"Oh yeah; he said he wished he could be there for it."

Conroy wonders if Sewell just took the first step toward implicating himself and responds, "Be careful what you wish for."

"What?" replies Sewell.

"Oh nothing" says Conroy, wanting to keep Sewell guessing, and then adds, "So, what else did he talk about?"

"Having to deal with a bunch of frickin' idiots, and getting screwed-over by them; he and I could definitely relate."

"Anything else?"

"No; not really."

"That was it... you had a few drinks, a few laughs, and went your separate ways?"

"Pretty much."

"*Really?* That's not what I heard."

"What do you mean?" replies Sewell, trying to figure out what *crap* this NCIS Agent is trying to accuse him of.

"You go by '*Willie*', correct?"

"Yeah... so?"

"So, the staff at *Davy Jones' Locker* said Colletti got into a heated argument with someone named Willie."

"That's an exaggeration... we had a *difference of opinion.*"

"Your history in Singapore and Australia indicates otherwise."

"Yeah... *whatever*" replies Sewell, getting frustrated that Conroy seems to know *every damn thing* that got him '*in the shits*' while on deployment.

"Then educate me."

"He started out being pretty entertaining, but it wasn't long before we realized he was full of BS... making himself out to be some Hot Shot that everyone '*had it in for*' because they were envious."

"I thought you said that you two could relate?"

"Not when he started referring to all enlisted guys as peons, and that *Mustangs* were just enlisted pukes masquerading as officers."

"*Mustangs*?" replies Conroy - he has no idea as to what Sewell is referring.

"Yeah" says Sewell, who then continues in a smart-assed tone, "Don't they teach you NCIS guys anything about the Navy?"

"Hey, we're civilians... we're not necessarily read-in on every slang term you guys use" says Conroy, starting to realize how Sewell keeps ending up with his face being used as a punching-bag.

"Well *Mustangs* are guys that had worked their way up from enlisted to officer... like a Warrant Officer."

Conroy's eyes light up at the mention of a Warrant Officer, thinking to himself, "*Holy crap, did Sewell just tip his hand here about Bauer?*"

Sewell then continues, "He said that Mustangs were not *real* officers and it was a joke that anyone had to salute them."

"And that bothered you?"

"Hell yeah, especially when he said that the only way three enlisted or former enlisted guys... Jerry, me, and Chief Warrant Officer Bauer... could come up with our Plymouth launch was to copy *his* launch from the ENTERPRISE... what a frickin' jackass!!"

"So, you and ol' Snuffy were no longer pals?"

"Snuffy... what a stupid nickname... we started calling him '*Snuff-Film*'" says Sewell in an almost sinister laugh, "That really pissed him off."

"*Snuff-Film*?" replies Conroy, "That says a lot - a Freudian Slip perhaps?"

"Say what??" replies Sewell.

"Oh, nothing" says Conroy, figuring the more *non*-answers he provides the more confused and agitated Sewell will become.

Conroy decides to take his first shot toward getting Sewell riled-up, "So after you two came to blows..." he says.

"Hey, I told you we never..." replies Sewell in an agitated tone.

Conroy cuts him off mid-sentence to add to Sewell's frustration... "Okay, after your *difference of opinion*, then what happened?"

"The old bastard left" replies Sewell in something of a huff, "and Jerry and I had a few more drinks."

"What about his cell phone?"

"He never came back to get it so I decided to get some use out of it. I mean, what idiot doesn't think to call his phone to find out where he left it? Anyway, like I told the Honolulu cops, I haven't seen the old fart since."

"Yeah, well that doesn't mean you don't know what happened to him. You know what I think?"

"I don't really give a rip."

"Well I'm going to tell you anyway."

Sewell expected Conroy's response, and replies in a resigned tone, "Okay... what?"

Conroy decides it's time to throw a barrage of '*conjecture wrapped in facts*' at Sewell in an attempt to get him to completely lose his cool. "I think Colletti represented everything you hate about authority... about having to take orders... about military life" he says, "And maybe you saw an opportunity to get back at one of those guys that consider someone like you a peon."

"What are you talking about?"

"I'm talking about you, your buddy Jamison, and the Warrant Officer getting ol' Snuffy a ride on the Ship under the guise of being part of the launch; and unfortunately for him, his *part* was that of playing the dummy. Jamison and Bauer would come up with a way to knock him out, load him in the car, and launch him... figuring his body would never be found."

"What? You're crazy!" says Sewell, clearly starting to percolate.

"Am I?" says Conroy, now going on the attack... "Chief Warrant Officer Bauer had nothing to lose, he was dying of cancer. You and Jamison lay low until Bauer's cancer gets the best of him and then there's nothing to tie you two to the murder, all the blame goes on Bauer."

"Wait a minute" says Sewell, "You're telling me that this *Snuffy* dude was launched in the Plymouth??"

"That's *exactly* what I'm saying."

"And Jerry and the Chief Warrant Officer are the ones who launched him??"

"You *know* they are" replies Conroy.

"I don't know *shit!!*" replies Sewell in major-defensive mode, "And you can't pin anything on me, I was in Hawaii!"

"No? Ever hear of the term *'accomplice'?*"

"No fucking way!"

"*No way?* Then why did you go UA at the *same time* that Colletti was murdered?"

"My going UA had nothing to do with Colletti... I got screwed out of three port visits! I was simply getting the liberty they frickin' owed me!"

"Oh, and here's that little *Freudian Slip* I mentioned" says Conroy as he gets up from his chair and leans over toward Sewell in an almost '*in your face*' manner, "The launch was filmed and put on the Ship's website... your own little 'Snuff-Film'" he says with air-quotes.

Conroy turns around and exits the conference room. Airman Apprentice Sewell sits there shaking his head... and fuming.

23

Approaching the entryway to the office Levine still has his head in the clouds, courtesy of his lunch date with Elise.

Passing the threshold of the doorway, and in particular the sight of Conroy with a goofy grin on his face, brings Levine crashing back down to earth.

Levine's sudden return to reality is not so much a reflection on Conroy, but rather the fact that Levine expected him to be on the SEADRAGON interviewing Airman Apprentice Sewell.

Levine looks to Conroy and asks, "I take it you haven't been able to arrange an appointment to interview Sewell?"

"Actually I just got back" responds Conroy, who then looks at his watch, "About twenty minutes ago."

"I'm assuming that's the reason you're walking around with a look of *'the cat that just ate the canary'*?"

"That's a fact; it was quite the experience."

"Well, let's grab Nic, we've got a lot of catching up to do" replies Levine as he starts heading toward Nicole's desk.

"No kidding... we've got Sewell, the Squadron guys, the Contractor, and whatever Nic dug up on Bauer."

"For sure; but before I forget, did you ever find out the maker of the mask used in those *'Grandpa Bandit'* robberies?"

"Not only did I find the news footage, but it also included a bonus story; the reporters followed-up the incident with an interview of the mask-maker."

"They interviewed the mask-maker?"

"Typical media hype trying to make something out of nothing to perpetuate their story; you know, crap like... *Didn't you consider that the person buying the mask might use it for some nefarious purpose?*"

"So did you get anything useful or not?"

"I passed the info to the guys at the Lab - no news yet."

"So you're telling me that you are *waiting* for the Lab?"

Conroy realizes that the term '*waiting* for someone or something' is not in Levine's vocabulary and replies, "I'll get an updated status from the Lab by close of business."

For the second time in just a few days Conroy narrowly avoids receiving 'The Look' from Levine.

"Hey Nic, time for an update" says Conroy as Levine and he arrive at Nicole's desk.

"Let's start with your info on Chief Warrant Officer Bauer" says Levine.

"Sure" responds Nicole as she points to the 42-inch screen, "I've got his info on the screen in anticipation of your arrival."

Levine and Conroy focus on the screen.

"Chief Warrant Officer Gordon Bauer" says Nicole, "Joined the Navy in 1988 as an Aviation Electronics Technician. He had an impeccable service record, climbing through the enlisted ranks to Chief Petty Officer in 2003. Two years later he was selected as Warrant Officer, and worked his way up to the rank of Chief Warrant Officer 3 by the time he retired. His duty stations included tours on the ENTERPRISE, KITTYHAWK, CARL VINSON, JOHN C. STENNIS, and finally the SEADRAGON. He retired the day the Ship returned from deployment."

"Anything in his records regarding issues with sailors that were under his charge?" asks Levine.

"Like sailors not making rate due to bad reviews, being assigned extra duty, being put on restriction... stuff like that?" asks Nicole.

"Yeah, *especially* the fact that Sewell worked for him and Bauer's evaluation certainly didn't help Sewell's career?" adds Conroy.

"Sewell being sent up to Captain's Mast on this last deployment, but nothing other than that" replies Nicole.

"Did you find anything of note *outside* of his military records?" asks Levine.

"Like?"

"Financial problems, credit issues, drunk driving, police reports, tickets, that kind of thing."

"A couple of speeding tickets and parking tickets, but that's it."

"So, the guy had a remarkably clean record" says Conroy.

"From everything that I was able to find" responds Nicole.

"Did you come up with any possible ties between Bauer and Colletti?" asks Levine.

"They both served on the ENTERPRISE."

"But Colletti served back in the late 70's and Bauer was what... late 80's or early 90's?"

Nicole looks at her notes, "Yep... '89 to '92."

"Colletti got out of the Navy eight years before Bauer *joined*, so clearly they never served together" remarks Conroy, "But maybe they met as part of the *Fightin' Tigers* Alumni Group?"

"Bauer couldn't be an alum" responds Levine, "The squadron was decommissioned before Bauer joined the Navy."

"Shit, that's right" replies Conroy, feeling like an idiot – yet again.

"They both lived in the San Francisco Bay Area back in '95 and '96 when Bauer was on the CARL VINSON in Alameda and Colletti was at *Digitech* in Sunnyvale" says Nicole, "but the two cities are about fifty miles apart and there is no indication they ever crossed paths."

"So, there are zero commonalities between the two of them" remarks Conroy.

"Other than the Tiger Cruise" responds Levine, "And their dead bodies."

"Well yeah - there's those two things" replies Conroy.

"And we're not finding anything that would point to this guy being a cold-blooded killer, either" says Nicole.

"Oh, we've got plenty of evidence *leaning* that way, but nothing pointing us in the direction of a motive" responds Levine.

"We've prosecuted cases without a clear-cut motive before" replies Conroy.

"Yeah, but those had overwhelming evidence to the perpetrator's guilt" responds Levine, "Our evidence thus far is extremely weak; nothing but conjecture and hearsay."

"And in reality Bauer has already been prosecuted in a sense" says Conroy, "by his cancer."

"The bottom line is that we've got a lot of investigating to do before we close the book on Bauer and this case" replies Levine.

Nicole looks toward Levine and says, "You ready for a briefing on our interview with the Contractor?"

"Let's hear it" responds Levine.

"Unfortunately, we didn't get a whole lot" replies Nicole.

"For one" adds Conroy, "the Contractor was so busy conducting training sessions that Colletti and he hardly ever crossed paths."

"That was the reason the Contractor rode the Ship... to conduct training sessions?" asks Levine.

"Apparently some technical upgrade was to start right after the Ship's return from deployment, leaving the Tiger Cruise as the only opportunity to train the sailors" responds Conroy.

"He said that the only thing he knew about Colletti was that he used to fly jets in the Navy, and that he was a guest of Chief Warrant Officer Bauer" replies Nicole.

"Does that mean that the *Contractor* knew Chief Warrant Officer Bauer; considering he mentioned him by name?" asks Levine.

"He said that Bauer coordinated the training sessions, and made sure all of his crew attended" responds Nicole.

"Did he know that Bauer was also the Launch Coordinator?" asks Levine.

"Yeah, in fact he scheduled the Contractor's training around the launch since some of his crew, including himself, were participants" responds Conroy, "And so that the rest of his crew could watch it."

"What about the fact that his roommate... *Colletti*... suddenly disappeared?" asks Levine.

"He said he figured Colletti must have moved to Bauer's stateroom since he was Bauer's guest in the first place" replies Nicole.

"Since he knew Bauer, even though his only interface was these training sessions, did he have any feedback on his state of mind?" asks Levine.

"He said he seemed a bit anxious, but he had no idea why he would have been that way" responds Conroy.

"Hmmm" says Levine as he thinks for a moment, and then remarks, "Sounds like you two thought of about every question I would have asked... good job."

"Thanks" responds Nicole.

Conroy responds with a smile, and then says to Levine, "How about the Squadron guys?"

"I can tell you there is no love lost for Colletti concerning all of his former squadron members" says Levine, "To a man he was pretty much a *self-serving* S-O-B."

"Geez... our list of people that had issues with Colletti grows every time we talk to someone that had any interaction with him" remarks Conroy.

"According to the Squadron guys, Colletti viewed *everyone* as being beneath him... subordinates, peers, and even superiors" says Levine.

"Hence the names you gave us that piqued your interest?" says Nicole.

"Well, there were a couple of crewmen that Colletti had specifically wronged" replies Levine, "One guy that, thanks to intervention from the Squadron Commander, luckily avoided Colletti's wrath; but the other guy, the one with the call-sign *'Rhino'*... well, he ruined the guy's career."

"What about the other names you mentioned?" asks Conroy.

"Both Kozinski and Baldwin to this day seemed extremely pissed at Colletti" replies Levine, "With one of them, when I told him Colletti had been killed, responded *'Holy crap – Karma finally caught up with him'.*"

"Wow, that's not a feeling of sorrow or condolences for a former shipmate, that's for sure" responds Nicole.

"And the *tipping-point* for the Squadron Commander was when Colletti apparently went on a tirade in front of a bunch of the kids during their Tiger Cruise" says Levine.

"I'm guessing *that* was the impetus for Colletti getting shipped-off to Adak?" says Conroy.

"That's exactly the action the Squadron Commander took" replies Levine.

"Did any of them offer any theories as to why the killer mimicked the ENTERPRISE launch?" asks Nicole.

"They seemed to be as surprised as we were to hear *that* news" responds Levine.

"Well, the preliminary research I did on Kozinski, Baldwin, and Caldwell didn't turn up anything that might implicate them as a person behind Colletti's murder" remarks Nicole.

"No?" asks Levine... looking for clarity even though Nicole's statement was rather obvious.

"Nope; although I can do some more digging if you'd like, but I focused my investigation on finding out the identity of the guy *'Rhino'* as you had requested."

"A former Lieutenant named either *Ryno*... as in *'R-Y-N-O'*, or possibly *'Rick Ryan'*?" says Levine.

"Not *'Ryno'*; but you're real close on the other one... *'Patrick'* vice *'Rick'*" she says. "Just a sec and I'll jump back to his page on my computer."

Nicole makes a couple of 'clicks' and a 'scroll' via her computer and states, "Here we go." She follows while reading the entry aloud, "Patrick, Ryan, Lieutenant Junior Grade."

"So, what do you have on him?"

"Like you had expected, he was with squadron RVAH-17, but because of substandard FitReps he wasn't picked-up for Lieutenant, and thus had to resign his commission."

"That matches what the Squadron guys said... with Colletti being the source of his substandard FitReps even though everyone else said he... this guy *Rhino*... was a top notch pilot."

"Are you shittin' me?? Colletti *purposely* ruined this guy's career??" responds Conroy, "I'd be frickin' livid!"

"The obvious reason they considered him to be the person with the biggest reason to hold a grudge against Colletti" replies Levine.

"That might be, but wait until you hear the punchline about this guy" says Conroy.

Levine looks confused and responds, "Something tells me it is either going to be really *good* news, or really *bad* news."

Conroy looks to Nicole as if to say, "*Go ahead, Nic.*"

Nicole gets the hint to continue the story... "So, besides having to resign his commission, those FitReps *also* kept him from getting work as a pilot" she says, "And his first job after the Navy was as a Merchandising Manager with JC Penney."

"He *did* eventually get part-time work as a flight instructor at a small airport" adds Conroy, "And picked-up side jobs as a sales-transfer pilot - flying planes from the seller's location to that of the new owner."

"But two years ago, while making a transfer, he had engine problems and his plane went down shortly after takeoff" interjects Nicole, "He did not survive."

"He died *two years ago*??" responds Levine in disbelief.

"That's right" replies Nicole.

"So *that's* the frickin' punchline you had for me" remarks a dejected Levine.

"Yep... sorry Jake" responds Conroy.

"Potential suspects keep turning up dead" says Nicole.

"No shit" replies Levine, "Every time we think we've gotten a break in this case we turn around and get sucker-punched."

"And with him dying *two years ago* we can't even consider a *murder-for-hire* scenario" responds Conroy.

Levine, somewhat exasperated at this point, takes a moment to think things through.

"Are you two ready to hear about my interview with Sewell?" asks Conroy.

"Give me a minute" replies Levine.

Conroy and Nicole look at each other while awaiting Levine's decision; they can understand Levine being perplexed, if not downright frustrated at this point.

Levine grabs his cell phone, scrolls through the contacts and hits '*Send*'.

Conroy and Nicole realize something must have clicked with Levine, but have no idea what it might be.

"Hey Doc" says Levine into the phone, "Can you get the Coroner's Report for Chief Warrant Officer Bauer?"

Conroy and Nicole are surprised... this move by Levine is unexpected, to say the least.

"What's on your mind, Jake?" asks the Doctor.

"Something just doesn't feel right" responds Levine, "His dying of cancer *right after* his Tiger Cruise guest gets launched via *his* orders? It's just seems way too convenient. I want to know *exactly* what was found during his autopsy."

"I'm afraid to say that there is a potential problem with your request, Jake."

"What's that?"

"Well, for *'one'*, there is no *Coroner* in this case unless for some crazy reason he was examined in San Bernardino County."

Levine responds in a confused tone, "What??"

"San Diego County is a *Medical Examiner* system, not a *Coroner* system."

"C'mon Doc, you know what I'm talkin' about."

"Understood; but for *'two'*, it's entirely likely that *no* autopsy was performed, just an examination of the external surfaces of the body."

"How the hell is *that* possible?"

"Standard procedure for a death due to natural causes like cancer. Now if we're talking a sudden or unexpected death, an accident, drug or alcohol related, suspicious circumstances..."

"It's suspicious in *my* mind" Levine interrupts.

"Well, had you been there at the time of Bauer's examination you might have been able to make a case for it."

Levine pauses in thought for a moment, and then continues, "So, even if my gut tells me there may be something more to Bauer's death, the ability to discover anything unusual that a Coroner... forgive me... *Medical Examiner*... might have missed, is pretty much a *lost cause?*"

"Unless the family specifically requested an autopsy your statement is entirely correct. But that would *not* have made much sense for someone who, by all accounts, died of cancer. Especially since the family would've had to pay for the autopsy out of their own pockets."

"Well, humor me and assess whatever the hell there is to assess; would you, Doc?"

"I'll let you know what I find."

"I appreciate that" responds Levine, and then hangs up his phone.

"Wow, we didn't see *that* coming, Jake" says Conroy.

"It will probably turn out to be nothing" replies Levine, "but this whole *'coincidental death due to cancer'* has been gnawing at me."

"You and me both" says Conroy, "but I was a little reluctant to bring it up."

"Never hold back when it comes to investigating a case."

"Got it."

"With that in mind Slade, what did you get out of Airman Apprentice Sewell?"

"You know how reports were that Sewell claimed to have *found* Colletti's cell phone?" says Conroy, "Which seemed to imply he just *happened across* the phone and never actually met Colletti?"

"Are you saying that he acquired the phone by either stealing it or by robbing Colletti?" asks Levine.

"The jury is still out on that, but both Sewell *and* Jamison *did* actually meet Colletti."

"A *planned* meeting?"

"A *chance* meeting according to Sewell… at *Davy Jones' Locker*."

"Where Colletti got into a heated argument with a guy named *Willie*?" says Levine, recalling the report from the Honolulu PD.

"Our man *Willie Sewell!*" responds Conroy in an affirming manner, "Although Sewell insists it was simply a *difference of opinion*."

"Difference of opinion over *what*?"

"About how worthless enlisted guys and Warrant Officers are."

"Colletti specifically called-out Warrant Officers?"

"Technically, Sewell said that Colletti used the term *'Mustangs'*."

"Same difference" responds Levine with a head-nod of understanding.

Nicole, however, is unfamiliar with the term and asks, "What exactly is a *Mustang*, and how does it equate to a *Warrant Officer*?"

"A *Mustang* is slang for an enlisted guy that worked his way up the ranks to become an officer" responds Levine, who then adds clarification, "It could either be as a Warrant Officer or as an LDO… Limited Duty Officer… which would be the same ranks as a Line Officer such as Ensign, Lieutenant, Commander - the ones we are all familiar with."

"I learn something new every day" replies Nicole.

"Anyway" says Conroy, "it sure had me wondering whether Sewell had '*tipped his hand*' as far as Chief Warrant Officer Bauer being involved."

"Based on the fact that Colletti had an intense dislike for Warrant Officers?" responds Nicole.

"Yeah, we're talking statements like '*they were not real officers and it was a joke that anyone had to salute them*'" replies Conroy.

"But Chief Warrant Officer Bauer wasn't even there when this confrontational conversation was going on, correct?" asks Levine.

"There was no mention of that from Sewell" replies Conroy, "but he may be keeping tight-lipped about Bauer in order to avoid any ties to him."

"Yeah" says Nicole, "If the three of them were '*in on it*' together, with Bauer dying of cancer, and Sewell and Jamison feigning ties to him, all the blame goes on Bauer."

"And get this" says Conroy, "Then they started harassing him about his nickname 'Snuffy', calling him '*Snuff-Film*'."

This information catches Levine and Nicole off-guard.

"Wow, that sounds like a Freudian Slip if I've ever heard one" says Nicole.

"That's *exactly* what I said to Sewell" responds Conroy, "And boy did it piss him off."

"But not enough to inadvertently incriminate himself?" replies Levine.

"No, but we could always take another crack at him" responds Conroy.

"Perhaps" says Levine, "But one thing is awfully curious."

"What's that?" asks Conroy.

"We know Sewell and Jamison told Colletti about the launch, but we haven't found a single piece of evidence of him actually being invited to ride the Ship… no phone call, no letter, no email… nothing" says Levine, "So, how the *hell* did he get aboard?!"

24

Honolulu – Six Weeks Ago

Off in the distance the *Sunset Dinner Cruise* boat, a very popular attraction for couples on vacation, beached itself at its designated mooring on the sands of Waikiki. Down came the boat's attached gangway; with a crewman leading the seemingly endless flow of happy travelers, along with the slightly tipsy and the unfortunate few who succumbed to seasickness, down the ramp and onto the sand… still warm from the afternoon sun.

"It's 'Go Time'" he said to himself as he turned back to the entryway of *Davy Jones' Locker*; a relatively small bar that, being somewhat secluded, managed to avoid all of the fanfare that defines the majority of Waikiki Beach.

He entered the dimly-lit bar. The thought of 'mood lighting' might come to mind, but *Davy Jones' Locker* was not exactly a haven for women; for *that* you'd need to make your way down the beach to *Duke's Canoe Club*… the Waikiki *"hot spot"* perfectly nestled between the two iconic hotels on the beach… the *Royal Hawaiian*, and *Moana Surfrider*. No, *Davy Jones' Locker* catered primarily to the sailors in town… those stationed at Pearl Harbor, those whose vessels were making a liberty stop in Hawaii, and retired seadogs that frequented the joint.

"Hey Stranger" said the barkeep, "Welcome to *Davy Jones' Locker*… sit anywhere you'd like."

The Stranger looked around and realized that even in the light of day the bar would be cave-like dark as it was mostly below ground, akin to the daylight basement of a home from the 1930's or 40's, or that of a more contemporary split-level; with a row of narrow windows virtually hugging the ceiling.

Behind the bar was a huge window, so to speak. Specifically, it was a large area of thick glass containing an aquarium of sorts, as if the bar had been built adjacent to a swimming pool. It reminded him of a public aquarium he had seen... not the large aquarium on Seattle's waterfront, but more like the smaller one at the *Point Defiance Zoo* in Tacoma, Washington. However; this aquarium was devoid of sea-life, with exception of the periodic bikini-topped beauty swimming about in a mermaid outfit.

"An interesting way to make a living, or more likely, an extra buck" he thought to himself as he watched the *'mermaid'*, *"providing entertainment of the visual kind to the male patrons of the bar."*

The "aquarium" also contained a sunken galleon, several sets of skeletons clad in pirate outfits, and a sunken 'treasure chest' with the lid open displaying its 'booty' of gold coins.

The bar was abuzz with sea-stories, laughter, and colorful language. He scanned the room, drifting between *'getting lost in the crowd'* and *'lurking in the shadows'*... he was sure that his *reason for being here* was somewhere within the crowd.

He spied someone who appeared to be in his mid-sixties doing his best to be the center of attention... animated and flailing about... entertaining a couple of twenty-something guys with stories of his adventures *'back in the day'*. This self-proclaimed hero was clad in shorts and the ubiquitous Hawaiian shirt, which was barely visible beneath an aviator jacket - his *'cloak of honor'* as it were. His audience, the two twenty-somethings, were dressed in civvies but exhibited all the signs of sailors on liberty... their stories of long days at sea, port visits focused more on strip clubs than experiencing the various cultures, and the bad-mouthing of the U.S. Navy hierarchy being the tell-tale indicators.

The Stranger made his way over to the vicinity of the trio... close enough to eavesdrop on their conversation and get a better bead on the aviator, while still being inconspicuous... *just another face in the crowd.*

As The Stranger was about to settle-in to his preferred listening post he inadvertently stepped into the glare of an overhead track light. *"Shit!"* he said to himself as he immediately receded back into the shadows and looked around for a new vantage-point. He spied a small high-boy two-topper tucked away in a nearby corner and slithered over to it. It was perfect... close enough to eavesdrop, yet dark and secluded so as to minimize any chance of detection as he stalked his potential prey.

"You're a fucking maniac, Snuffy!" proclaimed one of the young men in a fit of laughter, with the trio clinking their beer bottles together as a toast to the Gods of Barley and Hops.

The nickname sealed it... The Stranger had found the person of whom he had sought.

He sat there taking-in the conversation; with Snuffy's stories getting progressively more ridiculous as the night wore on. The way Snuffy told it you'd think he was the inspiration for Tom Cruise's *'Maverick'* character in *'Top Gun'*.

"I can't believe these impressionable sailors are buying this load of crap" The Stranger quietly said to himself aloud.

The conversation turned to *the Plymouth launch* the young sailors had planned for the SEADRAGON. Snuffy's eyes lit up and he metaphorically salivated like Pavlov's Dogs. This was the scenario The Stranger had planned for... the sailors were baiting the hook... the next step was to find the perfect moment to reel Snuffy in.

Snuffy 'went off' like an egotist who had just been given an award for being *'all that'*. Building himself-up to be the brains behind all things awesome, Snuffy explained to the sailors how he alone had engineered *the Plymouth launch* back on the ENTERPRISE. The sailors listened, almost in awe, as Snuffy described the event in excruciating detail. However, as he spun his web of tales the more outlandish they became, and the sailor's responses transitioned over time from "Really? How cool!" to "That's a bunch of bullshit!"

After several beers and a lot of bellowing the scene suddenly took an interesting turn... Snuffy's disdain for enlisted sailors had revealed itself. Apparently ol' Snuffy forgot the company he was keeping, or no longer gave a shit.

It started with Snuffy bragging about how he had put lowly '*bluejackets*' in their place, riding their asses, and making sure they cowered in his presence. "They'd give me the respect I deserved as a Naval officer or they'd pay for it!" Snuffy proudly proclaimed, "I'd show those worthless uneducated peons who was boss."

The sailors were taken aback, and tried to point out that it was the enlisted guys who actually did all of the physical work... operating the equipment to ensure a safe launching and recovery of the aircraft. But it was to no avail; in Snuffy's opinion a trained monkey could perform such duties.

And Snuffy's wrath wasn't confined to your everyday run-of-the-mill enlisted sailor. An enlisted sailor that had worked his way up to Officer... well, *that* was the *worst* because they were actually receiving *salutes*... a complete abomination in Snuffy's eyes.

The sailors were visibly agitated at this point, and they were not alone; The Stranger was finding that his calm and cool demeanor was being quickly heated toward the boiling point, courtesy of the rambling diatribe spewing-forth from Snuffy's pie-hole.

Snuffy went on to brag about how he had ruined a young Lieutenant's career for having the gall to question his orders. The moral according to Snuffy: *Don't fuck with me or I'll screw you over by a factor of ten.*

"*Some of us aren't handed our lives on a silver platter you fucking asshole*" said The Stranger to himself in response to Snuffy's continuous onslaught.

When Snuffy remarked that the sailors were too stupid to come up with their *own* Plymouth launch, and thus were relegated to copying *his* launch from the ENTERPRISE... well, *enough was enough*...

"I'm about to launch this fuck-head right out of his chair" one of the sailors whispered to the other.

"You want to get your ass thrown in the slammer? Remember that there's a time and a place... and this ain't it" responded his shipmate.

"I can't just sit here and take this shit while we wait for *'the right time'*."

"So, do what you always do; throw some shit right back at him. I'm sure you can think of a way to fuck with his head."

It turned out Snuffy had met his match... the young sailor had an equal disdain for officers, *especially* a *former* officer who still thought he had some sort of rank over him. The sailor may not have had a comeback in regard to Snuffy's rank, but he quickly pounced on his nickname, and started referring to him as *'Snuff-Film'*. This did the trick, with Snuffy growing increasingly agitated at the use of his newly-acquired moniker. The Stranger had to hand it to the young sailor, having to hold back his own laughter upon hearing the *'Snuff-Film'* reference.

The decibel level of the verbal exchange between Snuffy and the sailors was quickly escalating; and although The Stranger would've liked nothing more than to see ol' Snuffy get his comeuppance right then and there, he realized that would *not* be a good thing. *"Don't screw up the plan, Boys"* he said to himself.

Fortunately for The Stranger, before things got completely out of hand, the more-reserved sailor sent the smart-assed hot-head over to the bar to get the two of them another beer... a strategic move in the hopes that an interruption of the verbal sparring might cool down the situation; or better yet, that Snuffy would get the hint and get his pathetic ass out of there.

Snuffy saw this as an opportunity to save face; to finish things on *his* terms. He grabbed a few bills from the pile of cash that had accumulated on the table, got up, and without a single word to the remaining sailor, headed toward the exit.

"See you later... *Snuff-Film!*" echoed across the room as Snuffy made his exit.

Following, while maintaining a distance, The Stranger subtly made his way to the exit as well.

As the Stranger stepped into the dark of night outside of *Davy Jones' Locker* he saw Snuffy, looking a bit lost, standing several feet down the pathway.

The Stranger realized he'd let Snuffy get into his head... that he needed to quickly regroup, regain his composure, and become the *Snake Oil Salesman* necessary to execute *Phase Two* of his plan.

The Stranger approached. "Excuse me" he said as Snuffy turned to see who was there, "You wouldn't happen to be Vincent Colletti would you?"

Snuffy looked somewhat surprised, and responded "The guys call me *Snuffy.*"

"Well, I'm glad I finally found you, Sir" said The Stranger as he reached out to shake Snuffy's hand, "You're the last of the *Fightin' Tigers* I was hoping to catch up with before the SEADRAGON departs in the morning."

Snuffy was caught off-guard, "I am? I don't understand."

"I don't know if you are aware" said The Stranger, "but the SEADRAGON is going to perform the launching of a car just like you and your Squadron did back on the ENTERPRISE."

"Yes, I've heard of that" replied Snuffy, who then pointed toward *Davy Jones' Locker* and said, "In fact, I was just telling a couple of sailors at *Davy Jones'* here that I wished I could be there to see it."

"Well, today is your lucky day, Sir" responded The Stranger, "It just so happens that I am the coordinator for the launching and at the behest of the Ship's Captain you and a number of your *Fightin' Tiger* Squadron members are requested to be the Official Guests of Honor."

Snuffy responded with both disbelief and joy, "Do you mean me and..." thinking for a moment, "...*Condor?*"

"Yep" responded the Stranger.

"...and *Jaguar?*"

"Sure."

"...*Spades?*"

"Oh yeah."

"...*Warlock?*"

"Uh huh."

"...*Rhino?*"

"Yep."

"...and the rest of the guys?" said Snuffy as he was drawing a blank on the names of any remaining former Squadron members.

"Actually that's pretty much it" replied The Stranger.

"*Wait a minute...*" said Snuffy as he realized something was amiss, "Now that I think of it, I thought I heard that *Rhino* died a couple of years ago?"

"Oh, you're right" replied The Stranger, quickly covering his tracks, "I was just remembering the guys on the list and had forgotten what I'd learned about *Rhino.*"

"So, we all get to ride the SEADRAGON as guests of the Captain?" asked Snuffy, still in disbelief as to such an opportunity presenting itself.

"Not only *that* Sir, but I also heard that you were the *mastermind* behind the car launch on the ENTERPRISE" replied The Stranger as he took a major step toward feeding Snuffy's ego.

"Yes I was" responded Snuffy with his chest pumped-out in a showing of pride.

Fortunately for The Stranger the darkness of the night masked his '*rolling-of-the-eyes*' response to Snuffy's false bravado.

"That means that *you* will be the *Featured Guest* for our launching" replied The Stranger.

"I'll be the Featured Guest?! Wow, then I can tell everyone all about *my* launching!" responded a highly-excited Snuffy.

"That's exactly what we were hoping, Sir" replied The Stranger, adding another puff of air to Snuffy's overinflated ego. "But none of the launch-guys know that you will be in attendance, it is set up to be a *huge* surprise to be revealed immediately following the launch."

"That would be fantastic!"

"With that being the case though Sir, you will have to *lay-low* until just before the launching."

"I'll have to lay-low?" asked a disappointed Snuffy.

"It will only be a couple of days, Sir. And you can still enjoy aspects of the Tiger Cruise that do not involve the Flight Deck and the launch crew."

"I guess that wouldn't be so bad."

The Stranger looked at his watch and said, "And I apologize that it is such short notice, but the Ship gets underway early in the morning."

"You mean I have to go home and pack *right now??*"

"I'm sorry, but yes, that is the case. I'll drive you home, wait while you throw together a small suitcase, and we'll head to the Ship."

"But how will I get back home?"

"I have your return plane ticket from San Diego right here" replied The Stranger as he held up a ticket, "First Class."

Snuffy's concern subsided and he suddenly lit-up like he had just won the lottery.

"By the way" added The Stranger, "do you happen to have your old flight suit?"

"Yes, I do."

"Perfect."

"This is going to be the best time of my life" said Snuffy.

"And mine" replied The Stranger.

25

Levine sits at his desk and jots-down the agenda for the day via his favorite writing implement – a mechanical pencil with a 0.7mm lead. The 0.5mm lead is too sharp and too fragile, resulting in either ripping right through the paper or in multiple shards of broken lead filling up his trash can. And the 0.9mm is much too thick… you might as well be writing with a crayon. As Levine is prone to making minor tweaks to his agenda a suitable eraser is equally important, with a cylindrical mechanical pencil-like devise being his eraser of choice.

As Levine captures the first couple of items on his agenda he is interrupted by the ringing of his desk phone; the Caller ID showing that it is the Director on the com-line. Considering there was no hint of conversation to be heard from the Director's office Levine figures this can only mean one thing – the Director needs a quick update before his weekly call with the mucky-mucks back in D.C.

"Hey John" says Levine as he picks up the phone.

"Yeah Jake, can you swing by my office?" asks the Director.

"On my way."

Levine barely makes it through the doorway of the Director's office when the Director says, "I don't need a lot of detail, just a brief update on the *Colletti* case. The last I had was that your prime suspect had died of cancer, and you were trying to come up with enough evidence to confidently identify him as the perpetrator and close the case."

"We've interviewed several people with ties to Colletti: The guy that was his stateroom-mate during the Tiger Cruise, his former Squadron members, and one of the two missing sailors that we considered a person of interest."

"Judging by the sound of your voice you still have nothing definitive."

"We have yet to find *one true tie* between Colletti and Chief Warrant Officer Bauer – the prime suspect."

"But didn't you say that he was the one who *sponsored* Colletti on the Tiger Cruise?"

"Yeah, but that's just another one of the conundrums. We checked both Colletti's and Bauer's phone records and there is not a single call between them, *so how the hell did Bauer make contact and invite him to ride the Ship??*"

"So, the bottom line is that we've made a lot of progress, but we have a number of leads yet to follow-up on?"

"That's it exactly. You always know how to put the proper political spin on things; thank God you're the Director and not me."

"Alright, I've got it" replies the Director, "Keep me posted."

Levine gives the Director a thumbs-up acknowledgment and makes his exit.

As Levine heads back toward his desk he checks his watch; he has seven minutes until his 7:15 Team Meeting.

"Luckily today's agenda is mostly fluid… only a couple of specific items to address" Levine thinks to himself as he passes Conroy and Nicole – the two of them having arrived while Levine was briefing the Director.

Levine jots down the last item on his list and then speaks aloud toward Conroy and Nicole, "Hey Slade… Nic… you two ready?"

Conroy and Nicole walk over and seat themselves across from Levine.

"So, Slade" says Levine, "You were going to get the *latest and greatest* about the mask by 'close of business' yesterday."

"Indeed I did" says Conroy, "The guys at the Lab found the maker of the mask, a prop and costume shop in Burbank called *Hollywood Props.*"

"And?"

"It took a lot of digging, but we were able to verify that the mask *and* dummy were purchased together."

"Please tell me the buyer used a credit card."

"Nope; cash."

"How do we know the mask and dummy purchased are the ones used in support of the Plymouth launch?"

"When the buyer called to reserve them for purchase and pick-up he had to give a name."

"Finally a frickin' break!" responds Levine.

"Not exactly" replies Conroy as he hands Levine a printout from *Hollywood Props* that identifies buyers in chronological order by date of purchase. One particular name on the list is yellow-highlighted.

"*'Snuffy Savoy'??* Are you fucking kidding me?!!" responds Levine.

"The name of the victim… and the horse he rode in on" replies Conroy, trying to elicit a small amount of humor in light of the situation.

"*The car he was launched in*" responds Levine with a very *non*-humorous look, "I get it."

Nicole is taken aback; this is the first she has heard of this news as well.

"Purchased ten months ago" says Conroy as he points to the associated item on the list Levine is still holding.

"I suppose it's too much to ask if any of them remembered the buyer and have provided us with a description?"

"They said these are extremely popular items, selling dozens of them every month, mostly to local film studios and playhouses. And with this particular sale occurring almost a year ago, none of them could recall anything about the buyer."

"I said it several days ago and it still holds true" says Levine, "We've got our work cut out for us trying to catch *this* fucking bastard."

"I think the descriptor you used several days ago was *'son-of-a-bitch'*" responds Conroy.

"Well he's been upgraded" replies Levine, "Or downgraded; depending on one's perspective."

Levine, visibly frustrated, throws the list back toward Conroy. The list's forward motion ceases almost immediately after leaving Levine's hand and then starts a pendulum-like descent toward the floor. Conroy reaches out and catches the list as it is about to kiss the carpet.

"Okay" says Levine as he recaptures his composure, "The mask and dummy were purchased ten months ago... what does that tell us?"

"It was purchased *before* the Ship deployed overseas" replies Nicole.

"*Exactly*" responds Conroy, "So the killer apparently *knew* a car was going to be launched during the Tiger Cruise."

"Or he had something else altogether in mind and the Tiger Cruise launch was Plan-B" says Levine.

"Damn Jake, you always come up with an alternative I hadn't thought of" replies Conroy.

"Actually Slade I agree with your assessment that the killer knew there was going to be a launch" responds Levine, "I just want to make sure we keep an open mind to other possibilities."

"And the timing makes sense because the mask, and surely the dummy, had to have been brought aboard the Ship before they departed" says Nicole.

"That's right" replies Conroy who then looks toward Levine, "Because Jake, weren't you saying that the launch guys had all seen the dummy and mask *well before* the launching?"

"Well yeah, there's that" responds Levine, "And with the dummy being the size of an adult male it's not like it was going to show up in some sailor's '*care package*'."

"When you think about it" says Nicole, "It just confirms what we had already expected."

"That the killer was someone who had been on the Ship the entire time, and not someone who just showed up for the Tiger Cruise, killed Colletti, and then disappeared" replies Conroy.

"Let's see if we can put any of our *persons of interest* in the vicinity of *Hollywood Props* on the date the mask and dummy were sold" says Levine.

"Got it" replies Conroy, jotting it down on the infamous list of buyers from *Hollywood Props*.

"What's next on your agenda, Jake?" asks Nicole.

"I'm glad you asked, Nic; how about putting the launch footage on the screen?" replies Levine.

"Is there something you think we might have missed?" responds Nicole.

"We have not yet zeroed-in on Petty Officer Jamison" responds Levine, "I figure it's high time we take a closer look at his actions during the launch."

"Sure thing" replies Nicole.

Nicole manipulates her computer keyboard and mouse, clicks on the 'launch' icon, and the footage appears on the 42-inch screen.

Nicole looks toward Levine and says, "Ready when you are."

"Go ahead."

Nicole hits the *'Play'* icon and the footage starts to run.

"Zoom-in so we can get a closer look at Petty Officer Jamison" says Levine.

Nicole zooms-in while the footage continues to run; up to the point where Petty Officer Jamison starts performing the final checks of the car in preparation for the launching.

"Stop" directs Levine.

Nicole stops the footage and Levine then says, "Now zoom-in closer; I want to see *exactly* what he's doing."

Nicole zooms-in and starts the footage. We see Petty Officer Jamison scanning the car back-to-front, jumping under the front near the axle to check the catapult connection, and finally at the driver's-side door. This up-close look reveals a detail that was not nearly so evident before... that Jamison doesn't merely back away from the driver's-side door; he is *jumping back* and away.

"Holy crap!" says Nicole, "He jumped back like he just saw a ghost."

"Son of a Bitch" replies Levine, "Time to find our missing Petty Officer."

26

At the entrance to the NCIS Office a familiar sound is heard... 'beep-beep-beep-beep-beeeeep'. It is the sound of an authorized-user swiping their ID and entering their associated pass-code on the security keypad. The long beep is followed by "click" and the opening of the door.

The Office Administrative Assistant, Erin Larson, mid-thirties with curly bright red hair and a professional appearance so polished most visitors assume she's the Boss, looks up from her desk to see who has entered. Erin sees a familiar face and elicits a welcoming "Good Morning Doc" as Doctor Watson enters.

"Ms. Larson" replies the Doctor with a head-nod as he acknowledges her greeting and continues on toward Levine's office.

Levine, hearing a familiar voice, looks up from his desk to see Doctor Watson rounding the corner and heading his way.

"Hey Doc" says Levine, "I wasn't expecting you to stop by."

"I was over at the Naval Medical Center at Balboa Park and figured I'd pay you a visit" replies the Doctor.

"Balboa Park?"

"Chief Warrant Officer Bauer's post-mortem examination results" replies the Doctor as he holds up a manila envelope.

"And?" replies Levine.

"We're in luck – of sorts."

"*Of sorts?*"

"Even though the Chief Warrant Officer was retired and thus *should have* fallen under the jurisdiction of the San Diego County Medical Examiner's Office, he was treated as if he was still Active Duty Military."

"I'm at a bit of a loss here, Doc."

"He was examined by an Armed Forces Medical Examiner representative at the Naval Medical Center."

"I take it that's a good thing?"

"It means he received more of an examination than just the external surfaces of the body."

"Now you're talkin'."

"Well, be advised that it may give us nothing more than we already know."

"You haven't seen it yet?"

"Being *confidential information* it was sealed when I received it, so I figured I'd wait until I was in a secure area such as this to open and review the contents."

Doctor Watson opens the report and commences his review.

Levine sits and stares at the Doctor as he is reading. Judging by the level of anticipation you'd think Levine was a High School Class Valedictorian waiting for Dad to read him the results of the letter that just arrived from Harvard.

The Doctor stops suddenly, and with a perplexed look on his face says to himself aloud, "This can't be right." He flips back to the first page to see the name of the victim, figuring they *must* have given him the wrong report. However, the name is right… the description is right, but…

Levine can tell something's amiss, "What's the problem, Doc?" he asks.

"The Chief Warrant Officer had an inoperable brain tumor, and certainly would have been dead within a matter of weeks."

"What do you mean *would have* been dead?? Are you telling me that the Report identifies something *other than* cancer as the cause of death?"

"In my opinion, yes… digitalis in his system at a toxic level - surely causing cardiac arrest."

Levine is agitated to say the least, "So why is *that* not listed as the cause of death?!" he rails, "Is the Coroner... or M.E. or *whatever the hell he is*... complicit in a murder, or merely incompetent?!!"

"Your guess is as good as mine Jake, but you've got to look at the positive here."

"The *positive*??" replies Levine, clearly not in the mood to '*look at the bright side*'... whatever that could possibly be under the circumstances.

"Yes. Remember that there was *no reason* for the Doctor to perform an autopsy in the first place, and even more so, there was no reason to conduct a Tox Screen. Had he followed protocol we never would have discovered this anomaly, and this cause of Bauer's death never would have been discovered."

"Okay, I'll grant you that. And I realize it could be a major break in the case, but this guy's *still* got some frickin' explaining to do."

"I concur; I'll let you know as soon as I have him on the line."

"You can use my office; I'd like to get to the bottom of this as soon as possible."

"Understood."

As the Doctor attempts to contact the attending pathologist Levine gets up and takes a stroll around the office space to clear his head.

Levine's sojourn lasts about ten paces when he encounters Conroy and Nicole returning from a coffee-run. The two of them stop in their tracks at the sighting of Levine, and they can see the look of displeasure on his face.

"Your dark roast" says Conroy... handing Levine a sleeve-wrapped latte' cup.

"Thanks" replies Levine.

"Some bad news about the case?" inquires Nicole to Levine.

"You could say that" replies Levine, "It turns out that Chief Warrant Officer Bauer did *not* die of cancer."

Nicole and Conroy are taken aback.

"But the Death Certificate..." responds a very confused Nicole.

"Was a cover-up, gross misconduct, a conspiracy, complicit in a murder, incompetence - take your pick" replies Levine before Nicole can finish her statement.

"But how could that be?" replies Nicole, still trying to wrap her head around this news.

"That's what the Doc is trying to find out" responds Levine, "He's on the phone in my office as we speak, trying to get hold of the pathologist that conducted Bauer's autopsy."

"Are *you* planning on talking to him?" asks Conroy.

"The pathologist?" replies Levine, "Hell yes!"

Conroy and Nicole remain silent as they ponder the issue with diametrically-opposed thoughts regarding Levine's impending chat with the pathologist. In Conroy's case it's *"This is gonna be good"*, and in Nicole's case it's *"Thank God I'm not the pathologist."*

A voice emanates from the direction of Levine's office…

"Agent Levine, I have the pathologist on the line" says Doctor Watson.

"On my way, Doc" replies Levine.

27

Levine walks into his office and sees that Doctor Watson is on a video feed with the pathologist.

"Doctor Corwin" says Doctor Watson as he speaks toward the video screen, "I have Special Agent Levine here with me."

Doctor Corwin is in his mid-thirties with dark hair. He is wearing his U.S. Navy khakis, with a gold oak-leaf on his right collar lapel identifying his rank of Lieutenant Commander, and a taller and slimmer *'oak-leaf with acorn'* on his left collar lapel identifying him as being in the Medical Corps.

"What can I do for you Doctor; Special Agent Levine?" asks Doctor Corwin.

"There is an item on Chief Warrant Officer Bauer's report that is, shall I say, rather troubling" says Doctor Watson.

"I assume you are referring to the Tox Screen results?" replies Doctor Corwin, continuing with clarification, "The digitalis being identified in his system?"

"Yes Doctor" begins a very perturbed Levine, "How is it that you discover digitalis at a toxic level in his system and *then* denote his cause of death as cancer?"

"I surmised he must have taken his own life so that he wouldn't have to go through a prolonged and painful death due to his advanced-stage cancer" replies Doctor Corwin.

"Then why list his cause of death as *cancer* and not *suicide*?" asks Doctor Watson.

"I didn't want to tarnish the reputation of a decorated serviceman by ruling his death a suicide when his cancer was so advanced he likely would have died in a matter of weeks anyway."

"You didn't consider he might have been *murdered?*" asks Levine.

"*Murdered??*" responds Doctor Corwin, "That possibility never entered my mind."

"And why is that, Doctor?" replies Doctor Watson.

"His doctor reported he didn't want his family to see him deteriorate into a frail, bedridden man" responds Doctor Corwin, "In fact, he had hoped that he might gasp his last breath during this deployment... serving his country."

"You talked to his doctor?"

"Yes; I wanted to do my due diligence regarding my assumption of suicide by obtaining an understanding of his state of mind."

"And where did you *surmise* he got the digitalis?" asks Levine in a condescending manner.

Levine's question catches Doctor Corwin off-guard, and he hesitantly attempts to respond, "Well I...", but he finds himself stumbling on the attempt, which results in nothing but a pause.

Levine jumps at Doctor Corwin's obvious lack of an ability to articulate an answer, and responds in an agitated manner... "Exactly what I thought" he says, "Deciding to protect his reputation in lieu of stating the *facts* may have covered up a murder."

Doctor Corwin quickly backtracks, responding, "That wasn't the case at all, Sir."

Conroy makes a mental note to himself as he listens to this exchange between Levine and Doctor Corwin... *"It's amazing how, when you start yelling at someone, they suddenly start calling you 'Sir' - even when they are a doctor."*

"Then what was it??!!" asks Levine of Doctor Corwin, awaiting some defensive response full of medical mumbo-jumbo in an attempt to save face.

"I specifically asked Chief Warrant Officer Bauer's doctor if anyone in his family might have had digitalis prescribed" replies Doctor Corwin.

"And he told you *'Yes'*?" responds Doctor Watson, surprised that a physician would have agreed to reveal confidential medical information.

"He said that *'he wasn't at liberty to say'*" replies Doctor Corwin, "Which I took as an *implied* affirmation."

"Oh, I can't take any more of this, Doc" says Levine to Doctor Watson, and then turns and walks out of the office.

Doctor Watson thanks Doctor Corwin for his time and then hangs up the phone.

"Well, *now* we need to add Chief Warrant Officer Bauer's *murder* to our investigation" proclaims Levine to Conroy and Nicole.

Doctor Watson gives Levine a nudge and says, "Technically Jake, we don't have enough evidence at this point to rule out a suicide."

"Correction" says Levine to Conroy and Nicole, "We need to add Bauer's *'death'* to our investigation. Start looking into anyone that might have had a reason to kill him."

"*Colletti's killer* if Bauer was the accomplice and wanted to silence him - for one" responds Conroy.

"Or *Bauer's accomplice* if he... Bauer... was Colletti's killer" adds Nicole.

"I'm not talking about nameless phantoms" says a frustrated Levine, "I'm talking about coworkers, neighbors that he might have had an issue with, so-called 'friends', his wife's lover if such a person exists..."

"Got it" replies Conroy.

Nicole nods her head to indicate agreement with Conroy's statement.

Levine turns to Doctor Watson and says, "Your thoughts, Doc?"

"Since we can now consider Chief Warrant Officer Bauer's death as a possible homicide" says the Doctor, "that changes our ability to obtain medical information regarding any of his relatives; at least when it comes to a prescription for digitalis."

"That's something you'll look into?"

"Of course."

"And also from the perspective of a possible homicide" says Levine, "We need to figure out how a killer might have administered the digitalis."

"Well, it's available in both tablet and liquid form."

"*Liquid* form?? You mean like cough syrup? That seems like a dangerous option… a high risk for an overdose I would think."

"You wouldn't use a spoon or one of those little plastic Nyquil dose-cups; the liquid form utilizes an eye dropper so as to regulate the dosage."

"A liquid would sure make it easy to slip the drug into someone's drink" says Levine as he envisions such an act.

"As you know Jake, some killers will incapacitate their victim and then use *injection* as the means to introduce the fatal concoction."

"But isn't that pretty much just in those cases where the drug is only available in a vial specifically designed to have the contents withdrawn through a needle?"

"That's exactly right. Adding the drug to someone's drink is the most common method of introduction, so that's what I'd expect in this case."

"Does Bauer's autopsy identify his estimated time of death?"

"Yes it does."

"So, we just need to find out who was with Bauer near the time of his death and we've narrowed our suspect list down to a few, if not just one, person" responds Levine with a tone of optimism for the first time in days.

Thinking back to his initial frustrations in finding out the true cause of Bauer's death, Levine realizes that Bauer's autopsy results from Doctor Corwin is actually a *good* thing.

"And if we find that *no one* was with him near the time of his death?" replies the Doctor.

"Then I'll *consider* suicide as a possible option" responds Levine.

28

Alternating between a bite of a club sandwich and a sip of coffee, Levine has about a dozen things running through his head.

The ponderings at the forefront of his mind are those that are the most recent - *how was Chief Warrant Officer Bauer slipped the digitalis that killed him? ...who was his killer? ...and why was he killed?* The other items of note concern Petty Officer Jamison - *what was his involvement, if any, in either or both of Colletti's and Bauer's murders? And if he had no such involvement, what reason could he possibly have for going UA?*

Levine jots down the aforementioned ponderings on a notepad; his way of ensuring that no thought, concern, or item of interest gets overlooked or gets lost within the larger aspects of the investigation. After all, it is often a single detail... one minor piece of the puzzle... that solves the case.

"Hey Slade - Nic" says Levine loud enough to reverberate from his desk to theirs, "Any luck tracking down Petty Officer Jamison?"

Conroy and Nicole stroll over to Levine's desk.

"Shall we start with the *not-so-good* news?" says Conroy.

"Your statement tends to imply that there's some sort of *good* news?" responds Levine.

"Well" replies Nicole somewhat hesitatingly, "*Potentially.*"

"Okay" says Levine, "Let's hear what you've got."

"The only telephone number the Ship had for Jamison is no longer in service" responds Nicole, "Which is a primary reason why they haven't gotten him back in the fold."

"He had an apartment with Sewell and Petty Officer Simmons" says Conroy, "but they gave that up prior to going on deployment."

"On the upside he's still using his ATM and credit cards" says Nicole, "but on the downside he does all of his banking electronically, like a lot of us these days."

"And, unfortunately, the address that the bank has for him" adds Conroy, "is the Ship's FPO."

"So far you're not giving me any reason for a sense of optimism" remarks Levine.

"That's where we were as well" replies Nicole, "until Slade got an idea regarding the Honolulu PD's case file on Colletti."

"I decided to check the calls that Sewell made using Colletti's cell phone" says Conroy. "Most of them were 4-1-1 information and local calls there in Honolulu."

"But" says Nicole, "he *also* noticed a 619 area code."

"*San Diego County*" says Conroy with a drawn-out emphasis to make his point.

"And it wasn't the Ship's POTS line?" responds Levine.

"Nope; the number belongs to Regina Carlson, age 27, lives in La Mesa" replies Conroy.

"We're thinking she could be either Sewell's or Jamison's girlfriend" says Nicole, "Or possibly just a friend with whom Jamison might be staying."

"Or at the very least" says Conroy, "someone who might have information regarding Jamison's whereabouts."

"Not a slam dunk" replies Levine, "but certainly a possible lead."

"We've refrained from contacting her" says Nicole, "just in case she's in communication with Jamison."

"We don't want to run the risk of her tipping him off" adds Conroy.

"Good thinking" says Levine. "What say we make a surprise visit?"

Conroy and Nicole smile with a certain sense of pride – that's exactly what they were thinking, and hoping for.

Levine does a self-check at his belt above the left pants pocket to verify his badge is in place, dons his bullet-proof vest, and grabs his weapon.

Conroy is surprised that Levine had donned his vest and remarks, "You think we'll need a vest?"

"This guy is a possible killer and is on the lam" responds Levine, "We don't know *what* to expect, so we'd better be prepared for anything."

Conroy and Nicole follow suit, and the team heads out the office door.

29

A 25 year-old man, headphones covering his ears, is forming adjacent two-and-half-foot wide lines, parallel to the sidewalk, through the front lawn courtesy of a walk-behind mower. He is seemingly oblivious to his surroundings, focusing solely on the task in front of him... cutting perfect paths of green.

Having started at the sidewalk and working his way back up to the house, he has only a few swaths remaining when he is startled by the sight of a car pulling up to the curb.

He immediately ceases his motion and focuses his complete attention on the vehicle. Three of the car doors open, with two men and a woman exiting. He notices that the man and woman within his sightline, the passenger-side doors, are carrying guns.

With a look of panic on his face he shuts off the mower and quickly darts toward the front door of the house.

"Petty Officer Gerald Jamison, NCIS!" yells Levine as he sees the man making a break for it.

The man high-tails-it through the front door and latches the deadbolt behind him.

"Slade, Nic - the back" says Levine, nodding toward the house and transitioning to a trot, "I've got the front."

Nicole approaches a wooden gate on the left side of the house. She stops and peers through the small openings between the slats, reaches over the top to lift the metal clasp holding the gate shut, and then opens the gate. Stepping through the opening she draws her weapon and slowly starts walking along the narrow side-yard with a heightened sense of awareness.

Conroy approaches the right side of the house. He's not as fortunate as Nicole – no gated access on this side; he will be getting the pleasure of climbing over the fence. He peers between the vertical slats of the fence to ensure he is not about to make himself a target. With a clear view and no suspect in sight, Conroy makes a rapid ascent and descent over the fence like a steeple-chase runner in a track meet. He draws his weapon and proceeds in a manner virtually identical to that employed by Nicole at the opposite side yard - making his way toward the back of the house.

Levine positions himself at the side of the front door, making use of the multiple layers of the door jamb as shielding. He knows that a desperate perpetrator might start shooting directly at the door in the hopes of taking-out the agent on the other side. Unaware of Jamison's state of mind or intent, Levine is taking no chances.

"Petty Officer Jamison, NCIS!" yells Levine once again, hoping the Petty Officer will come to his senses and not make matters worse by continuing to flaunt authority.

Levine looks at his watch - Conroy and Nicole should be in-place and awaiting the Petty Officer in the event he attempts to flee through a back door or window.

Determining that he has waited a sufficient amount of time for Jamison to respond, Levine breaks open the door and enters the home with his gun drawn – no sign of the Petty Officer.

Hearing the front door being busted open, Petty Officer Jamison exits through the sliding glass door at the rear of the house. He takes but a single step onto the backyard patio before stopping in his tracks… Conroy is standing there, to his immediate right, with his gun drawn.

"Hands in the air Petty Officer" says Conroy in a stern and commanding voice.

Jamison makes a move to his left and sees the barrel of Nicole's gun staring him in the face.

"You heard him" says Nicole with an equally stern look on her face.

Jamison spins around and starts back toward the sliding glass door - Levine is there with his gun drawn.

"You don't listen very well, do you?" says Levine with an inflection that could be mistaken for Clint Eastwood in a Dirty Harry film.

The elusive Petty Officer raises his hands.

Petty Officer Jamison stands five-foot-ten with a slim build, and somewhat surprising for someone who had gone UA, he still looks the part of a spit-polished sailor... freshly shaven and shorn with a military-spec haircut that could pass Captain's Inspection. He is the antithesis of his pal Airman Apprentice Sewell.

"Hands behind your back" says Conroy while Levine and Nicole continue to have their weapons trained on Jamison.

Jamison complies - lowering his hands and then placing them hand-over-hand at his lower back.

Conroy cuffs Jamison and explains, "If you didn't run you would have avoided these bracelets."

Levine and Nicole lower their weapons.

"Why *did* you run?" asks Levine.

"I thought you might be hit-men or something" replies Jamison.

"Hit-men??" responds Levine, clearly not expecting such a response, "How do the letters N-C-I-S spell '*hit-men*'?"

"Could have been some kind of trick."

"And why would hit-men be after you?"

"Ummm..." murmurs Jamison, followed by a long pause as he attempts to come up with a viable response, "No reason... it's just your civilian clothes and guns... obviously you're not the Shore Patrol."

"That's not a very convincing answer" responds Levine.

Jamison remains silent.

"Tell me about Vincent Colletti" says Levine.

"Who?" replies Jamison.

"You may know him as *Snuffy*" says Conroy, "the guy you and your buddy Sewell hung out with at *Davy Jones' Locker*."

"I don't know anything about that guy" responds Jamison.

"We know better than that" replies Conroy, "You might want to re-think your response during our nice relaxing ride back to NCIS."

Conroy leads Petty Officer Jamison, hands cuffed behind him, toward the car; Levine and Nicole follow.

Conroy opens the rear driver's-side door and helps Jamison into the back seat, covering his head as he ducks.

Conroy has Jamison slide over near the passenger-side door. Conroy slides in next to him and then reaches over and buckles Jamison in, followed by buckling himself in.

Levine and Nicole then enter the car - Levine in the driver's seat and Nicole 'riding shotgun'.

Levine does a quick check via his car's control console to verify that the rear passenger inner door latches have been disabled; after all, the last thing he needs is the Petty Officer getting some crazy idea like jumping out of the car.

Levine decides to attempt to *'get into Petty Officer Jamison's head'* during the drive back to NCIS. He figuratively puts on his "Mr. Professional" hat and then directs a statement to Nicole, making sure he is loud enough to catch Jamison's attention…

"Special Agent McKenna" says Levine as he starts the car, "I'd like to have a nice little *'film session'* for the Petty Officer here when we get back to NCIS; can you arrange the Interrogation Room accordingly?"

"Yes Sir" replies Nicole, playing-along as she got the hint that Levine had directed her way.

Petty Officer Jamison has a look of confusion and concern on his face – exactly what Levine had hoped.

Levine puts the car in DRIVE and starts down the road. The entirety of the drive back to NCIS is embodied by a single word – silence.

30

Levine, Nicole, Conroy, and their "guest", Petty Officer Jamison, enter NCIS through a back entrance of the facility that avoids the Office area.

The entryway opens to two wide hallways – a long one directly ahead, and a much shorter one to the immediate right. The long hallway has two doors on the right side, one door on the left side, and a large door at the end. The short hallway has but a single door down near its end to the left.

"Special Agent Conroy" says Levine, "Can you take Petty Officer Jamison to the Conference Room while Special Agent McKenna preps Room One?"

"Of course" replies Conroy.

Conroy leads Jamison down the long hallway and into the door on the left - the Conference Room.

Nicole turns to Levine and says, "I'm assuming your cryptic message back in the car was telling me to upload the launch video on the screen in Interrogation Room One?"

"You decoded the message perfectly" replies Levine, "Set it up from the point where Petty Officer Jamison comes into view."

"Will do."

"Oh, and I want to be able to control the video... start, stop, and zoom... with a remote."

"No problem; it will take me just a couple of minutes."

"Great, I'm going to go get Jamison's file. Once you're ready, have Slade escort Jamison to the Interrogation Room, and then both of you meet me in the Observation Room."

"Got it."

Levine proceeds down the long hallway, exiting through the door at the end - emerging into the Office space. Lo and behold the Director is there to greet him.

"So, Jake" says the Director, "You found Petty Officer Jamison and brought him in for an interview?"

"In cuffs since the fool tried to run" replies Levine.

"That sure makes him look guilty."

"No kidding; and when I asked him why he ran he said it was because he thought we were hit-men."

"*Hit-men?* That's a new one" says the Director, who thinks for a moment and adds with a smirk, "Although you *do* resemble Sonny Corleone."

"You're on your game today John… or should I say *'Vito'?*"

"Couldn't resist."

"It will be interesting to get to the bottom of his *'hit-men'* remark, along with the reason we brought him here in the first place… his potential involvement in Colletti's murder."

"As always, keep me posted."

Levine gives a nod of comprehension toward the Director and then heads to Conroy's desk in search of Petty Officer Jamison's file.

Levine arrives at Conroy's desk expecting to have to sift through a pile of unorganized clutter – the usual state of affairs for Conroy's daytime domicile.

To Levine's surprise he immediately spies Jamison's file, along with Conroy's notes from his interview with Airman Apprentice Sewell, sitting on top of a portfolio. He grabs them both and returns to meet Conroy and Nicole in the Observation Room.

Levine enters the Observation Room; Conroy and Nicole are there awaiting his arrival. Through the privacy glass Levine can see Petty Officer Jamison seated at a table in Interrogation Room One - facing the glass. Jamison looks confused, almost disoriented, but not as nervous as Levine had expected. Not that Levine expected Jamison to be *'cool as a cucumber'*, but he thought he might be *'sweating bullets'* at this point.

"Everything's set up, Jake" says Nicole as she hands Levine a remote control.

"Great" replies Levine, who then turns to Conroy and asks, "Did Jamison share anything with you?"

"He's definitely confused as to why we brought him here" replies Conroy, "Especially our questions about Colletti."

"What did you tell him?"

"That we'll make all of that clear to him during our interview."

"Perfect" responds Levine, who then holds up Jamison's file while simultaneously handing a notepad to Conroy, "I grabbed Jamison's personnel file for my interview" he says, "I'd like you to observe from here and compare Jamison's responses with those you received from Sewell... I figured you'd want your notes."

"Thanks" replies Conroy.

"Either of you need to make a Pit Stop before we get started?" asks Levine in the direction of both Conroy and Nicole.

Conroy and Nicole look at each other and then nod their heads toward Levine indicating *'no'*.

"Then let's get the show started" says Levine as he exits the Observation Room.

31

Levine enters the Interrogation Room. Petty Officer Jamison turns his head to see who has entered.

Levine walks around the table where Jamison is seated, sets his file down, and grabs a seat directly across from Jamison. To Levine's back is the privacy glass, and to his right, a wall-mounted flat-screen television monitor.

Noticing the remote control unit in Levine's hand, Petty Officer Jamison's eyes bounce between Levine and the remote.

"You look like you have a question for me?" says Levine.

"I don't understand why NCIS would be involved in a sailor going UA" replies Jamison.

"Funny" responds Levine, "that's what Airman Apprentice Sewell said."

Jamison is surprised. "Why would you talk to Willie?" he asks.

"The same reason we're talking to you" replies Levine, "The timing of your going UA coincides with a murder, and we've got you at the scene."

Quietly, barely above a whisper, in a manner of comprehension laced in disbelief, and while lowering his head into his hands, Jamison responds, "Son of a bitch..."

"Apparently you know what I'm talking about" says Levine, "so how about I just cut to the chase?"

Levine grabs the remote and points it toward the television screen.

"In fact" says Levine, "what say we have the little *film session* Agent McKenna and I spoke about earlier?"

Levine hits the *'Play'* icon on the remote. The video of the launch commences, zoomed-in on Petty Officer Jamison, and Levine immediately hits *'Pause'*.

Looking directly at Petty Officer Jamison, and pointing to the screen, Levine says, "That's you; correct?"

"Yes, Sir" responds Jamison.

"Okay; so when I restart the video how about you give me the play-by-play?" asks Levine.

"Sir?"

"You explain to me what's going on... what you're doing" Levine clarifies.

"Yes, Sir" responds Jamison.

Levine hits *'Play'*. The video recommences, and Jamison details his actions...

"Right here I'm directing the car being moved into position...

"Here I'm checking the connection to the catapult...

"Here I'm checking the position of the steering wheel, along with the placement of the dummy...

"And now I'm backing away to clear the launch zone."

"Backing away??" responds Levine as he stops the video, "You're *jumping* back and away like you just saw a ghost. What's that about?"

"I did a last check inside the car and heard a moan; it scared the hell out of me and I realized that was *no dummy* in the car."

"So why didn't you stop the launch?"

"I tried to!" responds Jamison emphatically, "If you continue the video I'll show you."

Levine recommences the video.

"See where I am raising my hand?!" says an impassioned Jamison while pointing to the screen, "That's the STOP signal! But Chief Warrant Officer Bauer gave the LAUNCH signal!"

"Your gesture is not the LAUNCH signal?" replies Levine.

"No" reiterates Jamison, "Like I said, it's the STOP signal."

"So the arm-wave by Chief Warrant Officer Bauer is the LAUNCH signal?" says Levine in a tone of comprehension with a hint of a question.

"Yes Sir."

"What about right after the launch? Maybe he could have been saved?"

"Out in the middle of the Pacific?? The car disappeared in a matter of seconds. Besides, if the killer knew that *I* knew, I could be next."

"And you figured the killer was Chief Warrant Officer Bauer?"

"I couldn't imagine him doing it, but I figured he had to be the one who loaded the guy into the car, so who else could it be?"

"Oh yeah?" says Levine looking to poke holes into Jamison's response, "Maybe you were jumping back because you were Bauer's accomplice in this whole thing and the guy you *thought* you had knocked-out was now waking up?"

"What??" replies Jamison at such an accusation, "Why would I want to kill the guy? I didn't have anything against him."

"What about you and Airman Apprentice Sewell getting into a heated argument with Colletti and referring to him as *'Snuff-Film'*?"

"Are you telling me the guy in the car is the dude that calls himself *'Snuffy'*?"

"Don't play dumb with me, Petty Officer."

"I'm serious; I had no idea that's who you were talking about."

"And the heated argument you and Sewell had with him?"

"There was no heated argument" replies Jamison. "And the *Snuff-Film* thing was all Willie... he's always looking for ways get under someone's skin."

"Let me lay out the facts, and then you can explain to me how you are nothing more than an innocent bystander" says Levine.

"Okay" Jamison nervously replies.

"Both you and Sewell *knew* Colletti" says Levine, holding up his thumb on his right hand to denote his first item of note.

"When you told Colletti about your Plymouth launch he said he wished he could be there for it, and surprise-surprise his wish came true" he says, holding up his pointer finger.

"No matter how you want to phrase it, you and Sewell got into some kind of tiff with Colletti" he says, holding up his middle finger.

"Chief Warrant Officer Bauer *sponsored* Colletti" he says, holding up his ring finger.

"According to you and your shipmates the Chief Warrant Officer loaded Colletti into the car" he says, holding up his pinky finger.

"The Chief Warrant Officer was in failing health; so there's *no way* he dragged a knocked-out Colletti into the car all by himself... he must have had an accomplice" he says, now holding up his thumb on his left hand.

"You and the Chief Warrant Officer were the leaders of the launch, and you even said you knew that was *no dummy* behind the wheel" he says, holding up his left pointer finger.

"Your shipmates said you were acting strangely right after the launch *and* for the remainder of the Tiger Cruise" he says, holding up his left middle finger.

"You went UA as soon as you got back to shore" he says, holding up his left ring finger, and then adds... "Shall I continue? I'm running out of fingers."

"No Sir. But can I respond to some of your points?"

"By all means; that's why we're here... to determine the facts."

"So yes, Willie and I met the guy one night in *Davy Jones' Locker*, but that's it, we never saw him again" responds Jamison.

"And sure, I figured-out that there was a real person behind the wheel" he adds, "but only right before the launch. And as I said, I tried to stop it."

"And knowing that a person had been launched and thus surely murdered, and the realization that the killer might be after *me* next" he continues, "then of course I was on edge the rest of the cruise. And as I said, that is the reason I went UA."

"But I had no idea Chief Warrant Officer Bauer sponsored the guy, or even how he knew him" Jamison proclaims.

"And there's *no way* I helped the Warrant Officer kill the guy" Jamison finishes, "Check my Service Record, I've never even gotten into a fight, let alone be involved in someone's murder."

"So you, Sewell and the Chief Warrant Officer didn't plan this thing together?" says Levine.

"Absolutely not!"

"And the only reason you went UA is because you thought you'd be next?"

"Or that I'd be a suspect; and if Chief Warrant Officer Bauer *was* the killer who would believe a Petty Officer's word over a Warrant Officer? Either way I was screwed."

"You know that Chief Warrant Officer Bauer is dead."

"What?? Had I known that I wouldn't have thought you guys were hit-men he had hired, and I would have returned to the Ship."

"So *that's* what your '*hit-men*' statement earlier was all about?"

"I was afraid to say anything at the time" Jamison says, "in case the Chief Warrant Officer might be on the lookout for me."

"If you want me to take into account *anything* you say as being genuine and truthful you need to be forthcoming with *everything*."

"Yes Sir."

Jamison thinks for a moment and then adds, "You said the Chief Warrant Officer was in failing health?"

"That's correct."

"There were rumors he had cancer. I guess that's how he died?"

"He was murdered."

"*Murdered*?? Whoa, I had nothing to do with that! All I did was *go into hiding* so that I didn't become the next victim."

"Let's say I give you the benefit of the doubt and assume you're telling the truth" says Levine, "There isn't anyone *other than* the Chief Warrant Officer who could have pulled off the death-launch, or more likely, an accomplice?"

"Not that I can think of."

"You didn't see or hear anything unusual leading up to the launch?"

"No, but the Contractor guy had an office near that end of the Hangar Bay... he may have seen something... you should talk to him."

"We already have."

"Hmmm... now that I think of it, right before the launch the Chief Warrant Officer had a meeting with the Air Boss he seemed concerned about."

"That doesn't make sense... he *worked for* the Air Boss; why would he be concerned about a meeting with his boss?"

"That's the same thing that we all thought, but word around the Division was that the Air Boss seemed bothered about something."

Levine thinks for a moment and then says, "You need anything Petty Officer... a head break, a snack, a cup of coffee?"

"I'm fine Sir, but can I call my girlfriend? She's going to *freak out* when she gets home, sees the front door busted open, and I'm nowhere to be found."

"We can make that happen. Hang on, I'll be right back."

Levine exits the Interrogation Room and walks into the Observation Room. He looks at Conroy and directs a question, "Any inconsistencies between Jamison's story and Sewell's?"

"Jamison gave us some new information, which is no surprise since Sewell wasn't there for the actual launch" replies Conroy, "But their stories that were consistent were... well... *consistent.*"

"In that case, did Honolulu PD's case file include a description of the guy named 'Willie' that Colletti was arguing with?"

"No, the report just mentioned the name Willie."

"In that case, make a call to *Davy Jones' Locker* and get a description of the guy."

"You don't think *Willie Sewell* is the guy?" asks Conroy.

"Both Sewell and Jamison said there was *no* heated argument with Colletti."

"True, but that's just *their* story."

"And the staff at *Davy Jones' Locker* said the guy 'Willie' left *before* Colletti; but didn't you say that Sewell found Colletti's phone…"

"*After* Colletti left" says Conroy jumping in before Levine finishes, "Shit, how'd I miss that?!"

"With everything leaning toward Chief Warrant Officer Bauer, and the fact that we will never have the opportunity to interview *him*" says Levine, "I think it's time we talk to his widow."

Nicole has a look of concern on her face and responds, "You're not going to tell a grieving widow that her husband may have been a murderer are you?"

"That's all up to her."

"Up to *her*?"

"If she's evasive, appears to be hiding something, acts suspicious… anything along those lines."

"Hey Jake" says Conroy, "While you're interviewing Bauer's widow should I get Petty Officer Jamison back to the Ship?"

Levine looks at his watch and replies, "It's too late to go talk to Mrs. Bauer right now, Nic and I will do that in the morning. So sure, get the Petty Officer back to the Ship and then call it a day."

"Sounds good" responds Conroy, "I'll see you two in the morning after your interview."

"Oh, and I told the Petty Officer he could call his girlfriend" adds Levine.

"Yeah, I guess we wouldn't want her thinking that Jamison got bagged by some *hit-men*" replies Conroy with a wry smile.

32

Levine and Nicole walk up to the front door of the Bauer residence, a nice but modest home in Oceanside. Levine rings the doorbell. A woman in her early forties opens the door. She looks tired; not as if she had just awakened, but as if it had been quite some time since she'd had a good night's sleep. She is dressed in black and Levine immediately wonders if she might still be in mourning at the loss of her husband, or if he is simply jumping to conclusions regarding her attire.

"Mrs. Bauer?" asks Levine as both Nicole and he hold up their badges, "Special Agents Levine and McKenna, NCIS."

"Yes?" responds Mrs. Bauer, who is something at a loss as to why NCIS might be visiting her.

"First of all ma'am, our condolences on your loss" says Levine.

"Thank you. You'd think that knowing a loved one was dying of cancer, and that you had prepared yourself for the inevitable, that it wouldn't be so difficult."

"I understand, ma'am."

"So, what can I do for you?"

"We were hoping you might be able to provide some information about an acquaintance of your husband. Did he ever mention a *Vincent Colletti*?"

"No, I've never heard that name."

"Perhaps the nickname *Snuffy*?" adds Nicole

"No, I'm sorry" replies Mrs. Bauer, "he never mentioned either name."

Mrs. Bauer then adds, "Forgive me... would you like to come in?"

"Yes, thank you" replies Levine.

Mrs. Bauer leads Levine and Nicole to the living room, which appears to be seldom used... probably only for formal gatherings or when unannounced guests like Levine and Nicole are welcomed into her humble abode. The room is centered by a fireplace, with a sofa on one side and a loveseat on the other, and a coffee table between them. At the far corner of the room is a display case, containing what appears to be memorabilia, likely from the Chief Warrant Officer's career in the Navy.

"Won't you please sit down?" says Mrs. Bauer as she holds her hand out toward the sofa.

Levine and Nicole make themselves comfortable on the sofa while Mrs. Bauer takes a seat on the loveseat directly across from them.

"Now, where were we?" asks Mrs. Bauer.

"We were asking about Vincent Colletti" says Nicole, "Do you have any idea why your husband would have sponsored him on the Tiger Cruise during his last deployment?"

"He *did* say that he was sponsoring someone as a *favor*" responds Mrs. Bauer.

"Did he happen to say who the favor was for?" asks Levine.

"He may have mentioned a name but I don't really recall" replies Mrs. Bauer, "Why do you ask?"

"Vincent Colletti went missing and we were hoping you might have known him" responds Levine, "and possibly, where we might find him."

"I'm sorry I can't help you" replies Mrs. Bauer.

"Not a problem at all, ma'am" responds Levine.

Nicole looks over toward the display case across the room and asks, "I notice you have a display case over there, is that a tribute to your husband?"

"Yes it is" replies Mrs. Bauer, "He started it years ago as a means of recognizing his long and successful career, along with all of the unique and varied assignments he'd had through the years."

"I imagine it's a very impressive display" says Nicole.

"A lot of Gordon's cherished memories... from his first days as a young Airman Recruit to his retirement as a decorated Officer... he was especially proud of that."

"Of becoming a decorated Officer?"

"Yes; but mostly how he worked his way up from an E-1 Airman Recruit all the way to Officer. Being someone who came from very modest beginnings, one whose life was not handed to him on a Silver Platter, it meant a great deal to him."

"That is certainly something to be proud of. Do you mind if I take a look?"

"Please do" responds Mrs. Bauer, "Both of you" as she glances toward Levine.

Nicole and Mrs. Bauer get up from their seats and walk toward the display case, with Levine right behind.

The case is filled with items from Bauer's career... his medals, awards, squadron patches, pictures taken over the years aboard various Ships and duty stations, and a large photograph in the center that is signed by a number of the Officers on the SEADRAGON, including the Ship's Captain.

"A very impressive display" says Nicole.

"Thank you" replies Mrs. Bauer, "He was very proud of all of his accomplishments."

"As well he should be, ma'am" responds Levine.

One item in particular within the case catches Levine's eye; it is a patch with a cartoonish toad as the centerpiece and says 'EE-30 Load Toads'.

"This patch here that says 'Load Toads'" says Levine as he points it out, "I've never heard of such a squadron, do you have any idea what it is?"

"Oh that's not a squadron patch; it was given to Gordon by his uncle" responds Mrs. Bauer. "He idolized his uncle; in fact he's the reason Gordon joined the Navy."

"Hmmm…" ponders Levine, "In that case I'm guessing that the *'Electrical Distribution'* at the bottom of the patch applies to the Engineering Department of the Ship and not Aviation Electrical."

"You're probably right Agent Levine" says Mrs. Bauer, "If I remember correctly his uncle Ken was a nuclear operator on the Ship."

Nicole notices something similar to a High School yearbook within the case and says to Levine, "Hey Jake; this manual here says 'USS ENTERPRISE WESTPAC 1978'… do you think it could be the Cruise Book you were mentioning?"

Mrs. Bauer responds to Nicole's question, "Oh yes, that's exactly what it is… a Cruise Book. His uncle Ken, the one who gave him the patch, also gave him the Cruise Book; it was a memento from their Tiger Cruise."

The potential implication behind this news surprises Levine, who asks, "You're not saying that your *husband* was one of the *Tigers* on that cruise are you?"

"Yes he was" responds Mrs. Bauer, "His uncle invited him."

"Really?" replies Levine.

"Yes" she responds, "Gordon was ten years-old I believe, and the way he tells the story… well… *told* the story… he had the time of his life."

"Do you mind if we take a look at it?" asks Nicole.

"Not at all" replies Mrs. Bauer as she opens the display case.

Nicole flips through the pages of the Cruise Book while Levine looks over her shoulder. The album is a chronological history of the cruise… port visits in Hawaii, the Philippines, Hong Kong, Australia, and Singapore; shipboard activities like talent shows, boxing matches, and the initiation of *'polywogs'* to become *'shellbacks'*… a longstanding tradition when crossing the equator; and ending with a synopsis of each of the numerous Departments on the Ship.

After flipping through a good hundred pages or more Nicole suddenly stops and points out to Levine, "Wow, here's the Plymouth they launched" she says, and then points to the adjacent page, "And here's the photo of the launch that we saw on the internet."

"Are you familiar with that event?" asks Mrs. Bauer.

"Yes we are" replies Levine, "And it's identical to the 'Plymouth launch' that the SEADRAGON did recently."

"That was Gordon's plan" responds Mrs. Bauer, "As the coordinator for the launch he was hoping it would be just as entertaining for *this* group of Tigers as it was for him when he was a youngster."

"The Ship's Captain commented to us that the Tigers loved it" replies Levine.

"That makes me so happy" responds Mrs. Bauer.

"I'm curious ma'am, were you familiar with the launch car at all?" asks Levine.

"Not very well Agent Levine. Gordon had it here briefly, over on the side-yard, before it was towed to the Ship."

"So, your husband was the one who purchased the car?"

"No; he said it was one of the guys he worked with, but they didn't have a place to store it."

"He didn't mention a name?"

"No, he didn't."

"Did you happen to see him when they dropped-off or picked-up the car?" asks Levine, hoping he might at least be able to get a description of this person of interest.

"The guy who owned the car?" she asks, looking to receive clarification to Levine's question.

"Yes" says Levine.

"No; I got home from work one day and it was here, and then about a week later it was gone."

"I don't suppose your husband mentioned where they found the car?"

"No, I'm sorry."

Levine thinks for a moment and realizes he has exhausted all of the questions regarding the car that he had in mind.

Levine decides to follow-up on another item that came to light during the interview. "Mrs. Bauer" he says, "do you happen to have a phone number for your husband's uncle Ken?"

"Sure" she replies as she scrolls through the contacts on her cell phone, "Here it is... Kenneth Cavanaugh. He was down here for Gordon's service but he lives up in the Seattle area."

"Thank you very much" says Levine as he inputs the number into his cell phone.

"Why would you want to talk to him; if you don't mind me asking?"

"The gentleman that your husband sponsored on this Tiger Cruise... Vincent Colletti... was on the ENTERPRISE back at that time as well. Even though I realize it's a long shot, perhaps his uncle knew him."

"That makes perfect sense, thank you."

"Well, we don't want to take any more of your time. Thank you very much for your time and your hospitality."

"Thank you for indulging my walk down memory lane."

"It is our pleasure, ma'am."

Mrs. Bauer escorts Levine and Nicole to the door.

"Good luck" replies Mrs. Bauer as Levine and Nicole walk through the door and head down the walkway toward their car.

Levine and Nicole get into the car and sit there for a moment pondering what they had just learned.

"Now we know at least *one* tie between Bauer and Colletti, the 1978 Tiger Cruise on the ENTERPRISE" remarks Nicole.

"Actually it's more like a *'coincidence'* than some *'tie'* between them" says Levine.

"The obvious *'coincidence vice tie'* being the fact that Bauer was a ten year-old kid at the time while Colletti was a thirty year-old adult?"

"Correct. *And* because Colletti worked up in the Air Department while Bauer's uncle was down in Engineering."

"Maybe the uncle and Colletti could have met at the Chow Hall, became friends, and then the uncle introduced '*his nephew Gordon*' to Colletti?"

"Only the enlisted sailors eat at the Chow Hall, the officers eat in the Ward Room" explains Levine.

"Well, the Ward Room then."

"Even if Bauer's uncle and Colletti were both Officers, they would have eaten at different Ward Rooms... Colletti and the other Airedales up in Ward Room *One* on the Oh-Two or Oh-Three Level in the forward-end of the Ship, and Bauer's uncle in Ward Room *Three* down on the Second Deck."

Levine thinks for a moment and then adds... "And I'm pretty sure the uncle was an enlisted sailor."

"What makes you think that?"

"Bauer's wife said that the uncle was a nuclear *operator*, and *that* term... *operator*... would imply he was enlisted."

"So that would make it even *more* unlikely that Bauer's uncle and Colletti would have known each other" Nicole realizes.

Levine is in contemplation-mode once again, considering the various possibilities, and then finally ponders... "I wonder if Bauer *somehow* got word that Colletti was part of the launch back in 1978, and perhaps *that* was the reason he agreed to sponsor him?"

"A third party involved?"

"It's a possibility; especially since we've been thinking that it would be difficult for a lone person to have pulled-off the murder and launching."

"So, are you going to give Bauer's uncle a call?"

"Hard to imagine he could give us anything useful, but then again, it can't hurt. Even if he can't give us a connection between Bauer and Colletti, he might provide us with that possible *third party*."

After a brief moment of silence Nicole points out to Levine, "I noticed that you didn't tell Mrs. Bauer that her husband is a potential suspect."

"There are just too many contradictions associated with Bauer" replies Levine, "On one hand everything points to him being not only a model sailor, but a model citizen."

"Yeah, his service record is impeccable."

"And the way he honored his years of service… collecting memorabilia, mementos, awards, photographs…" says Levine, "How could a guy like that be a cold-blooded killer?"

"But on the other hand" replies Nicole, "He *was* the guy who *sponsored* Colletti, *and* he was the guy that everyone says loaded the 'dummy', which was actually Colletti, into the car."

"And even though he seemed like a model individual" adds Levine, "how many times do you hear that some murderer or even serial killer is the guy that everyone says, *'he was the nicest guy… wouldn't hurt a fly'*?"

"And we all know that family members are *always* in denial about the person's likely guilt" says Nicole, "Even in the face of overwhelming evidence to the contrary."

"Another thing to consider is that, according to the Doc, Bauer had an inoperable brain tumor" says Levine, "So who knows how that might have affected his personality."

"That adds yet another dimension to this thing" replies Nicole, "Perhaps Colletti did something that angered Bauer to the extent of hitting his breaking point?"

"Yeah, except this was a deliberately planned and painstakingly detailed murder… definitely not a 'spur of the moment, sudden impulse, *he just snapped*' sort of thing."

"Great point."

"Wait a minute…" says Levine as he stops and realizes something he hadn't considered, "Son of a Bitch!"

"What is it?" replies Nicole, surprised at Levine's sudden emphatic nature.

"Colletti's former squadron members said he went on a tirade in front of a bunch of the kids during the Tiger Cruise back in '78."

"And you think that the ten year-old Bauer might have been one of the kids subjected to that outburst?"

"Well, it's one way to tie Bauer and Colletti together that we hadn't thought of."

"Yeah, but Bauer's wife said he had *the time of his life* on that cruise; it's hard to believe he could have had such a great time and yet have been scarred enough from Colletti's tirade to murder him thirty years later."

"True" says Levine as he finds himself agreeing with Nicole's assessment, and then adds, "Maybe the tirade didn't affect a young starry-eyed kid full of wonderment, but what about an overprotective uncle that witnessed it?"

"Another reason to talk to him" responds Nicole.

"But still" says Levine, "I can't get over the fact that Bauer *himself* was surely murdered - fed a fatal dose of digitalis; that he apparently sponsored Colletti as a *favor* to someone; and that there is no indication he *truly* knew Colletti in any other capacity before Colletti actually stepped onboard the SEADRAGON for the Tiger Cruise."

"You're right Jake; Bauer's story is nothing but a myriad of contradictions."

"So the big question..." remarks Levine, "Is Bauer just a poor unfortunate patsy? Or is he a cold-blooded killer?"

33

"Got it… thanks" says Conroy into the phone. He hangs up just in time to see Levine and Nicole heading his way.

He quickly commences to scribble a few notes related to his conversation, quickening his pace as Levine and Nicole approach, fearing his concentration will be broken and his train of thought *lost to all eternity* upon their arrival.

Still scribbling as Levine and Nicole arrive, Conroy's penmanship is transitioning from barely-legible to something resembling hieroglyphics.

He releases his pen from his grip and exhales – you'd think he just finished the last question of his SAT's before the proctor yelled "Time!"

"So Slade, a couple of things we learned from Chief Warrant Officer Bauer's widow" says Levine, "One is that Bauer, when he was a ten year-old kid, was actually one of the Tigers on the ENTERPRISE during their 1978 WestPac."

"No shit?" responds Conroy, "How the hell did *he* happen to be there?"

"His uncle was on the Ship" replies Levine.

"And he worked with Colletti?" responds Conroy in an optimistic tone.

"No such luck; he worked down in Engineering."

"Don't tell me that this is just another one of our *'ENTERPRISE Twilight Zone'* coincidences?"

"It appears that way, but we need to talk to him nonetheless."

"Why is that?"

"Remember how the Squadron guys said Colletti went on a tirade in front of the Tiger Cruise kids?"

"And you think that a ten year-old Bauer might have been collateral damage and scarred for life?" replies Conroy, adding, with a tone of improbability... "Enough that he'd want to exact some sort of revenge after all these years?"

"Unlikely; his widow said that he had the time of his life during that Tiger Cruise."

Nicole chimes in, "But an overprotective uncle who was with him... that might be a totally different story."

"Makes sense" replies Conroy, who thinks for a moment and then follows-up, "Did you check to see if this guy is on the list of 'Tigers'?"

"Crap" responds Nicole, realizing she had not thought of making that possible connection.

Nicole turns and starts to head toward her desk to grab the list of *Tigers* that rode the Ship.

"Hey Nic" says Levine, "You can check that once we finish updating Slade here."

Nicole stops in her tracks and returns to the conversation.

"Another item" says Levine to Conroy, "is that Bauer told his wife that he sponsored Colletti as a *favor* to someone."

"He didn't sponsor him because he *knew* him, but instead he did so as a *favor*?" responds Conroy.

"That's what she said. So with that in mind, who could *not* have been a sponsor and thus needed to ask Bauer to sponsor Colletti for them?"

"Someone on restriction... like Willie Sewell for example?"

"I can see someone on restriction having their ability to sponsor a guest revoked, but it's hard to imagine a Warrant Officer would agree to such a thing."

"That's true" says Conroy, reconsidering his initial statement, "It would be as if he was actually *rewarding* someone who got *'in the shits'* bad enough to warrant restriction in the first place."

"And it seems extremely unlikely that he would agree to do so for Sewell" adds Levine.

"Maybe that's the exact reason it would *work?*" says Nicole, "It's something you would never expect, and thus you fly under everyone's radar."

"And since Sewell didn't even ride the Ship during the Tiger Cruise" says Conroy, "That fact would keep any focus away from him."

"In *his eyes* maybe" replies Nicole.

"That's true" responds Conroy, "I could tell during my interview that he was completely surprised to be receiving the kind of attention and heat I threw at him."

"Speaking of your interview though" replies Levine, "didn't he say that he had never met Colletti before bumping into him at *Davy Jones' Locker?*"

"True, but who's to say he's not a chronic liar" responds Conroy.

"Okay, we'll keep all of that in mind, but remember that Sewell was not on the Ship when Colletti was murdered so the most we can get him on is conspiracy to commit murder" says Levine.

"Understood" replies Conroy.

"So, who else would be on the *non*-sponsor list?" says Levine.

"They had a limit of three personnel per sponsor" replies Nicole, "So someone who had already sponsored their limit."

"Maybe someone threatened or blackmailed him?" says Conroy.

"Or how about a superior *ordering* him to sponsor someone?" adds Nicole.

"Holy shit Nic, you may have stumbled onto something!" responds Conroy.

"What's that?" replies Nicole.

"The phone call I was on when you two walked in" responds Conroy, "I found out that the '*Willie*' arguing with Colletti at *Davy Jones' Locker* was an older guy. He was in uniform... a Navy Commander."

"I take it you were going to share that with us at some point?" says Levine, slightly perturbed that this news is *just now* getting promulgated.

"I was waiting until you two were done updating me about your interview with Bauer's widow" replies Conroy somewhat defensively.

Levine thinks for a moment; processing this new piece of information. Suddenly something jumps out at him, and he flashes back to his meeting with the Captain of the SEADRAGON... "Son of a Bitch!" he says.

"What??" responds Conroy; thinking that Levine is pissed at him regarding the timing of his information.

"As soon as you mentioned a Navy Commander named *'Willie'* it dawned on me that the Air Boss Commander Williams' flight jacket said 'Ray *"Willie"* Williams'" responds Levine.

"Shit, you're right!" replies Conroy, "And isn't he the one who *suggested* doing a launching of a car to the Ship's Captain in the first place?"

"Hell yes!" responds Levine.

Another light bulb switches 'on' in Levine's mind, "Hey Nic, there was an Airman Williams that Colletti almost screwed-over back on the ENTERPRISE who had been accepted to NESEP" he says, "Can you do a back-trace on the Air Boss - Commander Raymond Williams - and see if he and this Airman from the ENTERPRISE might be one in the same?"

"Sure" replies Nicole, who then immediately goes to her desk, jumps on her keyboard, and commences typing.

Levine barely has time to think when Nicole looks up from her computer screen and says, "Here we go."

"You've got something on Commander Williams already?" responds Levine.

"I set up a quick link to *U.S. Navy Records* when we started looking into Colletti, Bauer, and the Squadron guys" replies Nicole.

"I should have known you'd be on top of this stuff" responds Levine, "What have you got?"

"You were right, Jake" says Nicole as she commences to read aloud while attempting to paraphrase, "Raymond Williams was an Airman on the ENTERPRISE in 1978… was accepted to the NESEP Program… subsequently attending San Francisco State University."

She scrolls down the page and then continues, "Upon graduation from San Francisco State he received his commission, went on to flight school…"

"No offense Nic" interrupts Levine, "but we don't need his life history at the moment."

"Of course" replies Nicole as she scans the screen, finishing with… "He is currently a Commander assigned as the Air Boss on the SEADRAGON."

An idea pops into Conroy's head. He scurries over to his desk and grabs the case file on Colletti that he received from Honolulu PD. He does a quick scan through the file and says, "A credit card purchase was made by a *Commander Raymond Williams* at *Davy Jones' Locker* the same day Colletti was there."

"He has his rank shown on his credit card?" replies Nicole.

"Actually it's shown as 'CDR'" says Conroy, "but yes, he's got his rank on there."

"That lying bastard!" says Levine as he turns and starts to head toward the door.

"Where're you headed Jake?" asks Conroy.

"I'm going to pay the Air Boss a little visit."

34

Levine observes a wall-mounted display case of photographs in the Ship's passageway titled 'Air Department'. The photograph at the upper left is of the Ship's Captain, and to the upper right is the XO. Slightly below the pictures of the Captain and XO, but in the center of the display, is a photograph titled 'Air Boss – CDR Williams'. Below the Air Boss' photo are those of the Department's Senior Leadership: Division Officers, Tech Assists, Chief Petty Officers, and the Department Yeoman.

Adjacent to the display case identifying the Air Department hierarchy is a door with an etched metal plate that reads 'AIR BOSS'. Levine raps on the door – the traditional two-knock sequence to denote a request to enter.

"Enter" responds a voice from the other side of the door.

Levine opens the door and enters the office of the Air Boss.

"Agent Levine" says the Air Boss, "This is an unexpected visit; what can I do for you?"

Levine cuts to the chase, "You lied to me Commander."

"What do you mean?"

"You feigned ignorance about the squadron insignia and it turns out *you* are a former squadron member. And *worse,* you said you didn't know an Aviator called *Snuffy.*"

"No, I said that *we had no* Aviators with that call-sign."

"You're playing *word-games* with me Commander?! He was murdered on *your* watch, and *you two* have a history!"

"The *Snuffy* I knew was from thirty years ago" says the Air Boss on the defensive, "I didn't even consider it could be the same guy."

"What do you mean you didn't consider it could be him? How many frickin' *Snuffy's* do you think are out there? *And* you *met him* at *Davy Jones' Locker!*"

"Just because I met him at *Davy Jones' Locker* doesn't mean I had any idea he was on the Ship during the Tiger Cruise."

"You had no idea he was on the Ship?? Hell, you're the one that got him invited!"

"The hell I was! Check the list of Tigers the XO provided, you won't see my name on there as Colletti's sponsor."

"A mere technicality... you had someone else sponsor him *for* you."

"Oh yeah? And who might that be?"

"I'll get to that in a minute; as soon as you tell me about your visit with Colletti."

"Sure, we had a few drinks at *Davy Jones' Locker*... and we talked about our days back on the ENTERPRISE."

"I heard it was a lot more than just *talk*; a number of witnesses stated that you two had an argument."

"We had a few words related to him threatening to get my NESEP acceptance revoked back on the ENTERPRISE and I wanted to *rub it in* that not only did I get the commission that he tried to screw me out of, but that I was *now* the Air Boss on the SEADRAGON."

"So, how did a case of *'rubbing it in'* escalate into a full-fledged heated argument?"

"Even though he essentially got *fired* from the Navy, which should have given him a dose of humility, he hadn't changed a bit... placing blame on everyone else, including me, for his demise."

"That doesn't sound extreme enough to go full-on *'in your face'*."

"And then him saying that *he* got railroaded by guys like *me*... when *I* was the one that *he* tried to screw over... what a jackass!"

"And?" says Levine, expecting more based on the level of agitation the Air Boss was exhibiting.

"And, that all of *my* achievements were nothing more than gifts from clueless leaders with their heads up their asses."

"So that was the tipping point?"

"Sure, I *'hit the limiter'*; who wouldn't?"

"And that resulted in a few choice words directed his way?"

"Well, if you want the *verbatim uncensored version,* I told him *he was a fucking worthless loser and a pathetic excuse for a leader,* and *that* is why the Navy got rid of him… shipping him off to a frozen wind tunnel before ultimately kicking his ass to the curb."

"A frozen wind tunnel?"

"Adak."

"So, your verbal crucifixion was just a warmup to getting even… by launching him off the SEADRAGON."

"Absolutely not; I was in Pri-Fly prior to and during the launch… I have plenty of witnesses."

"What about late at night or early morning before the launch?"

"I was with my son the day before, through the night, and at breakfast in the Wardroom before heading up to Pri-Fly to oversee the launch."

"Your son?"

"Yes; my son Derek."

Just what Levine was looking for… a name to follow-up on, *"Another potential suspect or accomplice"* he thought to himself.

"You realize that a family member is never considered to be a solid or reliable alibi" says Levine.

"We were surrounded by others the entire time… up in Pri-Fly for Flight Ops, in the Wardroom, being involved in the Aircraft Display on the Hangar Bay, checking out the launch car… you name it; I have a plethora of alibis."

"When I talked to you in the Captain's In-Port Cabin you said you didn't see the launch car."

"I didn't; I merely dropped off my son with the launch guys so that *he* could see it."

"Oh, so there *were* moments you were *not* with your son and *not* up in Pri-Fly."

"Nice try Agent Levine; it doesn't take a rocket scientist to figure out that I couldn't kill Colletti and load him into the launch car while the crewmen are showing my son *that exact same car.*"

The wheels are turning inside Levine's head – he is well aware of '*the obvious*' that the Air Boss was pointing out, but that's not where Levine was going when he made the statement, it was merely a diversionary tactic. What the Air Boss had apparently *not* figured out is that he gave Levine *just* the piece of information he had hoped, now the trick is to make sure that the Air Boss has no clue that he just served up his son as a possible accomplice. To that end Levine makes a calculated move… to direct the Air Boss in a totally different direction, linking him to Chief Warrant Officer Bauer, and doing so in a manner to put him on the defensive.

"That doesn't mean you didn't get Chief Warrant Officer Bauer to perform the act when no one was around" says Levine.

"That's ridiculous! Why would a decorated serviceman, particularly one who was ready to retire, agree to such a thing?"

"Maybe you had something on him?"

"What could I have possibly had on him?"

"In my line of work I've found that the possibilities are endless."

"I'm thinking that if you *had* anything you'd be talking specifics and not various '*what if*' scenarios."

"Maybe the better question is… why *else* would the Chief Warrant Officer kill Colletti?"

"Who's to say he's your man anyway?"

"It's interesting how often you answer a question with a question, Commander."

"Just what are you implying Agent Levine?"

"Not a thing" replies Levine in a sarcastic tone.

"So, back to Bauer?" prods the Air Boss.

"I've got your curiosity piqued do I?" responds Levine, "The Warrant Officer loaded Colletti into the car, *and* he gave the LAUNCH signal... which was bad enough on its own, but he did so *despite* the fact that Petty Officer Jamison realized something was amiss and provided the STOP signal... now *that's* very curious indeed."

"So, that's why he's your man?"

"No, that's just part of the '*why else would he do it?*'."

"Come again?" responds the Air Boss.

"There's all of that against him and yet he had an impeccable Service Record" says Levine. "And the really weird part is that he *sponsored* Colletti, a person he didn't even *know*. But wait a minute... *someone* must have known Colletti... Oh that's right... *YOU* did."

"Try as you might Agent Levine, I had nothing on Chief Warrant Officer Bauer to compel him to commit a murder."

"No? Then what was the secret meeting you had with him just before the launch?"

"Secret meeting?? There was no secret meeting."

"His crew said you had ordered him up to your office and that the Chief Warrant Officer was very concerned about it. In fact, they said you seemed bothered about something, hence the Warrant Office's concern."

"I ordered him up to my office for a meeting all right; but the only reason it would have been considered a *secret* is because it was a *surprise*... a picture of the Ship, signed by all of us up in Pri-Fly... a '*Fair Winds and Following Seas*' retirement memento."

"*Crap*" Levine thinks to himself as he realizes this memento is the one that Nicole and he saw in the display case at Bauer's home. He also realizes that he needs to maintain his poker face, and adds, "What about the report that you seemed bothered about something in regard to the Warrant Officer?"

"That was all a part of the act - the *surprise*" replies the Air Boss, "Get him all concerned that I was pissed about something and then surprise him with the revelry and his gift."

"All part of an act, eh?" responds Levine, "Interesting..."

"Are we done here?" remarks the Air Boss, having had enough of Levine's accusations and innuendos.

"For now" replies Levine as he turns around and exits the space.

Departing the Air Boss' office, Levine heads directly to the Cat Shop, hoping to catch one or more of the crewmen he had spoken with previously that were involved in the Plymouth launch.

Levine enters the Cat Shop and is immediately recognized by Petty Officer Simmons and Airman Jones. The two sailors pop-tall as if a high-ranking Officer had walked into the room.

"Sir, what can we do for you?" asks Petty Officer Simmons.

"You two are *just* the gentlemen I was looking for" replies Levine.

"We are?" responds the Petty Officer with a look of concern on his face.

"Yes" replies Levine, "I heard a rumor that the Air Boss brought his son down to check out the Plymouth before you launched it."

"Yes, Sir" responds the Petty Officer.

"Can you provide me any details?" asks Levine.

"The Air Boss asked us to show his son the car, how it was painted like a squadron jet, how we were going to launch it, that kind of stuff" responds Airman Jones.

"Did you guys show him the dummy?" asks Levine.

"Oh yeah" replies Airman Jones, "He thought it was totally cool."

"Was the Air Boss there when you showed his son everything?" asks Levine.

"No, he left right after ordering us... I mean *asking* us... to show his son the car" replies Petty Officer Simmons.

"Were either of them around at any *other* time?" asks Levine.

The Petty Officer and the Airman look at each other while saying almost in unison, but slightly overlapping, "Not that I recall."

Petty Officer Simmons pauses for a moment and then adds, "But no one is on duty between 2200 and 0600 hours, so I suppose they could have checked things out again during that time."

"Interesting" says Levine as he turns to leave. "Thanks guys, you've been a big help."

"You're welcome, Sir" replies Petty Officer Simmons.

The Petty Officer and the Airman look at each other in a *"what just happened?"* manner. After Levine's line of questioning the two of them are just as confused, if not more so, than when Levine first arrived.

Levine pulls out his cell phone to make a call – no signal.

"I should have known there'd be no cell phone signal in the confines of the Oh-Three level" he thinks to himself, *"Nor most anywhere else within the skin of the Ship for that matter, now that I think of it."*

He hustles down to the Hangar Bay, pulls out his phone, verifies he has a signal, and immediately places a call to Nicole.

"Hey Nic, another name for you to look into: Derek Williams" he says, "Commander Williams' son."

"A possible suspect?" asks Nicole.

"You never know" replies Levine, "I'm just now leaving the Ship; I'll fill you two in when I arrive."

35

Levine walks into the office; heading directly to the vicinity of Conroy and Nicole's desks.

"Hey Jake" says Conroy as Levine approaches, "It sounds like you got some interesting info from the Air Boss?"

"The Air Boss has an alibi regarding his *own personal* whereabouts at the moment Colletti was launched – he was up in Pri-Fly surrounded by a gaggle of witnesses" says Levine.

"Pri-Fly?" asks Nicole.

"Primary Flight Control" responds Levine.

"I guess the name speaks for itself."

"Don't feel bad Nic, it took me years to learn the myriad of acronyms and nicknames the Navy uses and I still *'swing and miss'* on occasion."

"But hey" says Conroy, "the Air Boss still could've had an accomplice who actually performed the deed, correct?"

"Not only that, Slade" responds Levine, "but his alibi in the wee hours *before* the launch, which is when Colletti was surely knocked-out and loaded into the car, is his son Derek."

"His son?" replies Conroy, "That's a worthless alibi."

"That's what I said. And he tried to counter by saying that a number of people saw the two of them together."

"Even in the wee hours of the morning?"

"Of course not."

"So what did he say to that?"

"I didn't mention *that* fact. One doesn't want to reveal *everything* you're thinking... the key is to bait the hook and see if they bite."

Nicole jumps in, "But if the Air Boss was in Pri-Fly during the launch then somebody else *still* would've had to make sure the deed went off as planned, wouldn't they?"

"You would think" responds Levine, "Which pretty much leads us back to Bauer."

"Does that mean you've changed your mind about Bauer being a patsy?"

"I'm trying to wrap my head around Bauer's possible involvement based on this new information."

"The Air Boss and his son as possible suspects or accomplices?" responds Conroy.

"Well, Bauer was surely too frail to do it all on his own" replies Levine.

"Maybe it was the Air Boss *and* his son" says Nicole, "And Bauer was an *accessory after the fact*?"

"Like he was aware, but had to keep quiet for some reason?" says Conroy.

"That's why I was thinking that the Air Boss had something on Bauer" replies Levine, "But he had an answer for the issue that Petty Officer Jamison brought up."

"About Bauer being called up to see him right before the launch?" asks Conroy.

"Yes; it was to present him the *Retirement Memento* that Nic and I saw at Bauer's home" replies Levine, "The photo of the Ship signed by his peers and superiors."

"Maybe any threat or blackmail was directed toward Bauer's wife or someone else in his family?" asks Nicole.

"That would seem the most likely" says Conroy, "Since Bauer knew he was dying of cancer, any threat against him *personally* would be fruitless."

"I agree" responds Levine, "but unless the threat was made by letter or email, or was captured via text or voicemail, it will be almost impossible to prove."

"And I've been looking into potential enemies of Bauer, but came up empty" says Nicole, "So it sure seems likely that he was silenced as part of this whole *Colletti murder.*"

"What did you find on Derek Williams, the Air Boss' son?" asks Levine.

"He tried to follow in Dad's footsteps to become a Navy pilot" replies Nicole, "but he didn't make the grade."

"Flunked out of Flight School?" responds Levine.

"Yes; and apparently didn't take it very well. His Service Record states that he had a few choice words for the Flight Instructor when he got his walking papers."

"Like father like son... with the Air Boss *going-off* on Colletti at *Davy Jones' Locker.*"

"So Dad *almost* gets screwed over by a higher ranking Officer, and perhaps the son feels like *he* got screwed over by a higher ranking Officer" says Conroy.

"Interesting possibility" says Nicole, "Taking out his frustrations on an easy mark – Colletti."

"With Bauer being collateral damage" says Conroy.

"One of many reasons to consider Bauer as a patsy in lieu of a willing perpetrator" responds Levine.

"What's the son doing now, Nic?" asks Conroy.

"He's co-owner of a gym in El Cajon" replies Nicole.

"I assume that means he's physically fit enough to drag a knocked-out Colletti into the Plymouth?"

"He's listed as six-foot-two and 220 pounds on his driver's license, age 32; and he's pretty buff in his photos on his gym's website."

"It sounds like you're intrigued by his website photo" Conroy says to Nicole in a harassing manner.

"Don't even go there Slade" responds Nicole in a harsh tone along with a glare that could melt the polar ice cap.

"Okay" replies Conroy, "So he has the physical ability, and he had opportunity."

"But motive is still sketchy" says Levine.

"Although we *should* look into them as potential suspects, right?" says Nicole.

"Of course" replies Levine, "Including whether either one or both were in the vicinity of *Hollywood Props* when the dummy and mask were sold."

"Speaking of potential suspects, or at least *'persons of interest'*" says Nicole, "I checked the list of 'Tigers' for Bauer's uncle – no *'Kenneth Cavanaugh'* listed."

"Did you check for any pseudonyms like *'Snuffy Savoy'* or any garbage like that?" replies Levine.

"Yes I did as a matter of fact. I wanted to make sure we didn't fall into the *'Fool me Twice'* category."

"Good plan. But I take it nothing stood out?"

"Nope – unfortunately."

Levine's cell phone rings – he takes a glance and sees that it is Doctor Watson calling.

36

Observing the Caller ID on his phone Levine contemplates the possible news he is about to receive. He had been hoping for a call from Doctor Watson regarding Chief Warrant Officer Bauer's time of death, who was with him when he died, and whether or not anyone in Bauer's family had been prescribed digitalis... the murder weapon. A myriad of questions, possibilities, and options run through his head as he answers the call... *is it good news finally, or another dead end?*

"Hey Doc" says Levine, "Do you have some info for me regarding any of Chief Warrant Officer Bauer's family that had been prescribed digitalis? Or who was with him when he died? Or better yet - both?"

"The first news is that *none* of his family members were prescribed digitalis" replies the Doctor.

"So, that seemingly rules out suicide."

"Unless he got the digitalis from some other source."

"Which seems unlikely."

"Agreed. And the other news is that his wife was the only person with him when he died."

"Damn; I was hoping this might help us narrow-in on his killer, but it wouldn't make any sense for his wife to kill him when he was already *on death's door* due to his cancer."

"Unless it was a mercy killing, but as I said, no one in the family had a prescription for digitalis."

"Do you have the specific details about his death? You know... his wife's statement?"

"Yes" replies the Doctor, "Let me find it here."

The Doctor scans through the report and then states, essentially to himself but aloud, "Here it is."

He reads aloud, yet paraphrasing, "She said he was in a lot of pain that evening, took his pain medication, and then went to bed. When she came to bed about an hour later he was dead – apparently dying in his sleep."

"Holy shit!" says Levine.

Levine's abrupt response catches Doctor Watson by surprise, "What is it Jake?"

"His pain medication... maybe *that's* the source of the digitalis?"

"You make a great conjecture. If his pain medication was a capsule then the contents of one or more of them could have been replaced with the digitalis, and a liquid medication would have been even easier... just add the digitalis into the liquid."

"I'm going to call Mrs. Bauer and see if she still has his meds on hand" says Levine.

"And you'll call me back?"

"Of course; and if she still has his meds then you and I need to get over there ASAP."

"Agreed."

Levine hangs up and immediately calls Mrs. Bauer.

"Hello?" responds Mrs. Bauer as she answers the phone.

"Mrs. Bauer?" says Levine.

"Yes."

"This is Special Agent Levine from NCIS – I visited you yesterday with my fellow Agent Ms. McKenna."

"Yes Agent Levine, what can I do for you?"

"I was wondering ma'am, do you happen to have any of your husband's medications still in the house?"

"Yes I do, is there any particular one you are asking about? If so I can go grab it for you."

"No!" says Levine abruptly, and with emphasis continues... "Please do NOT touch any of them."

"I don't understand your concern?"

"I'll explain when I get there. Will you be there over the next hour?"

"Yes I will."

"Great, I'll see you soon."

"Okay" she says, "Goodbye."

Levine hangs up and immediately dials Doctor Watson. "Hey Doc, we're in luck; some of Bauer's meds are still in the house. I told Mrs. Bauer to be sure not to touch any of them and that we'd be right over to explain."

"That's great. You'll pick me up?"

"On my way."

Conroy, hearing aspects of Levine's conversation with Doctor Watson, asks Levine, "Some news about Bauer?"

"Yeah" says Levine as he starts to hightail it out of the office, "I'll provide you two details when I get back, right now the Doc and I need to get over to the Bauer residence."

37

Mrs. Bauer is about to pour herself a cup of tea when the sound of a car door shutting catches her attention. She glances at the clock on the microwave and realizes that it has been almost an hour since Special Agent Levine called.

Strolling over to the window and taking a peek out toward the street confirms her suspicion - Agent Levine is coming up the walkway; however, there is another gentleman with him that she does not recognize.

She takes a deep breath. She's had a bit of a sinking feeling in her stomach ever since Agent Levine called, running various scenarios through her head as to his sudden interest in her dear departed husband's medications – none of the scenarios are comforting.

The doorbell rings. Mrs. Bauer nervously and anxiously opens the door.

"Mrs. Bauer" says Levine, "It's nice to see you again."

"Agent Levine" responds Mrs. Bauer.

Levine then points to his comrade, "This is Doctor Watson ma'am; he's a forensic pathologist with the San Diego County Medical Examiner's Office."

"Doctor" responds Mrs. Bauer as she reaches out to shake hands with Doctor Watson.

"Ma'am" replies the Doctor as he gently shakes her hand and then releases his grip.

"Please come in gentlemen" says Mrs. Bauer as she steps aside to allow passage for her guests.

"Thank you" replies Levine as Doctor Watson and he step onto the slate entryway and close the door behind them.

"I was just about to pour myself a cup of tea, would you gentlemen care for any?" says Mrs. Bauer.

Levine and Doctor Watson look at each other. They realize if they say *"No thank you"* that Mrs. Bauer will likely avoid pouring herself the tea she had wanted, so at least one of them will need to accept her invitation whether they care for any or not.

Levine decides to make the gesture, "That would be nice, thank you."

"And you, Doctor?" says Mrs. Bauer.

"I'm fine ma'am, thank you" replies the Doctor.

"I have some Green Tea steeping in a pot Agent Levine" she says, "But I also have Earl Grey and Chamomile if you prefer?"

"Whatever you're having, ma'am."

"Green Tea it is then. Grab a seat on the sofa in the living room – Agent Levine you know where that is."

"Yes ma'am."

Levine leads Doctor Watson to the living room; the two of them take a seat on the sofa.

Levine points to the display case at the far end of the room and says to Doctor Watson, "That's the display case I was telling you about – a very impressive collection of memorabilia showcasing Chief Warrant Officer Bauer's career."

"Thank you for the kind words about my husband Agent Levine" responds Mrs. Bauer as she walks into the room carrying a small serving tray centered by a teapot; with two teacups at opposite corners diagonally.

"You're welcome, ma'am" replies Levine as Mrs. Bauer sets the serving tray on the coffee table between them, "Thank you for the tea."

Mrs. Bauer lifts her teacup off of the tray and takes a sip. She then looks directly at Doctor Watson. "Forensic pathologist" she says, "That doesn't sound very good in regard to my husband's death – no offense Doctor."

"No offense taken, ma'am" replies the Doctor, "I completely understand how you might be curious, or confused, or even have a certain amount of anxiety as to why I am here."

"It turns out that Vincent Colletti, the gentleman your husband sponsored during the Tiger Cruise, was killed" says Levine to Mrs. Bauer, "and as near as we can tell the killer was apparently trying to frame your husband for Colletti's murder."

"Oh my Gosh" replies Mrs. Bauer, "Why would anyone want to frame my husband? He didn't have an enemy in the world."

"We're thinking it was a matter of circumstances, ma'am" responds Levine, "With your husband dying of cancer the killer could frame your husband and he... your husband... would not be able to defend himself and thus the killer gets off scot-free."

"But what would all of that have to do with his medications?"

"We're looking for any evidence the killer might have left behind... fingerprints, DNA, that sort of thing."

"And that's why Agent Levine invited me to join him, ma'am" adds Doctor Watson, "To evaluate any forensic evidence the killer might have deposited on them."

"I'm glad you contacted me" says Mrs. Bauer, "Having my husband's legacy ruined by a false murder charge would be a horrible travesty."

"We completely agree, ma'am" responds Levine.

"Would you mind showing us your husband's medications?" asks Doctor Watson.

"Of course" replies Mrs. Bauer as she gets up from her seat, "I believe they are all in the medicine cabinet in the Master Bathroom... if you'll follow me."

Levine and Doctor Watson follow Mrs. Bauer down a hallway, through the Master Bedroom, and into the Master Bathroom.

Mrs. Bauer opens the medicine cabinet above the sink, "Here they are" she says as she points to various medications within the cabinet.

Doctor Watson puts on his gloves while Levine pulls out several zip-lock type plastic bags from his inner jacket pocket.

Doctor Watson reaches into the cabinet and examines a bottle of liquid. He notes that the prescription label says *'Hydrocodone'*.

The Doctor pulls the bottle out of the cabinet and holds it up to Mrs. Bauer, "Is this the pain medication your husband took the night he died?" he asks.

"To be honest, I'm not sure" replies Mrs. Bauer, "He had actually been avoiding all of his pain meds because they made him feel *'loopy'*, but he was having an exceptionally difficult time that evening."

Doctor Watson holds the bottle up toward Levine, "This prescription was issued by the Chief Medical Officer on the SEADRAGON."

Levine doesn't say a word, but he understands the implication.

"Does that have any significance?" asks Mrs. Bauer.

"It could" replies the Doctor.

"But we can't say anything beyond that, ma'am" adds Levine, "Considering the confidentiality of our investigation at this time."

"I understand" replies Mrs. Bauer.

Doctor Watson and Levine bag a few more items from the medicine cabinet, with the Doctor noting that the hydrocodone is the only item issued by the Medical Department on the SEADRAGON; all remaining medications are merely over-the-counter drugs.

Doctor Watson turns to Mrs. Bauer and asks "Is there anywhere else your husband might have kept medications, like the bedroom nightstand, a kitchen cabinet, out in the garage, places such as those?"

"Let me check the nightstand" replies Mrs. Bauer.

"If you point it out to me I'll check, if you don't mind ma'am."

"Oh yes… of course."

Doctor Watson and Levine follow Mrs. Bauer to her husband's nightstand. She opens the drawer – nothing but a cell phone charger, a couple of unopened pairs of shoelaces, a travel-sized pack of tissues, a writing pad, a ball-point pen, nail clippers, and some breath mints.

"Well, if you think of anything else please call me" says Levine to Mrs. Bauer, handing her his card.

"And be sure not to handle the item if you do find any, ma'am" adds Doctor Watson.

"Of course" replies Mrs. Bauer.

"We can see ourselves out, ma'am" says Levine, "Thank you for the tea and your hospitality."

"It was a pleasure to meet you" says Doctor Watson to Mrs. Bauer.

"Thank you" replies Mrs. Bauer, "Both of you."

"It's our pleasure, ma'am" says Levine as he and Doctor Watson walk out the front door and onto the pathway, heading toward their car.

"I'll get the Lab to analyze these post haste" says Doctor Watson to Levine as they climb into the car.

"I'm assuming the hydrocodone is the most likely source of the digitalis, if in fact any of these meds have been tainted?" asks Levine as he shifts his car into DRIVE and heads down the road on his way back to the Medical Examiner's Office in Kearney Mesa.

"That's true; being a liquid it would be the easiest to contaminate; and the most likely to be ingested."

"How's that?"

"The other items are some cold remedies... an antihistamine, a decongestant, and a cough suppressant... along with a muscle relaxant."

"Things that Bauer may not have felt the need to take for months or more, depending on developing a cold, or wrenching out his back, something like that?"

"Exactly. Assuming the killer wanted Bauer to die as soon as possible so as to not implicate him in a murder, he had to select something he was sure Bauer would take relatively soon."

"You'll let me know as soon as you have the results from the Lab, correct?" asks Levine.

"Of course" replies the Doctor.

38

Conroy and Nicole look up from their respective desks to a somewhat unfamiliar sight, at least one they haven't seen much of late - Levine appears to have a bit of a bounce to his step as he walks toward them. Not that he's *'bounding about'* like a teenager who just passed his driving test, but he definitely has the look of someone with a newfound sense of optimism.

"Some good news to share, Jake?" says Conroy.

"I may be getting ahead of myself" says Levine, "but it looks like we might have found a potential detour around all of these road blocks and dead ends we keep running into."

"Something stemming from Chief Warrant Officer Bauer's meds?" replies Nicole.

"I should know better than to get my hopes up" responds Levine, "but one of his meds… *hydrocodone*… was prescribed by the Ship's Chief Medical Officer."

"Do you think that's the source of the digitalis?" asks Nicole.

"And if so, does that mean we're adding the Chief Medical Officer to our list of suspects?" asks Conroy with a sense of disbelief at such a possibility.

"We'll see what the Toxicology Lab results tell us" replies Levine, "But if we find that the hydrocodone is the source, then one of the things we'll look into is *anyone* that might have had access to Bauer's meds."

"It would be crazy to think that the Ship's Medical Officer would have a reason to spike his pain meds" says Conroy, who thinks for a moment and then adds, "Unless Bauer specifically requested it."

"Bauer requesting it??" responds Nicole.

"Yeah, remember the Autopsy Doctor said that Bauer's wish was that he'd gasp his last breath while on this past deployment, serving his Country?"

"Chief Medical Officer *Kevorkian*? Hard to believe that might be a possibility."

"Obviously we'll look into that if it comes to it" says Levine.

"Wouldn't it be ironic if we discovered that *Colletti* had access to Bauer's meds?" says Nicole.

"Bauer kills Colletti, but not before Colletti had spiked Bauer's meds, and thus they end up murdering *each other?*" replies Conroy, "That would be Karma at its finest, wouldn't it?"

"Or something right out of a *Hitchcock* movie" says Nicole.

"Those are the best, aren't they?" responds Conroy, "Trying to figure out the plot twists of his movies is what got me interested in crime scene investigation at a young age."

Levine is tempted to flip Conroy and Nicole some crap for going off on a tangent about Hitchcock movies, but he realizes he'd be quite the hypocrite considering he made a crack about the movie "*Psycho*" to the Director just a few days ago.

"Okay Robert Cummings and Grace Kelly..." says Levine as a reminder to get the two of them back on track.

"*Dial M for Murder*" responds Conroy, "One of my favorites."

"I loved the whole mystery surrounding the passkey" adds Nicole, "Hitchcock at his best, that's for sure."

"Shall we get back to the notion of possible suspects?" Levine says in an '*enough is enough*' tone of voice.

"Of course" responds Conroy.

"In that regard, Slade" replies Levine, "Do we have results for persons of interest in the vicinity of *Hollywood Props* the day the mask and dummy were purchased?"

"Both Nic and I looked into Bauer, Sewell, Jamison, Kozinski, Baldwin, Caldwell, and the Air Boss - Commander Raymond Williams" responds Conroy.

"And his son - Derek Williams" adds Nicole.

"Any luck?" says Levine.

"Only one of them, Conrad Caldwell, can be placed in the vicinity on that specific date" replies Conroy, "At least by way of credit card purchases."

"Really?? *Caldwell??*" replies an almost dumbfounded Levine, "He's the last person I would suspect."

Nicole interjects... "And he probably still is. The '*vicinity*'" she says with air-quotes, "was the fact of being at Disneyland with his grandkids that day."

"Hard to imagine he would have picked up the dummy while he was with his grandchildren" replies Levine.

"Nic also sent photos of all eight of them to *Hollywood Props* in the hopes that they might remember one of them; unfortunately, they didn't recognize a single one" says Conroy, who then adds, "But here's something crazy..."

"This whole frickin' case has been about '*crazy*'" responds Levine, "So what the hell; let's add another crazy-ass item to the mix."

"All of our probing questions, photos, and such jogged their memory about something strange that occurred around that time frame" says Conroy, "At least from their recollection."

"What's that?" asks Levine.

"They recalled that a guy came into the shop in a lame-ass disguise: obvious wig, fake mustache, and with goofy teeth that were surely right out of a costume shop."

"Did they get video of the guy?"

"No such luck; but they said we could rule out the much older guys."

"How's that?"

"They said they couldn't pinpoint a specific age range, but there's no way the guy was in his sixties or seventies, so we should focus on the others."

"So, that leaves us with Sewell, Jamison, the Air Boss' son Derek Williams, and Bauer" interjects Nicole.

"*If* in fact the weirdo in the disguise is even the person that bought the dummy and mask" responds Levine, "Hell, we could be chasing a red herring here."

"How about Slade and I do a social media search on the four of them?"

"In search of??"

"Maybe one of them wore the disguise for a Halloween party or something?"

"Okay, you two see what you can find" responds Levine, "As for me, I think it's high-time I talk to Bauer's uncle."

Levine scrolls through the *'Contacts'* list on his cell phone. He stops at *'Kenneth Cavanaugh'* and hits *'Send'*.

39

Stepping away from a Conference Room table upon conclusion of a Project Planning Meeting, Kenneth Cavanaugh's cell phone rings.

"Perfect timing" he thinks to himself as he grabs his phone and checks the Caller ID.

He immediately recognizes the area code as it is the same as his project's Type Commander Representative, commonly referred to as *'TYCOM Rep'*, based out of San Diego. However, the specific number is unfamiliar; he assumes it must be an assistant to his TYCOM Rep.

"Hello?" says Cavanaugh as he answers his phone.

"Kenneth Cavanaugh?" responds Levine.

"Speaking."

"This is Special Agent Levine, NCIS."

As a high-level manager with the Department of Defense Cavanaugh is used to receiving phone calls from various factions associated therein... Project Management, Engineering and Technical Support, and Trades... along with outside agencies like the Prime Contractor's Laboratory, and Headquarters. But a call from NCIS? That's a new one, and quite unexpected.

"What can I do for you?" asks Cavanaugh.

"I have a few questions regarding Gordon Bauer" replies Levine, "I understand he was your nephew?"

"That's correct" responds Cavanaugh, now even more confused.

"When was the last time you saw him?"

"At his Memorial Service a couple of weeks ago. You *do* realize he passed away due to cancer a few weeks ago, don't you?"

"Yes, in fact that's part of the reason I'm calling; when was the last time you saw him *prior* to his Memorial Service?"

"Here at my place a year ago this past summer... when I hosted our family reunion."

"Has he ever mentioned a person named *Vincent Colletti*?"

"You're being rather cryptic with me Agent Levine, and as such I'm not feeling all that obligated to continue this conversation unless you want to show up at my door or my office with your credentials so that I know you are who you *say* you are."

"I understand Mr. Cavanaugh; I actually received your name and number from his widow, Angela Bauer."

"From Angie?"

"Yes. And I apologize, I should have provided you that information initially, but feel free to call her and verify if you'd like."

"To answer your question... *no*, he never mentioned a *Vincent Colletti*."

"I don't suppose *you* knew him?"

"Never heard of him before you mentioned his name five minutes ago; why do you ask?"

"I'll try to make a long story short: Vincent Colletti turned up dead and the last person to see him alive, as far as we know, was your nephew."

"If you're implying that Gordon might have had anything to do with this guy's death I can tell you that you are absolutely, without a doubt, mistaken."

"We have our doubts as well" says Levine, trying to allay Cavanaugh's defensiveness even though Bauer is still *'in-play'* as a suspect in Levine's mind, "But I'm sure you can understand the importance of any information received from the last person to see the victim alive?"

"Of course; but as I said, I've never heard of the guy."

"Well, ironically you served with him on the ENTERPRISE during the 1978 WestPac."

"There were over five-thousand men on the ENTERPRISE, so unless he worked in Engineering or Reactor Department it's highly unlikely we would have crossed paths."

"Air Department... he was a pilot."

"A pilot?? Hell, the closest thing to crossing paths with a pilot during a WestPac would have been observing Flight Ops on the television screen in Central Control while I was on watch."

"Speaking of that WestPac, I was told you took Gordon with you on the Tiger Cruise."

"Oh yeah, he had the time of his life. His favorite part was when they launched a car – catapulted it right off the Flight Deck."

"Were you privy to the tirade that went on just before the launch?"

"We heard some kind of commotion off in the distance. Some guy in khakis, I assume a Chief, ranting and raving like a *Boot Camp Drill Instructor dressing-down a Seaman Recruit.*"

"You and your nephew weren't in the midst of it all?"

"Fortunately, no; but it had to be awful for the young kids that *were* exposed to it."

"I'm guessing you were not aware, but the guy doing all the yelling and screaming was *Colletti.*"

"No kidding? You're not trying to talk to every single person that happened to be on a Tiger Cruise with the guy over thirty years ago, are you?"

"No... just those with a tie to Colletti."

"I don't see how Gordon would have any ties to him."

"We haven't been able to tie him to Colletti either; which makes one thing very curious."

"What's that?"

"Why would your nephew have sponsored Colletti on the *SEADRAGON's* Tiger Cruise?"

"*Colletti* is the guy he sponsored??"

"That's the case; why does that sound surprising to you?"

"He told me that the guy he sponsored never showed."

Levine's surprise overshadows Cavanaugh's at this point, and he responds, "When did he tell you that?"

"I gave him a call to congratulate him on his retirement and to hear some sea stories from his deployment, and one of the first things he mentioned was, *"Here I sponsor this guy for someone and then he never shows"."*

"Did he mention *who* or *why* he was sponsoring Colletti?"

"Not that I recall."

"Well if you *do* recall anything, anything at all no matter how trivial it might seem, please call me."

"I will."

"I greatly appreciate your time Mr. Cavanaugh, you've been a big help."

"No problem at all."

Levine hangs up and takes a moment to ponder this latest curveball thrown at him. His contemplation is interrupted by his cell phone ringing - it's Doctor Watson.

"Hey Doc" says Levine as he answers, "News from the Lab I hope?"

"You are correct Jake; the hydrocodone *was*, in fact, the source of the digitalis."

"Finally some of the pieces are falling into place. I don't suppose we had any luck with DNA or fingerprints?"

"Unfortunately; only the Chief Warrant Officer's."

"Well, this is a major step forward Doc, thanks!"

40

"Had an interesting talk with Bauer's uncle" remarks Levine to Conroy and Nicole, "And got some news from the Doc."

"Yeah?" responds Nicole.

"The uncle said he'd never heard the name *Colletti* before I brought it up" says Levine, "And he said that he and Bauer were not really privy to the tirade Colletti spewed during the '78 Tiger Cruise."

"No reason for him to hold a grudge then" replies Conroy, "Assuming you believed him."

"He didn't come across as being deceptive" responds Levine, "But one thing he said caught my attention; he said that Bauer told him that the guy he, *Bauer*, sponsored on this Tiger Cruise *never showed*."

"What the hell??" responds Conroy.

"So, that means that either Bauer *wasn't* involved at all" says Nicole, "or it was simply Bauer's attempt at fabricating an alibi."

"I wonder if Bauer told his wife the same thing?" says Conroy.

"You'd think that if he was fabricating an alibi he'd want to get the word out to a wide audience" says Nicole, "Figuring that the more people reiterate the story the greater the likelihood of *believing* the story."

"An implied corroboration when in fact they are unknowingly perpetuating a lie?" replies Conroy.

"Exactly" replies Nicole.

"You two make a great point" responds Levine, "And the fact that Mrs. Bauer made no such comment could be rather telling."

"Back to Bauer being a potential patsy?" asks Nicole.

"We may not know for sure until we catch his killer" replies Levine, "Patsy... accomplice... accessory after the fact... who the hell knows."

"So, Jake" says Conroy, "You said you had some info from Doctor Watson?"

"That I do" replies Levine, "The hydrocodone *was* in fact the source of the digitalis."

"So now we need to figure out who had access to Bauer's meds" says Conroy.

"And I have a sneaking suspicion it is going to be a short list" replies Levine.

"Normally that's a good thing" responds Nicole, "But by the tone of your voice I get the impression you're thinking otherwise?"

"I'm thinking we are going to find it to be the Ship's Medical Department, Bauer, his wife, and *maybe* his stateroom-mate depending on when the prescription was filled" replies Levine.

"All unlikely perpetrators" says Nicole.

"That's a fact" responds Levine.

"Shall I talk to the Ship's Medical Officer?" asks Conroy.

"I'll have our illustrious M.E. take care of that" responds Levine, who then asks, "Hey, did you two find out anything through your social media search for the '*doofus in disguise*'?"

"No such luck" replies Nicole, "Either *none* of the four... Bauer, Sewell, Jamison, or Derek Williams... were the guy in the disguise; or they simply didn't post their pic anywhere that we could find."

"I wasn't holding my breath on that one" says Levine, "but like you two said, we had nothing to lose beyond the time you spent searching."

"On a separate note" says Conroy, "Nic and I were thinking that perhaps we've had a bit of tunnel vision, you know, focusing on those with a *direct* tie to Colletti."

"And you're thinking we should redirect our focus?" says Levine.

"Actually we already have" replies Nicole, "We expanded our focus from those that Colletti had *personally* screwed-over, to their family members."

"Figuring they might have a reason for revenge" adds Conroy, "*Especially* if, in their eyes, Colletti's actions had dire results to their loved one."

"What did you use as your criteria for *dire results*?" asks Levine.

"We kind of used Ryan Patrick as our template" replies Nicole, "You know, how the Squadron guys said that Colletti had ruined his career."

"That's the guy with the call-sign *'Rhino'*, correct?" says Levine.

"Yep" says Nicole.

"Makes sense" says Levine, "But a ruined career? *That* was your criteria for *dire results??*"

"That was just one data point; and then we looked for guys that seemingly had a promising life *before* Colletti screwed them over" says Conroy, "and they ended up with drug or alcohol dependency, unable to hold down a job, on the streets, suicide, died by drug or alcohol overdose... those types of things."

"Millions of people suffer from those maladies" responds Levine, "but you can't blame them on someone in their life that happened to be a flaming asshole."

"True, but remember we're only talking a small sampling of people here" replies Conroy, "And our objective is simply to attempt to narrow the playing field."

"Alright, let's hear what you've got" responds Levine.

"We dug into all of our *persons of interest* and, for the most part, nothing stood out regarding Caldwell, Baldwin, and Kozinski" says Nicole.

"And Bauer, Sewell, and Jamison remain suspects based on everything we've already learned" adds Conroy, "but they were never subjected to Colletti's wrath, so we didn't include them in this particular search."

"Which leaves us with Derek Williams and Ryan Patrick?" responds Levine.

"Exactly" replies Conroy.

"The jury is still out on Derek Williams" says Nicole, "but we found some interesting stuff on Ryan Patrick. And go figure he's the guy that everyone said had the biggest reason to hold a grudge against Colletti in the first place."

"Something gave you a reason to think a family member might have blamed *Colletti* for Patrick's death?" says Levine, "That wouldn't make much sense; you said he died in a plane crash."

"True; but apparently his wife went into a deep depression after his death" adds Conroy, "and six months later she took her own life via an overdose of Lanoxin, a drug she was taking for a heart condition."

"An interesting turn of events there; don't you think, Jake?" says Nicole.

"Are we sure it was a suicide and not an accidental overdose?" asks Levine.

"She left a suicide note" replies Conroy.

"About how she couldn't go on without the love of her life... her husband" adds Nicole, "And that she hoped her son would understand."

"They have a son?" asks Levine.

"Yes; Patrick's obituary lists two survivors" replies Nicole, "wife Maureen and son Allen."

"So, if the son knew that Colletti ruined his father's career" responds Levine, "and then his mother commits suicide several months after his father's death..."

"Then maybe he... *the son*... hit his breaking-point with the death of his parents and went after Colletti" says Nicole as she finishes Levine's thought.

"Certainly *could* be a motive" says Levine.

"And we've got nothing to lose by digging deeper into such a possibility" says Conroy.

"I agree" replies Levine, "But before we forget about it, let's get that drug info to Doctor Watson."

"The Lanoxin?" asks Conroy.

"Yes" responds Levine.

"You got it" replies Conroy.

"And speaking of the son" says Levine, "Any chance he's a crewman on the SEADRAGON?"

"There's no *Allen Patrick* listed in the Ship's registry" replies Nicole, "And no such person is listed as a rider during the Tiger Cruise."

"But a cursory search online *did* find a *J. Allen and Cassandra Patrick* in Del Mar" adds Conroy.

"It's a long shot, Jake" says Nicole, "But who knows, maybe he's the son?"

"And since we have an address we were thinking we should go talk to him" adds Conroy.

"Sounds good, Slade" responds Levine, "What say you and I go while Nic performs some of her magic?"

"My magic?" responds Nicole.

"Your research expertise" replies Levine. "Dig up everything you can on this guy: If he knew Bauer or the Air Boss or his son Derek... if he made a purchase at *Hollywood Props*... if he owned a '63 Plymouth... you name it."

"Even though he may not have been the physical killer he could have been the *Puppet Master*?" replies Nicole.

"That's the angle I'm thinking" responds Levine, "So let's delve into his life as if such is the case."

41

The sun disappears over the horizon as Levine and Conroy approach the front door of the home of Allen and Cassandra Patrick.

Stepping onto the landing they ready their respective badges in anticipation of a greeting. Levine leans over and rings the doorbell.

A woman who appears to be in her mid-to-late thirties answers the door. She's five-foot four inches tall with a slim figure and strawberry blonde hair; she is dressed in business attire, as if she has just gotten home from the office.

"Can I help you?" she asks.

"Good afternoon, ma'am; Special Agents Levine and Conroy, NCIS" says Levine as Conroy and he hold up their badges, "We're looking for Allen Patrick."

"You mean Jay?" she replies, "I'm sorry he's not here."

Levine looks at his watch; he's thinking that anyone with normal work hours would be arriving home shortly.

"Do you expect him home anytime soon?" Levine asks.

"Actually, he's not living here right now."

"Do you know where we can find him?"

"Not really; we've been separated for over a year now and I only talk to him on occasion, and I hardly ever see him."

"So, you're his wife?" says Conroy.

"Yes; Cassandra" she replies, "I apologize for not introducing myself."

"Not at all, ma'am" responds Conroy.

"He didn't provide you a forwarding address?" asks Levine.

"When he first moved out he went to his parent's house" she replies, "But the house was later sold and he said something about moving into an apartment, but that was the extent of it."

"What about where he works?" asks Conroy.

"Isn't that why you're here?" she responds, "Something to do with his work?"

"In a sense, ma'am" replies Levine, "But there are other issues as well that we need to discuss with him."

"He worked for *Advanced Aviation Systems*, but I don't know if he's still there" she replies, "He went through a rough patch when his parents died and took an extended leave of absence."

"Our condolences" responds Levine.

"Thank you."

"Speaking of his parents; were they *Ryan and Maureen Patrick?*"

"Yes."

"What can you tell us about your husband?"

"Forgive me gentlemen, but I'm at a loss here with your questions" she replies with a sense of concern.

"We're working a case that involves a man named Vincent Colletti who served on the USS ENTERPRISE with your husband's father, and also had some recent experience on the USS SEADRAGON" responds Levine, "So we're interviewing anyone that might have knowledge of him."

"We are hoping that your husband might have information shared by his father that could help our investigation" adds Conroy, "Or perchance your husband has done some work recently for the SEADRAGON."

"That makes sense" she replies, "but bringing back memories of his father could be very difficult on him."

"He had a tough time dealing with the loss?" asks Levine.

"It was bad enough when his father died, but when his mother took her own life six months later the grief consumed him."

"And that's when your husband took a leave of absence from work?"

"Yes; his depression was so bad he rarely got out of bed the first week, and over time his depression turned into anger."

"That's not uncommon when going through the stages of grieving" responds Conroy.

"Yes, but he never achieved the final stage of *acceptance*" she replies. "In fact, he seemed more intent on *vengeance* rather than holding dear what he still had."

"How do you mean?" asks Levine.

"He couldn't accept that sometimes bad things happen to good people; in his mind someone was to blame and justice must be served for the loss of his parents."

"Upon whom did he place the blame?"

"He never said, but *getting justice* became an obsession with him; it was like he was a different person, and it took a toll on our marriage."

"Did he say in what manner he intended to obtain justice?" asks Conroy.

"I assumed he was doing his *own* investigation into his father's death" she replies, "He always said it was someone's fault, but that the police weren't doing anything."

"He didn't believe it was an accident?" asks Conroy.

"He refused to even *acknowledge* that word" she replies.

"And once he concluded his investigation?" asks Levine.

"I'm sure his plan was to turn any evidence he found over to a Federal Agency instead of the local police" she replies, "Like you gentlemen perhaps?"

"We're not at liberty to divulge specifics, but we *are* interested in his evidence" responds Levine.

"When was the last time you talked to him?" asks Conroy.

"About a week ago" she replies, "And the funny thing... in a good way... he seemed much better."

"Do you happen to have a phone number for him?" asks Levine.

"Yes" she replies as she grabs her phone and scrolls though the Contacts, "Here's his cell number" as she holds up her phone for Levine to view.

"Thank you very much" replies Levine, "We greatly appreciate your time."

Levine and Conroy step off the landing and start walking toward their car; Cassandra Patrick watches them for a brief moment and then shuts the front door.

Levine and Conroy get into the car and buckle-up.

"That was a telling conversation" says Conroy. "If we can somehow tie Allen Patrick to Bauer, or Derek Williams, or Jamison, or someone else on the SEADRAGON that we haven't thought of, we could have our killer."

"Hopefully we're able to tie him to one of those three" responds Levine, "I can do without another suspect we haven't thought of."

"Amen to that" replies Conroy.

42

"Sounds good Doctor; I'll see you soon" says Nicole as she ends her conversation with Doctor Watson and hangs up the phone.

She stands up to stretch her legs after spending the last couple of hours glued to her chair staring at a computer screen, talking on the phone, and taking notes.

She takes a sip of her latte'; "Damn - it's cold" she says.

She walks over to the office Coffee Mess area, puts her latte' cup in the microwave, punches in '27 seconds', and hits 'start'.

She contemplates the information she has learned about Allen Patrick as she stares at her latte' rotating on the turntable.

"Ding" goes the microwave.

She extracts her latte', takes a sip, and says to herself out loud, "Ahhh... perfect."

She starts back toward her desk, oblivious to the sound of the multiple beeps predicating someone's access into the office area.

"Pull any rabbits out of your hat, Nic?" says Conroy as Levine and he stroll up behind her.

"I've got a few surprises for you guys" replies Nicole as she turns to acknowledge them, "Any luck with Allen Patrick?"

"It was an eye-opening conversation, that's for sure" responds Conroy, "How about you?"

"I can't wait to compare notes with whatever story he told *you* guys" replies Nicole as they all arrive at her desk, "Because I found some intriguing items about him."

"Actually he wasn't there, but we *did* talk to his wife" responds Conroy, "and she refers to him as *Jay* instead of *Allen*... for whatever that's worth."

"Hmmm..." says Nicole as she ponders the information, "That fits right in with some of the info I've dug up."

"Interestingly enough, she was making a case against her husband without realizing it" says Levine.

"She incriminated him right there in your interview?" responds Nicole.

"No, she didn't outright incriminate him, and she gave no indication that she was familiar with the name *Vincent Colletti*" replies Levine, "It was more a matter of providing specific details regarding his state of mind."

"His state of mind?" says Nicole.

"She said he was extremely depressed after his parents' death, which became a desire for vengeance" says Conroy.

"Vengeance?" replies Nicole, "Did she say whom?"

"No; she said he never told her the target of his quest for justice" responds Conroy.

"And she seems to think his *quest for justice* involves him doing his own investigation into his father's death and turning the evidence over to the authorities" adds Levine.

"And what do *you* think?" asks Nicole.

"I think his '*justice*'" says Levine with air-quotes, "involved murdering Colletti."

"She also said that recently he seemed to be back to his old self" says Conroy, "I'm thinking that's because *all was right in the world now that he'd gotten his revenge.*"

The conversation is interrupted by a familiar voice, several feet away, ringing-out... "I was hoping you all would be here."

"Hey Doc" says Levine as Doctor Watson approaches, "I wasn't expecting you to stop by."

"I hope I'm not interrupting, but Agent McKenna and I have been exchanging information over the past hour or so" responds the Doctor,

"Plus, I just had a little chat with the SEADRAGON's Medical Officer, so it only made sense to swing by while on my way home."

"Not at all; in fact we're all ears, Doc" replies Levine, "What did you learn from the Ship's Medical Officer?"

"Chief Warrant Officer Bauer had been in a fair amount of pain" replies the Doctor, "To the extent that the Medical Officer tried to convince the Warrant Officer to depart the Ship early, but Bauer would have nothing to do with that idea."

"Too proud of a Naval Officer to essentially quit on his crew?" asks Nicole.

"Or that he still had a job to do" says Conroy, *"Launching Colletti."*

"Either of those could be the case" replies Doctor Watson, "But from the Medical Officer's perspective it was solely a matter of *'can he still do his job effectively?'"*

"Obviously the Doctor felt he *could* since he remained on the Ship throughout the deployment" remarks Levine.

"With that in mind he prescribed the hydrocodone to deal with his pain; small dosage... liquid... utilizing an eye dropper."

"And the digitalis?"

"It could *not* have been introduced via the Ship's Medical Department, not even accidentally."

"No?"

"It's not a drug that they carry in their inventory; and according to their records none was ordered in support of a specific sailor's health issue."

"Did the Medical Officer have any theories regarding the tainting of the hydrocodone?"

"Nothing beyond those we've already postulated, except we both figured that the tricky part with spiking Bauer's meds is that the perpetrator had to do so *after* the launch so that Bauer would be the one implicated."

"Either because he needed Bauer's assistance; or because he chose Bauer to be the fall-guy" responds Levine.

"And you can't say *'Bauer did it'* if Bauer was already dead" adds the Doctor.

"So Doc, Nic was going to fill us in on the information she's compiled on Ryan Patrick's son" says Levine, "Did you want to stick around?"

"Of course" replies the Doctor, "Since she and I have been in communication I may have information to add."

"Great" responds Levine, who then turns to Nicole and says, "You're up, Nic."

"It gets crazy right off the get-go" says Nicole.

"Not more screwed-up *'crazy'* crap" replies Conroy in a disheartened tone.

"Crazy *'good'*" responds Nicole with an almost impish grin, "Digging into *'J. Allen Patrick'* I discovered that the letter *'J'* is for *'Jason'.*"

"*That's* crazy-good??" replies Conroy, not comprehending anything positive from Nicole's proclamation.

"It is when you add in the fact that his wife is the former Cassandra *Kirk*" responds Nicole.

"You're frickin' kidding me" replies Conroy, "Are you saying what I *think* you're saying?"

"I'm thinking that the *Contractor,* who roomed with Colletti, is the son of *Ryan Patrick* whose Navy career was *ruined* by Colletti" responds Nicole.

"And the name Kirkpatrick is really a hyphenated *Kirk* and *Patrick*?" replies Levine.

"It makes sense, don't you think, Jake?" says Conroy.

"Right now it is only a theory" responds Levine, "We need some facts."

"Here's a fact for you, Jake" says Doctor Watson as he jumps into the conversation, "The drug that Maureen Patrick used to commit suicide is the *same* drug that killed Chief Warrant Officer Bauer."

"I thought he died of a digitalis overdose?" replies a somewhat confused Levine.

"As did she" responds Doctor Watson, "*Lanoxin* is merely a *trade-name* for digitalis."

"And here are some more facts for you, Jake" says Nicole, "Kirkpatrick used to work at *Advanced Aviation Systems*."

"That's where the wife... Cassandra Patrick... said her husband Allen, or should I say '*Jay*', used to work" responds Conroy.

"*Advanced Aviation Systems* was competing for the contract that was eventually awarded to *Tech-Star Avionics*" says Nicole, "And Kirkpatrick jumped ship to *Tech-Star* almost immediately after *they* were awarded the contract."

"I'm guessing the training that Kirkpatrick was conducting during the Tiger Cruise is in support of that contract?" responds Levine.

"He's the *Lead* for the installation on the West Coast Carriers" replies Nicole. "And the contract was awarded a year ago, with the SEADRAGON slated to be the first Ship to receive the work."

"So, Kirkpatrick could have set up the training with Bauer *before* the Ship went on deployment?" says Conroy.

"That's *exactly* when he started communicating with the Ship" replies Nicole.

"The son of a bitch implied that he *barely knew* Bauer" responds Conroy.

"Believe it or not, it gets crazier" says Nicole.

"You've piqued my interest" replies Levine.

"Talking to local law authorities" responds Nicole, "there were two complaints from women who thought Kirkpatrick had given them a date-rape drug."

"Such a drug could have been used to knock Colletti out in order to launch him" remarks Doctor Watson.

"Why wasn't he charged with a crime?" says Levine.

"The women were not physically assaulted" replies Nicole, "So there was not sufficient evidence to charge him."

"Why would he take a woman home, be enough of a low-life scum-bag to give her a drug to knock her out, and then sit and wait until she woke up?" says Conroy, "And to do it more than once??"

"Perhaps he is so cold and calculating that he was using these women as trial runs in order to determine the amount of the drug needed to knock someone out" postulates Doctor Watson.

"Well, his calculations were off" responds Levine, "Colletti was *coming out of it*' according to Jamison."

"I'm sure he didn't consider the increased body weight and mass of a male when he was conducting his trial runs" replies the Doctor.

"Trial runs??" says Nicole with disgust, "More like *lab rats!*"

A lightbulb illuminates inside Conroy's head… "Hey Jake" he says, "Someone we hadn't thought of who could *not* sponsor a guest for a Tiger Cruise."

"Who's that?" responds Levine.

"A Contractor" replies Conroy.

"Shit, you're right" responds Levine.

"That would explain a few things" says Conroy, "Not only Bauer sponsoring Colletti, but him being assigned a stateroom with Kirkpatrick."

"On the flip-side" says Nicole, "If Bauer was merely a patsy then Kirkpatrick could have talked him into sponsoring a former aviator who had been a part of the *original* Plymouth launch back on the ENTERPRISE."

"That's a great point, Nic" replies Conroy.

"What about Derek Williams?" says Levine, "Have you been able to tie him to Patrick… or *Kirk*patrick… or whoever the hell he is?"

"No" replies Nicole, "But I haven't been able to eliminate him from having some level of involvement either."

"Time to bring his ass in for questioning" remarks Levine.

"Williams?" says Nicole.

"Kirkpatrick" responds Levine, "But hey, maybe he'll serve up Williams while he's at it."

"I doubt he's still at work at this hour" says Nicole as she looks at her watch and sees that it's 5:30pm.

"Call his office first thing in the morning to be sure he's going to be there" says Levine to Nicole, "And let's tentatively plan for a nine-o'clock visit."

"And who knows" replies Nicole, "I may have some more ammo for you by then."

43

The twilight sky outlines a silhouette passing through the glass doors at the entryway of the building. The vision catches his eye, and suddenly his complete attention is focused therein. His initial *interest* quickly transitions to *intrigue* as she approaches.

"Damn" he thinks to himself as he realizes she is quite stunning. And based on her attire she is certainly not a current client... too professional, too business-like... definitely not appropriate for rope climbing, scaling a rock-wall, pull-ups, plyometric-jumps, or dead lifts.

"Welcome to *'Warrior Gym'*" he says, "Are you here for a tour of the facility, information regarding our Training Programs, or to sign-up for one of our upcoming Competitions?"

Although she recognizes him from his website photo she responds, "Actually I'm looking for Derek Williams" as she glances at the *'Derek'* emblazoned on his polo shirt and then back to make eye contact.

"That would be me" he says, smiling and pointing to the *'Derek'* on his shirt.

"I thought so, but you never know... you could have more than one *Derek* here."

"So, how can I help you?" he says.

"Special Agent McKenna, NCIS. I was hoping you might be able to answer a few questions in regard to a case I'm working."

"You're a Fed? You guys are supposed to be in pretty damn good shape, I bet you can *kick some ass* when you need to."

Nicole responds with merely a half-smile agreement with his statement.

"And I assume you have a first name" he says as he reaches out to shake hands.

"Nicole" she responds, firmly shaking his hand.

"A pleasure" he says, "Derek." He pauses for a moment and then adds… "I guess I already said that, didn't I?"

"Yes" says Nicole as she releases her grip.

"How about we talk in the Conference Room?" he says as he nods toward a nearby doorway.

Nicole follows him into the Conference Room, which appears to double as the Break Room, complete with a sink, microwave, refrigerator, a blender, and an array of oversized vitamin-style containers full of powdery muscle-building concoctions… *"I guess the ability to make your own Protein Shake is a 'must' around here"* Nicole thinks to herself.

"Have a seat" he says, gesturing toward the table.

Nicole sits down, with Williams following, directly across from her.

"Since I'm not in the Navy or Marines I don't really see how I can possibly be of much help to your case" he says, "Unless one of my Swabby or Leatherneck clients *beat the shit* out of some poor sap or something?"

"No; the case involves the recent Tiger Cruise on the SEADRAGON."

"What would that have to do with me?"

"Someone was murdered during the cruise; and you were there."

"And thousands of other people. What's the deal; you guys botched the crime scene or are so lacking leads that you're interviewing every damn one of us that rode the Ship?"

"Just those few who had the means… opportunity… motive. And persons of interest that might be able to provide relevant information."

"I don't see how I can provide any relevant information, but go for it."

"You aren't familiar with the crime?"

"Not at all, why should I be?"

"Despite requests to keep things *under wraps* during an investigation, word tends to get out. In this particular case, the victim was inside the car that was launched."

"No shit? A *dead guy* was in the car?"

"Yes."

"That's some screwed-up shit; but I still don't see what role I might play in helping you solve it."

"It turns out that you were one of the last people to see the car before the victim was knocked-out and loaded into it."

"Me??"

"Yes; when you received your private tour of the car, including the dummy that was *supposed* to be behind the wheel."

"Yeah, but I wasn't *the last* person to see it, so shouldn't *they* be the ones you're talking to?"

"We have... all of them. And some of them remain within our pool of suspects. But like *them, you* have no alibi during the timeframe of the act."

"What do you mean I have no alibi; I was with my father."

"An interesting thing about alibis... sometimes they become exactly the *opposite*. Here the person thinks the alibi gets them *off*, when in fact it is providing evidence *against* them."

"How could that be?"

"If we have evidence of someone at the scene, and you say *they* are *your* alibi... well, now that places *you* at the scene."

"There's no way you can place my father at the scene."

"Maybe we have evidence of *you* at the scene and your *'alibi'* is now implicating your *father?*"

"Say what??"

"And by the way, it doesn't help that your father had a heated argument with Colletti the night before he mysteriously shows up as a guest on the SEADRAGON; and then a couple of days later *he... Colletti...* is murdered."

"My father has an argument with this Colletti guy, and based on that you're equating it to *murder??* That's ridiculous, no one's going to buy that load of crap!"

"Maybe... maybe not."

"And I know for a fact that *I'm* the only person my dad sponsored on the cruise; did you idiots even *think* to look at the guy who sponsored the victim?"

"Of course; but here's the thing – Chief Warrant Officer Bauer, the guy who *sponsored* the victim, *didn't even know* the victim; in fact the only person that *did* know him was your father, and Bauer *worked for* your father... Do you see where I'm going with this?"

"I told you my father *wasn't there,* so you're going to have to look elsewhere for your sacrificial lamb."

"We have; and guess what... YOU are the perfect accomplice for Bauer."

"How the hell do you figure *that* crap?!"

"Your father's disdain for Colletti, *your* disdain for the Navy, your physical ability to pull it off, and whatever your father had on Bauer to make him do it."

"My father told me you fucks were trying to pin it on him. So, you failed at *that* and now you're trying to pin it on *me??* That's fucking bullshit!"

"I thought you said you weren't familiar with the crime?"

"That's because I wanted to see what tricks you had up your sleeve... and sure enough you sneaky fucking Feds are playing games with me."

"Lies and changing your story only enhances your appearance of guilt."

"Screw you assholes."

"And I'm just trying to do my job here, a foul mouth and berating my co-workers and me is unnecessary."

"Or what, you're going to kick my ass?"

"I guess I shouldn't be surprised, your personnel file from the Navy mentioned how you had a hot temper and even *went off* on your Flight Instructor."

"Fuck you and this bullshit! You wanna see a hot temper??! You ain't seen nothin' yet... so you'd better get the hell out of here before things get ugly!"

Nicole remains silent and seated in the hopes that Williams is merely blowing off steam. She figures once he *cools his jets* she can continue to pry information out of him, or better yet, get him to incriminate himself, or his father.

But Nicole has miscalculated her assessment of the situation – Williams' face is growing increasingly red with fury; and his eyes are seemingly ready to hemorrhage, with a glare that could burn a hole through her skull like a laser.

"NOW!!!" screams Williams as he slams his fist on the table.

Nicole jumps back in her seat and starts to reach for her weapon... just in case.

Williams notices Nicole's sudden hand-motion toward her waist. "What are you going to do, *shoot me?!*" he says, "Go ahead, draw your fucking piece and see what happens!!"

Nicole slowly gets up from her seat while maintaining eye contact with Williams, with her hand remaining *'at the ready'*.

She slowly makes her way through the doorway of the Conference Room, into the reception area, and then out through the front door; all while keeping an eye on Williams.

Fortunately, her car is but a few feet from the gym entrance. She quickly jumps in, locks the doors, starts the car, and drives away – frequently checking her rear-view mirror.

Williams, shielded from Nicole's view by the reflection of the glass, stands motionless inside the entryway – fixated on her car as she drives away. He steps through the doorway before Nicole disappears from sight; she glances back, and steps on it.

44

As she makes her way down Main Street Nicole's emotions are an odd mixture of *relief* combined with *a heightened sense of awareness.*

"What if he's following me?" she thinks to herself.

In hindsight she wishes she would have learned the make, model, and color of Williams' car as part of her investigation, but who knew she might be dealing with a potential violent stalker; or worse, a murderer who figures she is on to him.

The downside of nightfall: You get nothing more than a mere glimpse of a vehicle behind you as it passes under the glare of a streetlamp, *and* you happen to be lucky enough to have glanced in your rear-view mirror at that brief moment in time. The next best thing: Making out the pattern of the headlights and driving lights from the vantage point of the mirror, but trying to determine a vehicle via that method is nothing but a crap shoot.

"Shit" she thinks to herself as she ponders this dilemma.

Her mind wanders to an episode of *The Twilight Zone* where a woman keeps seeing a hitchhiker as she travels across the country. It's not the fact of frequently seeing a hitchhiker that's so creepy; it's that it is always *the same* hitchhiker. *How is that possible?? He gets a ride right after she drives by, and then when she stops for food or gas he passes her by and gets dropped-off down the road?? That's the only likely possibility... but to happen time and time again??* When the woman returns to her car after making a late-night call from a pay phone she is surprised by the sight of a figure in her rear-view mirror - the hitchhiker is sitting in the back seat. "Going my way?" he says. She suddenly realizes he is not a hitchhiker; he is '*death*'... waiting to take her '*home*'.

Nicole's wandering mind is conjuring up all kinds of scenarios with varying degrees of drama, mystery, and even horror. Fortunately, in a manner of speaking anyway, her thoughts akin to a nightmare are suddenly interrupted by the illumination and associated "ding" of an orange light on the dashboard – it's the *fuel* light.

"Dammit" she says aloud. Her plan to gas-up immediately after work had become buried under the weight of the opportunity to interview Williams before he closed-up shop.

She decides she wants to put more distance between Williams and her before stopping, so she continues down Main Street as it transitions to El Cajon Boulevard.

A few miles down the road, just before the interchange with the Kumeyaay Highway, more commonly known as I-8, she sees a gas station on her side of the road.

She decides to turn in to the station and pulls up to a pump near the associated mini-mart so that she is in a well-lit area with plenty of potential observers.

She exits her car and approaches the automated pay device, selecting 'Pump No. 1' and then 'cash'. As she is about to hit 'enter' she notices another car pull into the station, but to her unease they pull directly into a poorly-lit area away from the gas pumps and stop – the motor still running.

"Is someone in there staring at me? Is it him? Dammit I can't see shit!!" she says to herself as her eyes remain fixed on what *would be* the driver of the mystery vehicle, save for the reflective glare of the glass.

The glare suddenly recedes as the upper-portion of the window is being replaced by an increasing void of darkness – the mystery occupant is rolling down the window.

"Screw it!" she says aloud and immediately jumps back into her car and speeds away, frantically watching the rear-view and side-view mirrors for any sign of the mystery vehicle.

"Do I stay on El Cajon Boulevard, or jump onto I-8?"

She recalls that El Cajon Boulevard quickly transitions to Murray Drive right near Jack Murphy Stadium, and at this time of night there are too many spots during this stretch where some maniac could run you off the road with potentially no witnesses.

That seals it – she jumps onto I-8 and floors it. She figures if she gets pulled over by the Highway Patrol she can adequately explain her case. Besides, she'd prefer the CHP's company over Williams any day, even if it means a few dollars donated to the State's coffers.

She continues down I-8 at breakneck speed for only a few miles and decides to jump back onto El Cajon Boulevard at La Mesa. She figures this little maneuver would outfox any potential tail... either he never saw her jump onto I-8 earlier and thus trudged along El Cajon Boulevard to Murray Drive while she was flying down the freeway at 80 miles per hour; or he jumped on I-8, but is so far behind her that he never saw her return to El Cajon Boulevard and thus ends up at Ocean Beach wondering *where the hell she went.*

Back on El Cajon Boulevard Nicole continues on her journey, feeling somewhat relieved at this point.

Just before passing over the 805 Freeway Nicole spots two gas stations on her side of the boulevard, about a block apart. One station is lit up like a slot machine, with a flurry of activity both at the pumps and inside the mini-mart. The other is a Mom & Pop station with a small dimly-lit sign and one lone car filling-up. She opts for the slot machine.

Her eyes are glued to El Cajon Boulevard as she fills up the tank – no sign of her possible stalker.

As she exits the station Nicole ponders, *"What a story I have to tell... whew!"*

Her sojourn takes her to essentially the end of El Cajon Boulevard, becoming Normal Street for a few blocks, and then Washington Street, which becomes W. Washington Street.

Approaching I-5 she makes a right turn onto San Diego Avenue, and continues until she finds a parking spot near her final destination - in Old Town.

45

Nicole walks into *Old Town Bar and Grill* in San Diego's Historic District. Brandi is seated at the bar, swirling a glass of red wine as if she's sampling wines at a Tasting event.

As she grabs the stool to Brandi's immediate left Nicole notices that Brandi's glass is three-quarters of the way empty.

"You're late" says Brandi.

"Sorry."

"It sucks when *'Girls night out'* appears to be *'Lonely girl out on the town'* to the guys at the bar; you have no idea how many drinks I had to turn down."

"None of them were drink-worthy?"

"Sure, but that kind of defeats the purpose of *'Girls night out'.*"

The bartender approaches Nicole and asks, "What can I get you?"

Nicole turns to Brandi and says, "What are *you* drinking?"

"A Reserve Pinot Noir – a little pricey but it is *most excellent.*"

"A glass for me as well" says Nicole to the bartender, "And another one for my friend here."

"Of course" replies the bartender.

"Thanks" says Brandi to Nicole.

"It's the least I could do."

"So what held you up?" asks Brandi.

"I just had a rather unpleasant interview with Derek Williams."

"Why does that name sound familiar?"

"The Air Boss' son."

"Didn't you say that your research showed him to be hot-tempered with a disdain for anything to do with the Navy?"

"Yes I did; and his true colors shone through."

"And Jake was okay with you interviewing him alone?"

"I didn't tell Jake I was going."

"Are you kidding me? He's going to be pissed."

"I was trying to surprise him with some new evidence before we go to pick up Kirkpatrick in the morning, but yeah… I screwed-up on this one."

"Well, did you get anything? Maybe that will lessen the pain of Jake's wrath."

"As you know, 'wrath' is not really Jake's *M.O.* …it's more the tone of disappointment, which is worse."

"Very true… it's right up there with 'The Look'."

Nicole smiles at Brandi's descriptor just as the bartender arrives with two glasses of Pinot Noir. While the bartender is dropping off their drinks Brandi chugs the remainder of her current glass and slides it toward the bartender.

"Thanks" says Brandi to the bartender.

"My pleasure" he responds.

"Anyway… yes" says Nicole to Brandi, "I did get some interesting info, and it could be vital to the case, but at the moment something else has me concerned."

"What's that?"

"It seemed like someone was following me on my way here."

"Do you think it was him? …*Williams?*"

"I don't know who *else* it could be. But luckily I think I lost him."

"Well maybe you're just paranoid after your unpleasant exchange with him."

"Perhaps; but you know how the saying goes?"

"How's that?"

"Just because you're paranoid it doesn't mean that someone's not out to get you."

"Your double-negatives are messing me up, but I see what you mean."

Nicole takes a sip of her wine, "You're right" she says, "This is one of the best Pinots I've had."

"It's from a winery in the foothills of the Santa Cruz Mountains" replies Brandi.

"Cheers to that!"

"To what?"

"To great wine" says Nicole as she holds up her glass.

"To *'Girls night out'*" says Brandi.

They take a sip of their wine and Nicole starts to glance around the room while asking Brandi, "So, who are the guys here that attempted to buy you a drink?"

"Near the end of the bar to my right" says Brandi somewhat quietly as she head-nods in that direction, "The designer jeans and white shirt."

"Mister GQ" responds Nicole.

"And the guy back behind us in the lounge chair" Brandi continues, "The dark suit and light shirt with no tie."

"Mister Professional" responds Nicole. "What do you think, lawyer? Hedge fund manager?"

"How about HR Director?" replies Brandi.

"Or how about the CEO of some computer startup company??" says Nicole.

"I like that possibility" responds Brandi, "Oh, and the guy at the end of the counter to your left - Padres baseball cap."

Nicole looks and starts to respond when her focal point shoots right past the guy at the counter and directly to a shadowy figure sitting at a small table just beyond.

"Shit!" says Nicole as she quickly turns back to face Brandi, "That's him!"

"Who?!" responds Brandi.

"Don't look!" says Nicole, "I don't think he saw me."

Brandi cannot help herself as a male figure in her peripheral vision quickly jumps up, and he's in the vicinity of Nicole's previous glance. She is startled with what she sees – the look of rage on his face.

"Too late!" Brandi says, "And he's headed this way!!"

Williams is racing toward them, and Nicole barely has a chance to turn around when he is on top of her.

"Are you fucking following me?!?!" says Williams as he grabs Nicole by the throat.

Nicole attempts to reach for her weapon, but it is wedged between her body and the seatback of her barstool due to the weight of Williams on top of her.

The sudden commotion startles the bartender, knocking over a drink in mid-pour. "What the fuck Dude?" he says, "Get your hands off of her!"

Williams stays on the offensive; and the bartender yells out, "Code Red!"

The bartender quickly grabs a liquor bottle out of the rack of well drinks, but he doesn't like the feel of it. He does a quick scan around his area for something more suitable and grabs a full bottle of wine by the neck. He raises the bottle in the air like a club as he moves toward Williams.

This motion catches Williams' attention and he repositions himself; attempting to use Nicole as a shield to deflect the bottle.

"I told you to get off of her!" says the bartender with the wine bottle reared-back and ready to strike.

"This is none of your business, asshole!" yells Williams.

As Brandi is ready to throw herself into the fray in Nicole's defense, Williams is abruptly ripped-away by a forearm choke-hold courtesy of the bouncer.

Nicole draws her weapon just as the entryway to the bar is suddenly filled with flashing red and blue lights.

With the bouncer still restraining Williams, and the bartender nearby with his wine bottle 'club', Nicole returns her weapon to its holster.

A pathway through the crowd is cleared by two officers from the San Diego Police Department entering and taking over the scene.

Nicole identifies herself to the officers and provides a statement. Brandi, the bouncer, the bartender, and a number of onlookers provide statements as well.

"Do you wish to file charges, ma'am?" asks one of the officers.

"Absolutely" replies Nicole.

"We'll provide you the footage from our security cameras" says the bouncer to the officers.

Nicole and Brandi watch Williams as he is hauled away in handcuffs; he is ranting and raving as he goes, "*SHE* was following *ME* you assholes, I was just protecting myself."

"Yeah, *right*" responds one of the officers, "You're a two-hundred pound *Gym Rat* and she weighs what... a buck twenty-five?"

"Don't let her size fool you; she's a Fed... with all kinds of tricks up her sleeve... including trying to pin some bogus murder on me."

"A *murder* to add to your assault charges?" says the officer, "It sounds like you'll be opting for our *long term* accommodations."

"Oh I get it, you fucking cops stick together – you're *ALL* in on it."

The officer guides Williams into the back seat of his cruiser. "You have the right to remain silent" he says, "So shut the hell up."

Nicole and Brandi collectively exhale a sigh of relief as the flashing red and blue lights of the police cruiser fade out of sight.

"My heart's racing about a thousand miles per hour" says Nicole to Brandi as they sit back on their barstools.

"You hide it well" replies Brandi, "I'm shaking like a eucalyptus tree in a windstorm."

Nicole grabs her wine glass, takes a huge swig, sets the glass down, and says, "Time to make the dreaded phone call."

"I feel for you" replies Brandi.

Nicole grabs her phone, does a quick scroll, and hits *'Send'*.

"Hey Jake" she says into the phone, "I screwed-up."

46

"Williams *'lawyered-up'*" says Levine to Nicole and Conroy as they are driving toward *Tech-Star Avionics*, "so, we'll have to see if Kirkpatrick serves him up as an accomplice."

"And in the meantime?" asks Nicole.

"He gets to sit and stew in San Diego police custody for assaulting a Federal Officer."

"What do make of his *'Are YOU following ME?'* statement last night?"

"I think it was just his way of trying to deflect the fact that HE was following YOU" replies Levine, "You know... trying to make *you* out as being the bad guy in order to give himself a lame-brained excuse for a confrontation."

"I guess you're right."

Levine pulls into a parking space in the lot for *Tech-Star Avionics*, and the team exits the vehicle.

"You take the lead, Slade" says Levine as they approach the entryway to the building.

Conroy is the first to enter the reception area, with Nicole and Levine right on his heels. He glances over toward Tara, the receptionist, who looks up from her desk and makes eye contact. She lights up like a schoolgirl whose first crush has just walked into the room.

"Nice to see you again, Agent Conroy" she says with a big smile and a flirtatious voice as Conroy approaches her desk.

"Nice to see you as well" Conroy replies.

"I assume you're here to see Mr. Kirkpatrick?" says Tara.

"Yes, we are" responds Conroy as he nods toward Levine and Nicole who are standing back in the reception area.

"He's in with Ms. Fairchild at the moment" responds Tara as she gestures toward a closed office door adjacent to the reception area.

"Has he been in there very long?"

"About fifteen minutes. He shouldn't be much longer, unless you want me to interrupt them?"

"That's fine… we'll wait. Thanks."

"My pleasure" replies Tara in a breathy voice.

Conroy turns around to relay the information to Levine and Nicole. Just as he is about to speak, the sound of a door unlatching and opening draws the attention of Levine and Nicole away from Conroy.

"That's him" says Nicole to Levine as Kirkpatrick walks through the doorway of Ms. Fairchild's office.

Conroy turns around at Nicole's prompt.

Kirkpatrick glances over toward the three individuals in the reception area and immediately recognizes Nicole and Conroy. He gestures a subtle wave of *'Hello'* and walks over to greet them.

"Agents Conroy and McKenna, back with more questions I assume?" says Kirkpatrick, adding, "And I see you've brought a coworker" as he spies Levine in the background.

Levine steps forward, holds up his badge, and says, "Special Agent Levine, NCIS… you need to come with us."

"But I already told your Agents everything I know" replies Kirkpatrick.

"Not by a long-shot Mr. Kirkpatrick" responds Levine, "Or should I say *Jason Patrick*, son of *Ryan Patrick* who served on the ENTERPRISE with *Vincent Colletti*."

47

Observing Kirkpatrick through the privacy glass between the Observation Room and Interrogation Room, Conroy and Nicole can tell that he is getting fidgety, if not downright frustrated.

"What do you think is running through his head right now?" says Nicole.

"He's trying to figure out exactly what we have on him" responds Conroy, "And trying to come up with plausible answers for each possible scenario."

"Notice how he keeps checking his watch? How long do you think Jake is going to let him just sit there?"

"Long enough until his head is about to explode from all of the different scenarios he needs to come up with."

Nicole grabs a file folder that was lying next to her. She holds it up and says, "I brought a little gift for Jake's interrogation."

"I was wondering what that was" replies Conroy.

Nicole opens the folder for Conroy to see.

"Oh, that is fucking awesome!" responds Conroy as he almost breaks into laughter.

"I thought you'd like that" replies Nicole, sporting a mile-wide grin.

Levine enters the Observation Room. Conroy and Nicole are surprised to see that the Director is with him.

"Jake... Director" responds both Conroy and Nicole.

The Director gives a nod of acknowledgment and says, "Pay no mind to me; I'm just here to observe the interrogation."

"How's our *guest* doing?" asks Levine.

"He's been percolating for a while now" responds Conroy, "And I think he's about ready to blow a gasket."

"Good" replies Levine.

"Here's the item I was telling you about, Jake" says Nicole as she hands him the folder while also making a brief glance the Director's way. She's having a hard time 'paying no mind' to the Director; after all, he's 'The Big Boss' and she's never known him to observe an interrogation.

Levine takes a look, replies "Perfect", and then slides the folder into a much larger file folder he's carrying.

"I assume our game plan is exactly as we rehearsed?" asks Conroy to Levine.

"You got it" replies Levine, "Every time he thinks he's gotten us to buy-in on his response, we immediately throw him off-track."

"Either by debunking his response, calling his bluff, or throwing the 'BS Flag'" responds Conroy.

"The 'BS Flag'?" says Nicole.

"BS... for 'Bullshit'" replies Levine, "A football analogy."

"Like a penalty flag?" responds Nicole.

"Exactly" replies Levine.

"But what if he gives you a sensible and honest answer?" says Nicole.

"Then we immediately ignore it and throw something brand new at him" replies Levine. "The key is to keep his mind jumping so much that he is unable to keep track of his lies, and then we pick them apart one-by-one."

"Or better yet" adds Conroy, "he gets so frustrated that he spills his guts just to shut us up."

"And remember" says Levine, "If we get to the point where he refuses to say any more, that's when we inundate him with facts, conjectures, innuendos, and most importantly, all of his inconsistencies."

"Anything to add, John?" says Levine to the Director.

"Nothing at all" responds the Director. "It sounds like you've got your game plan dialed-in and ready to go as always."

"Alright Slade, let's do this" says Levine as he walks out the door. Conroy turns and follows right behind.

48

"Fucking finally" Kirkpatrick mumbles to himself as he hears the door open to the Interrogation Room. Still seated, he turns to see who is entering – it's Levine and Conroy.

Levine walks over toward the far side of the table, directly across from Kirkpatrick. But before he gets to his chair he drops a large file onto the table near his seat. The file smacks loudly as it hits – the sound echoing around the room like a slap in the face.

Conroy recedes to the corner of the room, remaining standing, while Levine sits down - staring at Kirkpatrick but not uttering a word.

"What is this, *'Good cop – Bad cop'*?" says Kirkpatrick as he nods first toward Levine and then Conroy, "Or are you afraid I might 'fly off the handle' and he's your henchman to keep me in line?" he says with a thumb-point toward Conroy.

Kirkpatrick awaits a response, but Levine remains silent.

"I have a training session to get back to Agent Levine" says Kirkpatrick, who is quickly losing his patience, "Are we here to play stare-down or what?"

"You're going to be a bit late for that" replies Levine, "say... *'25 years-to-life'.*"

"What the hell are you talking about? What have I supposedly done?"

"How about two murders?"

"*Two* murders???" responds Kirkpatrick – he didn't see that coming.

❅ ❅ ❅

"I'm sure he expected that we'd to try to pin Colletti's *murder on him" says* Nicole *to the Director as they observe the interrogation, "but did you notice that inflection in his voice? He had* no idea *that we figured out that* Bauer *was murdered."*

"Good read on his tell Agent McKenna" replies the Director, "And that's Jake for you... right out of the gate he throws Kirkpatrick a scenario he hadn't expected."

❊❊❊

"That's crazy!" adds Kirkpatrick, responding to Levine's contention, "You've got nothing on me."

"We've got you connected to *both* victims. For starters, how about the fact that Colletti was somehow offered to be a guest for the Tiger Cruise, *and* that you two were assigned to the same stateroom?"

"Yeah, so? I couldn't have gotten him assigned there."

"But Chief Warrant Officer Bauer could; and he did so as a favor to *you* since a Contractor could not be a sponsor."

"That's a crock... Colletti was *his* guest."

"If *that* was the case then why wouldn't Colletti have roomed with the Warrant Officer?"

"How should I know? Probably because his roommate was there."

"His roommate was on leave; so there was no reason for him to be rooming with *you* unless he was really *your* guest."

"Under your scenario" Conroy interjects, "it's nothing but a *crazy coincidence* that your roommate *just so happened* to serve with your father thirty some-odd years ago."

"That's *exactly* what it is" responds Kirkpatrick, "just a coincidence."

"And he also *just so happens* to be the person who ruined your father's career?" says Conroy, "That's just another aspect of the *coincidence* I suppose?"

"I wouldn't know anything about that" replies Kirkpatrick.

"Do you *seriously* think that Bauer didn't tell anyone he sponsored Colletti for *you*?" says Levine.

Kirkpatrick decides to go on the offensive in an attempt to deflect and diminish the accusation, "That's all you've got; the guy assigned to the same stateroom as me happened to serve with my dad?!" he says, "That's not even worth showing up at my office, let alone dragging me down here!"

"Oh, we're just getting started" responds Levine.

Kirkpatrick remains silent, waiting to hear what crap Levine is going to throw at him next.

"You worked in an office adjacent to the Plymouth" says Levine, "The *same* office where the *real* dummy was stored."

"That means nothing" replies Kirkpatrick.

"Oh it means a lot… but we'll get to that in a minute."

"And I don't know anything about a dummy" replies Kirkpatrick.

"The dummy, and mask, that *you* bought from *Hollywood Props* in Burbank?" says Levine, "Nice touch giving them the name of '*Snuffy Savoy*.'"

Kirkpatrick is taken aback by this news, but he stays on the offensive, "That's a bunch of crap" he replies, "There's no way you can tie that to me."

"Because you thought you were being smart by paying cash?"

"Because I didn't pay for them at all!"

"Oh, so you stole them?"

"Stop trying to put words in my mouth; I had nothing to do with the purchase of them."

"We have you *in the vicinity* on the date of purchase."

"And I have *you* in the vicinity of my *ass*, but that doesn't mean you bought me my underwear" replies a smart-mouthed and agitated Kirkpatrick.

"You're pretty quick with a witty response" says Levine, "But here's a little loose-end you failed to clean up that has come back to haunt you."

Kirkpatrick has a look of confusion on his face as Levine pulls an 8 x 10 photograph out of his file folder. He places it in front of Kirkpatrick – it's a picture of the guy that Levine refers to as '*the doofus in disguise*' who made a purchase from *Hollywood Props*.

"Nice selfie" says Levine with a '*Got ya*' grin.

"That's not me" replies Kirkpatrick.

"That's the best you can come up with? Then how do you explain your *name* right here?" he says as he points to the identifier underneath the person in disguise.

"Somebody faked the name."

"I can have the social media page brought in here if you'd like, but we both know it's legit."

"You should consider revising your settings so your friends can't *'tag you'* on their page" says Conroy.

Kirkpatrick has a look of dejection mixed with frustration, and has no response.

"And then there's the fact that you were giving women a date-rape drug" says Levine.

"What the fuck are you talking about, I've never assaulted a woman" responds Kirkpatrick now on the defensive, "And what would that have to do with Colletti?"

"You were using them as guinea pigs."

"Guinea pigs??"

"To determine the amount of drug you'd need to knock-out Colletti in order to launch him."

"Now you're just grasping at straws... inventing outlandish accusations to fit some lame-ass theory you're trying to sell."

"Oh, so you gave them the drug in order to *rape them?*" counters Levine.

Kirkpatrick is speechless, but his clenched teeth and piercing eyes speak volumes.

"When we told you about Colletti you said you were sickened by the idea that he was behind the wheel of the Plymouth during the launch" says Conroy.

"That's true... I was" replies Kirkpatrick.

"All we said was that he was in the car" responds Conroy, "We never told you that he was *behind the wheel.*"

"Where else would he be?" replies Kirkpatrick, "Besides, there was supposed to be a dummy behind the wheel."

"You said you didn't know anything about a dummy" responds Levine.

Kirkpatrick tries to think of a response, but now he's second-guessing himself at every turn.

❋❋

"Jake is leading him exactly where he never knew he didn't want to go" says Nicole to the Director in the Observation Room.

The Director pauses for a moment as he processes Nicole's statement; finally realizing it might sound a little crazy, but it makes perfect sense... "You have a way with words Agent McKenna" replies the Director, "and you're exactly right."

❋❋

"Your wife said you wanted vengeance against the person responsible for the death of your parents" says Conroy.

"You talked to my wife??!!" responds Kirkpatrick with sudden anger, "She had nothing to do with this!"

Levine and Conroy's eyes light up as Kirkpatrick's words surely seem to have tipped his hand toward his guilt. Nicole and the Director take notice in the Observation Room as well.

❋❋

"Did he just implicate himself by attempting to keep his wife clear of any possible involvement?" says Nicole to the Director.

"That's sure what it sounded like."

❋❋

"Oh, we talked to her alright" responds Levine, "And I wonder what she'd think about the date-rape drug?"

Levine pauses for a moment, just long enough to let Kirkpatrick ponder his statement, and then adds, "I'll get back to that."

"So, if revenge against *Colletti* was your motive" says Conroy, "why kill Chief Warrant Officer Bauer?"

"He died of cancer" replies Kirkpatrick, "You guys said so yourselves."

"He was murdered" responds Levine.

"That's not true" replies Kirkpatrick, "I read his obituary right after he died and it said he died of cancer."

"I thought the first time you had heard of his death was a few days ago when we told you?" responds Conroy.

"Yeah, that's right" replies Kirkpatrick, "I looked it up online right after you guys told me about it."

"You *just now said* you read about it *right after he died*" responds Levine with great emphasis, "And that was *three weeks ago!*"

Kirkpatrick remains silent.

"And here's another problem with your *obituary* story" says Levine as he pulls out a sheet of paper from his folder and places it in front of Kirkpatrick.

Kirkpatrick's head remains motionless, but his eyes drift down to spy the paper.

"Bauer's *'Obit'*" says Levine as he lifts up the paper and sticks it in Kirkpatrick's face, "No mention of *cancer* whatsoever."

"I have nothing else to say" responds Kirkpatrick, realizing that Levine has called his bluff, *and* that every time he speaks he just digs himself a deeper hole to try to climb out of.

"No?" says Levine, "Let *us* say it for you."

Conroy realizes that Levine is about to unleash the barrage, and readies himself to join in the fray.

"You got Colletti down to your office near the Plymouth at zero-dark-thirty" says Levine, "Probably to give him a private tour of the launch car."

"You knock him out with some drug like Rohypnol; the drug you *'tested'* on those women" says Conroy.

"You put him in the mask and flight gear of the dummy, but with his own flight suit from his days as an Aviator on the ENTERPRISE... *the cloak of your father's tormentor*" says Levine.

"You load him in the car, and the launch team assumes he's the dummy" says Conroy.

"The launch is successful, or so it appears; except that one of the Petty Officers notices it's a *real person* behind the wheel and tries to stop it" says Levine. "But it's too late, the car gets launched and Colletti plunges to the bottom of the sea."

"And the Petty Officer keeps silent about what he has discovered; figuring he'll be the next victim if the killer knows he's a witness" adds Conroy.

"But Chief Warrant Officer Bauer is *not* so lucky since he's the *one* person you *know* can tie you to Colletti, and is now a potential liability" remarks Levine.

"So, you silence him using the same drug your mother used to commit suicide" says Conroy.

"Spiking his hydrocodone since you knew it was only a matter of time before he would use the drug to try to ease the pain of his cancer" adds Levine.

"An interesting thing about forensics" says Conroy, "They're your best friend when you're innocent, but they're your *worst enemy* when you're guilty."

"I guess you didn't consider a toxicology report as part of Bauer's autopsy" says Levine.

"And an Internet search on *Lanoxin* using your company computer back when you were at *Advanced Aviation Systems*... not too smart" adds Conroy.

"You should reconsider *burning your bridges* when you leave a company" says Levine, "They were more than happy to accommodate us in our investigation."

"You had motive, the means, and opportunity" says Conroy.

"And you almost pulled-off the perfect crime" says Levine, "Except a fishing trawler cast its net and dredged up Colletti's sarcophagus... a 1963 Plymouth Savoy."

Kirkpatrick cannot believe this is happening, that all of his planning and scheming, his trials and tribulations, have just blown up in his face. His frustrations finally get the best of him… "How the Hell does a car get fished out of the middle of the ocean??!!" Kirkpatrick yells out in disbelief, "And who does an autopsy and toxicology test on a corpse riddled with cancer??!!"

Kirkpatrick, with his mouth shut, starts breathing so heavily that his chest visibly expands and contracts with each inhale and exhale.

"I've hated the bastard ever since that day on the ENTERPRISE" says Kirkpatrick, essentially to himself, in an almost trance-like state, staring into space.

"The ENTERPRISE?" says Levine with a mixture of surprise and curiosity.

Kirkpatrick turns his head toward Levine and, with a demon-like stare, responds, "When he verbally crucified my father in front of all of us kids."

"The Tiger Cruise back in 1978?" replies Levine.

"Can you imagine a six year-old kid seeing his father treated that way??!! And making the other kids think that my dad was a worthless low-life??!! I wanted him launched in *that* Plymouth!!"

"He ruined the Tiger Cruise for you and your father."

"Oh, it wasn't enough for him to ruin our Tiger Cruise; his goal, which the scum-sucking bastard achieved, was to ruin my Dad's career - forcing him to resign from being a Navy pilot!"

"But your dad *did* eventually get work as a pilot."

"Yeah, teaching fucking *'pilot wannabees'* how to fly Piper Cubs! My dad was a Fighter Pilot for crying out loud! And then he dies flying one of those silly little planes??!! He should have gone out in a blaze of glory serving his country!!"

"And that pushed you over the edge?"

"Not me, but it did my mother. My dad was the love of her life, and Colletti took that from her. And then he took *her* life!"

"He was responsible for her suicide?"

"Hell yes!! If it wasn't for *him* my dad would have been one of the best the Navy had ever seen, and my mother would have been the proud wife of a Navy hero."

"So, it was time for Colletti to pay."

"You bet your ass it was time for him to pay... for being the worthless, cruel, and heartless fucking bastard that he was!"

"So, you found out he was in Hawaii, made an elaborate plan to get him launched, and approached him at *Davy Jones' Locker*."

"Davy Jones' Locker was just an opportunity to stalk my prey. Go figure he was hanging out with 'Goody Two Shoes' Jamison and his smart-mouthed sidekick Sewell. And the little shits almost caught me there, but I slithered into the background like a snake."

Kirkpatrick pauses briefly, and then with an evil-sounding semi-laugh continues, "I couldn't believe my luck, frickin' Sewell and Jamison were baiting the trap without realizing it."

"Baiting the trap?"

"Telling him all about the Plymouth Launch" says Kirkpatrick. "Colletti was so stoked I knew he'd be an easy mark."

"Then you approached him?"

"Not yet; too much risk that *'Mr. Can't Keep His Fucking Trap Shut'* would tell someone he'd be catching a ride on the SEADRAGON... and that would *totally* screw up my plan."

"Your plan?"

"His disappearance" Kirkpatrick explains. "Lucky for me he had no wife, no kids... no *life* for that matter. No one was going to miss him... one day he's here; the next day he's gone... without a trace."

Levine remains quiet; taking it all in.

"I waited until he left the bar; just a few hours before the ship got underway" Kirkpatrick continues, "And spoon-fed his ego with bullshit."

"In what manner?"

"I told him I was the coordinator of the launch and that *he* was the *Honored Guest,* but that it was a big surprise so he had to lay-low until the actual launch."

"And he took the bait?"

"He ate it up like a toddler with an ice cream cone; practically drooling on himself. And with the ship's imminent departure he barely had enough time to throw together a small suitcase and get the hell out of there."

"How'd you get Chief Warrant Officer Bauer to go along with your plan? What did you have on him?"

"Bauer??" responds Kirkpatrick, almost offended that he needed anyone's help to pull off his crime, "He had no clue what was going down, he was just the perfect sap to take the fall if the body was ever found."

"He had to be more than just your fall-guy."

"Well, he was a means to an end... a way to get Colletti shipboard."

"You pulled off this complex scheme all by yourself? No help from Bauer or Derek Williams?"

"*Williams*?? Who the hell is that?"

"The Air Boss' son."

"Never heard of the guy" says Kirkpatrick. "And sure, I needed Bauer to get the car onboard, get it painted like the one from the ENTERPRISE, get the dummy stored... all of that crap."

"What about loading Colletti into the car?"

"I didn't need any help hauling his sorry ass into the car; the fool climbed behind the wheel without me even asking. So I climbed into the passenger-side seat and we celebrated the upcoming launch with a few drinks."

"A special concoction in his case" replies Levine.

"Of course; enough to put him to sleep for hours."

"So why drug him? Why not just break his neck?"

"And have him defecate all over himself? That would have been totally obvious; everyone realizing the guy was a real-life *shit sandwich*."

"Well, your drugging almost backfired; he was coming out of when he was launched."

"Really?? That's even better. I can only imagine what went through his head as he realized he was getting launched."

"And what if he came out of it *before* he was launched?"

"Plan-B" replies Kirkpatrick.

"Plan-B?"

"I explain to everyone that he snuck some booze onboard and had too much to drink, which is why he was passed out in the car. And then sometime later he suddenly has a heart attack."

"A heart atta..." Levine starts to say before realizing exactly what Kirkpatrick is saying, "Oh, so *Colletti* gets the digitalis instead of *Bauer*."

"It would have been a letdown" replies Kirkpatrick, "but sometimes you have no other choice than to rely on your backup plan."

"How did you get the digitalis into Bauer's meds?"

"I met him in his stateroom after the launch to go over my remaining training; and when he started asking me '*why my guest Colletti never showed up*' I knew it was time to take action. So I rambled on so long that he had to go take a piss, and once he walked out the door I dumped the entire contents into his hydrocodone."

"But it was weeks later before he finally took his meds; that had to be concerning."

"Yeah, that really screwed me. Had he died when he was *supposed* to, before we got back to port, I wouldn't be sitting here with you assholes right now."

"Karma's a bitch, ain't it?"

"Yes it is... just ask Colletti." Kirkpatrick then pauses momentarily and adds... "Oh wait, you can't, *the fucker's dead*."

"I can see you having a vendetta against Colletti, but why kill Bauer; he had caused you no harm?"

"Like you said, he was the only one who could link me to Colletti. Besides, he was going to die of cancer anyway; the digitalis was more humane, it kept him from a slow and agonizing death."

"I see… so you're a humanitarian" Levine sarcastically responds.

49

"Great job on the interrogation today, Jake" says Nicole as she looks up from her computer screen when Levine and Conroy walk up to her desk.

"Thanks" replies Levine, who then gives a nod toward Conroy, "Slade held his own as well."

"Yes he did" replies Nicole.

"It's nice to know that Chief Warrant Officer Bauer wasn't involved" says Levine, "Although it sucks that Kirkpatrick took advantage of Bauer's willingness to help out a former Aviator."

"Yeah" says Nicole, "A true patriot who almost got railroaded and his legacy ruined."

"And considering Derek Williams' actions yesterday, it's a bit of a shame that Kirkpatrick didn't serve him up as an accomplice."

"I guess I got him all 'spun up' for nothing."

"All you did was lay-out the facts, right?"

"True."

"Then it's not your fault that the guy was a powder-keg ready to explode. But the *next* time..."

"I know... *two Agents minimum* when interviewing a potential suspect outside of an Interrogation Room."

Levine gives Nicole a smile of approval.

"All I can say is that this was one *pain-in-the-ass* case" remarks Conroy.

"Which makes it that much more rewarding when we solve such a mystery" says Levine.

"That's true" admits Conroy.

"You know what comes to mind when I look back on this case?" says Nicole.

"What's that?" says Conroy.

"Are you familiar with the movie *'Jason and the Argonauts'*?" says Nicole.

"That's a little before your time, Nic" responds Levine.

"I love the old classics" replies Nicole, "Especially when the guy on the Classic Movie channel provides insights regarding the film."

"Yeah, those are great" responds Conroy, "So, what about the movie?"

"Remember where the God Neptune rises from the sea and holds back the rocky banks to allow passage of the Ship?" says Nicole.

"Yeah?" says Conroy.

"Well, it was like he... *Neptune*... came rising out of the sea to deliver the Plymouth and Colletti to the fishing trawler for us to solve his murder."

"You've got a wild imagination there, Nic."

"Maybe so; but you see what I mean, right?"

"All I see is someone spending too much time watching SciFi-Mythology-Fantasy flicks."

"I have to admit, that's an interesting perspective" says Levine.

"Thanks, Jake" says Nicole.

"I was talking to Slade" replies Levine with a grin.

"I should have known better than to try to bring up a unique observation with you guys" says Nicole.

"We're just flipping you crap" replies Conroy, "It often seems that some obscure or almost unexplainable event occurs that leads us down the path toward justice."

"Fate, karma, divine intervention... call it what you will, it's always a welcome addition to solving a case" adds Levine.

"So Nic" says Conroy, "What the heck are you perusing there on your computer?"

"Just some of the files I collected on the case."

"You *do* remember that we just solved it... right?"

"Yeah, I'm just... Holy crap!" says Nicole as something jumps out at her while staring at her computer screen.

"What??" replies Conroy at Nicole's sudden outburst.

"I had compiled a bunch of info as we were trudging through the case" Nicole says.

"And you found something we missed?" asks Levine.

"Well, yes and no" replies Nicole, "I found an article from the Alameda Gazette, dated October 30th 1978."

"And?" replies Levine.

"A person went missing off of the ENTERPRISE right around the time of their Tiger Cruise launch."

Nicole and Conroy, with perplexed looks on their faces, look toward Levine...

"Dedicated to the Men and Women who served on 'The Big E' - the USS ENTERPRISE (CVN 65).

Commissioned November 25th, 1961;

Inactivated December 21st, 2012"

Author's Note:

Yes, there actually was a 1963 Plymouth launched off of the deck of the USS ENTERPRISE during their 1978 WestPac Tiger Cruise.

But no, a person did not go missing around the time of the launch; that statement was merely creative license taken by the author for the entertainment of the reader.